PARTICULAR PASSAGES 3

WEST WING

Particular Passages 3: West Wing
Copyright © 2022 Knight Writing Press
Additional copyright information for individual works provided at the end of this
publication.

Knight Writing Press
PMB # 162
13009 S. Parker Rd.
Parker CO 80134

KnightWritingPress@gmail.com

Cover Art and Cover Design © 2022 Knight Writing Press

Interior Art © 2022 Knight Writing Press

Additional Copyright Information can be found on page 261

Interior Book Design and eBook Design by Knight Writing Press

Editor Sam Knight

First Publication July 2022

Paperback ISBN-13: 978-1-62869-051-4
eBook ISBN-13: 978-1-62869-052-1

Dedication

Welcome, intrepid reader.

This book is for you.

Thank you for venturing down unknown passages alongside us.

May your bravery bring you that for which you search.

May your search be that which brings you the most pleasure.

And may your search be never ending.

Table of Contents

But I'm Real

by
J. A. Campbell

But I'm Real

Y ou're not one of us."

I stared at Ryan and twisted my hands together. Seriously? They'd invited me to the meet last month. "But..."

"No." He shut the door in my face.

I swiped at my eyes and backed away from the solid carved oak door of the Victorian mansion where the meet was held. The house was set back into the old growth forest a ways, and I just wanted to disappear into it forever. Embarrassment warred with anger and rejection, the emotions tightening in my chest until I turned and ran for my car, fighting sobs.

I didn't fit in anywhere. I never had, and I was starting to think I never would. Wasn't there anyone else out there like me?

I wrenched the car door open and all but threw myself in. The old Focus grumbled to life after a couple of protests. I really needed to get a new car. It was on the list. The long list. Graduating college was supposed to provide opportunity, right? I mean, I didn't regret my education at all. I just wished I saw more prospects in my future. Maybe it was simply that I felt I didn't belong anywhere, and that feeling made it hard to settle into anything.

I'd been happy in college. No one had known, or cared, about my differences and I'd been too busy to try and find a community, but now...now people cared. They either didn't believe I was real, or they thought I was a freak, and either way, they didn't want me around.

For a bunch of shifters to tell me I wasn't real...well, that was ridiculous.

The rabbits didn't want me, and the deer. Well, they'd told me they were changing their meet location just so I'd never find them again. Seriously, like I was going to tell anyone?

We had to be careful. Discovery was probably worse than just not belonging anywhere in the first place.

The full moon—the traditional were meetup time—rose as dusk settled through the rolling countryside. It was beautiful, this Virginia wilderness. Green. Lush. Full of life. I'd hoped to be spending it with the were rabbits on this hundred-acre estate where, in theory, we—no, they—were safe from the intrusions of humanity.

Honestly, there was no point trying with any of the other communities. I knew what they'd say. They'd take one look at my shifted form and sneer. Large lagomorphic body, antelope horns protruding from my skull, certainly a freak. I looked like a large, leggy jack rabbit with horns, and no one wanted me around.

I needed to drown my sorrows, but I wasn't a drinker. Even with my were metabolism, I was a lightweight, and I just wasn't feeling the hangover tomorrow. I'd mostly quit drinking after a few experiences in college anyway. No, what I needed was the best hot chocolate in town and a friend to share it with.

Fortunately, I knew just where to go.

It didn't take long to make it to my favorite coffee shop, despite how far out in the country I had been. Maybe I had driven a little fast.

The coffee shop was housed in part of an old house, built around the turn of the last century. The floor creaked whenever someone walked across it, and I loved the old wooden floor almost as much as I loved the hot chocolate.

My friend from college, Caroline, worked the late shift. While she didn't know what my issue was, she knew I felt different, felt like I'd never fit anywhere, and that I'd thought I'd found a group finally.

She looked up from the counter she was wiping down, took one look at my face and sighed.

"Erica, honey, grab a seat. I'll be right over."

"Thanks, Caroline." I almost burst into tears as I found my way to one of the corner tables.

We weren't quite alone in the small coffee shop, but the other patron seemed engrossed in his book, and I put him out of my mind after a cursory glance.

Minutes later, Caroline joined me, setting two steaming mugs down on the table. She slid one over to me and I clutched it in my hands. I could no longer stop the tears.

"Honey, what happened?"

"They said I didn't belong, that I couldn't go to their meet. I'm never going to find a group to belong to," I sobbed.

"Erica, I obviously don't understand why this is so important to you, but I know it is. Just, remember, you have friends that love you no matter what. Do you want to talk about it?"

She put a hand on my shoulder, and I took a sip of the melted chocolate bliss. It helped calm me, and I shook my head.

"I can't talk about the things that make me different, Caroline. There's just…no one else like me, and I don't understand why."

"Have you thought about going home?"

"Um, Virginia Beach?" I took another drink of my chocolate, my tears drying.

"No. Wyoming." She leaned her elbows on the table and stared at me.

"I wouldn't exactly call Wyoming home. I haven't been there since I was a kid." I downed the last of my chocolate.

The floor creaked and I glanced up, but the other patron—a guy—was just putting his drink in the dirty dish tray. He gave us a curious look on his way to the door but then he was gone, and we were alone.

"I moved out here when my parents were killed. You know that." I'd been old enough to know I couldn't tell anyone about my were nature. It came down my father's side, and my mother's sister had raised me, so she didn't even know. Still, I'd considered it before, and the idea dwelled in the back of my mind. Maybe someday I would.

"You should go. Even if it's just for a visit."

"Maybe." I sighed and ran my hands through my hair.

"Erica, I need to close up, but if you want to wait, I'll keep hanging out after I'm done."

"No, that's fine. I really appreciate the hot chocolate, Caroline." While weres didn't have to shift with the full moon, it tugged at the animals inside us, and I wanted to answer the call. Even if that animal was a freak and I didn't know what it was.

"On the house tonight. Think about it, going home that is. I'm not trying to get rid of you, but I think it might be a good idea."

"Yeah, maybe," I conceded.

I gave Caroline a quick hug and headed outside. It was truly night at this point, and I wondered where I should go. I tried to vary the locations I went to shift so as not to attract attention. Most humans had no idea shifters existed, but the ones who did could be very dangerous to us.

The car's engine turned over, caught, and I released the breath I was holding. I pulled out of the small parking lot, noting another pair of headlights leaving the curb when I did. That wasn't particularly unusual, even this time of night, so I didn't pay much attention.

I wound my way through the historic district, not really looking at the beautiful old homes and businesses. I saw them nearly every day, and right now I was wracking my brain for a place to go shift. Normally I had this planned out days in advance, but I'd thought I'd known where I would be tonight.

Grinding my teeth in frustration and trying to push down the anxious feeling in my chest, the feeling of a prey animal without a safe place to be, I searched for a haven for the evening. I needed to stretch my legs and really run.

Finally, I remembered a trailhead that allowed night hiking. Risky, but at least I wouldn't have to worry about my vehicle being towed. I'd shifted there once when I'd first moved to the area.

The trip was short. There were a couple of other cars in the parking lot and it didn't seem strange when another car pulled in not long after me. Still, I gave it a quick glance, and frowned when I recognized the man from the coffee shop.

I froze when he met my eyes. His lips curled into a smile, and he whispered something that chilled my blood. "I found you, little were."

I quickly unfroze, diving to the ground when he pulled a gun.

I'd seen enough pictures of them over the years to recognize an animal tranquilizer gun when I saw one. It was a hunter's primary weapon when they weren't completely sure their target was a were, but they felt confident enough to go hunting anyway

Gravel crunched as he moved closer.

Fortunately, my keys were still in my hand, and I'd seen him before I'd moved away from my car. Staying low, I opened my car door, got in and prayed that it would start.

For once, the Focus caught on the first crank, and I threw it into reverse, almost nailing another car in the process, but ultimately making it out of the parking lot without hitting anything.

It wasn't even safe to go home now. Even if this had been some run-of-the-mill sicko, they wouldn't stop until they'd caught me. *Damn it.*

Rent was paid for the month. I could get Caroline to collect my things once I figured out what I was going to do.

Had the guy heard us mention Wyoming? I couldn't remember. It was a big state. Surely, I could lose myself in it?

I guess there was one good thing to come out of all this. Someone believed I existed. I laughed bitterly through my terrified tears. Yeah, someone who wanted me dead.

Maybe I'd have better luck in the west, and now I had no choice but to leave Virginia. I hit the interstate and slowed to a normal speed. I did not want to get a ticket. The itch to shift grated against my nerves, but it helped me stay awake as I drove into the night.

I ran out of steam somewhere in Ohio. The need to shift was too great, and I had to stop or I was going to wreck my car. I pulled off the interstate on a random exit that looked like it led into the endless rolling farmland. Shifting in the open like this was risky, but I could probably find one of the treelines, the remnants of the forest that had once covered much of the eastern US, and change there. I wouldn't be able to run like I normally did but I could at least graze and fill my belly. I hadn't eaten much recently, and it was starting to catch up to me.

Aware that it was the middle of the night, I didn't want to get noticed. I tried to drive normally while looking for a place to pull off the road and park. Finally, I thought I saw a treeline in the distance and went down a dirt road a ways. The crunch of gravel under my tires was loud, rivaled only by the screaming cicadas. I found a place where I could pull off the road near the stand of trees and turned off my car.

I rolled down the window, letting in the muggy air, and listened for sounds of discovery. I sat that way for almost a half an hour, barely moving, muscles quivering with tension. Everything screamed at me that I was making a mistake, shifting in unfamiliar territory, but the need to change was overwhelming, and I couldn't deny it any longer.

Finally, satisfied that I was alone, I got out of my car and gently shut the door. I stashed my keys under the bumper and moved into the trees. Still listening, tense, ready to bolt at any moment, I shed my clothing. Then, again before I committed to the shift, I stretched every sense I had, wary of detection.

At last, satisfied that I was alone as I could manage, I sank to my knees and committed to the shift. My bones tingled, limbs stretching and shrinking. My skin itched as fur sprouted. I rubbed at my scalp with my paws as horns and ears jutted from my head.

I lay there for a minute, panting and catching my breath after the change. As soon as I had my breathing under control, I listened again. Still nothing but the cicadas.

If this form had been capable of tears, I would have been weeping right now. This was no way to live. Hiding from everything, rejected by everyone. My only hope was finding someone else like me in Wyoming.

Heart heavy, I hopped around a little bit to stretch my legs before finding a patch of lush greens and doing my best to fill my belly.

The rest of the trip was like that. Stopping only when I had to. Sleeping in my car to conserve money and staying ever watchful for pursuit. By the time I'd made it to the Wyoming border, I had almost relaxed. I was running low on money, but so far it seemed like I'd gotten away. Now if I could just find some clue as to what I was, or some hint of a shifter like me before my money ran completely out, I might be okay after all.

My luck held until Laramie, Wyoming. Then the engine light came on, and I had to stop. Not holding out much hope for the life of my car, I left it at a shop and walked over to a diner. At least I could get some food and wait for the bad news.

The décor was, well, taxidermy. It wasn't quite what I was used to, but I supposed it had some charm to it. The hostess sat me at a table and handed me a menu. Though I was extremely hungry, I settled for coffee and a salad. Something cheap. I had no idea how much the car was going to cost me.

Once I had ordered, I studied the animals throughout the diner. I was no expert, but the taxidermy seemed well done, and I did enjoy seeing animals I'd only ever read about, though I'd have preferred to see them alive.

Finally, my gaze settled on something I'd never seen before, except in mirror smooth water on moonlit nights, and I froze. This one was tiny, but the resemblance was unmistakable. What was it?

The waitress returned with my coffee and caught me staring at the creature. She laughed. "Normally I'd mess with you a bit, honey, but you look done in, so I won't. Isn't real. Just a jackrabbit taxidermied with antelope horns."

"What is it?" I couldn't help the quaver in my voice.

"Call it a jackalope. Local legend, story, whatever you want to call it. Local to Wyoming anyway."

"I…" I didn't know what to say. My hands shook as I stared at the jackalope, and contemplated how like my own form it appeared, just in miniature. Knowing the name for my species was huge. Clearly at least one other were like me existed, or they never would have thought to put horns on a rabbit.

Still, even here they didn't believe we were real. I rubbed my arms and turned my attention back to the waitress. She frowned as she studied me. Something about her seemed familiar to me, and I wondered if maybe she was a shifter of some sort. I couldn't always tell, but sometimes there was a certain familiarity. Maybe that was what she was feeling. If it was, I hoped she didn't ask. I'd had a shit day and I didn't think I could handle someone else telling me to my face that I didn't exist.

"You okay, honey?"

I took a breath and shook my head. "Yeah, I'm okay. Car is broke. Not sure what I'm going to do." I shrugged. "It'll be fine."

"You got a place to stay?"

I shook my head, gaze drifting back to the jackalope sitting perched on a tree branch on the wall.

"I'm assuming, since you didn't know what a jackalope was, that you're not from around here?"

I refocused on the conversation, not wanting to say anything that might cause me danger, but not seeing why I couldn't admit to being from here originally.

"My parents lived in Tie Siding when I was a kid. Well, I guess I lived there, too. They were killed. Car accident in the winter. Pretty bad." So bad that even my father who could heal nearly anything, had perished. "I grew up with my aunt and uncle back east."

"Not much in Tie Siding. You heading back there?"

I shrugged. "I don't know. I guess I was just looking for something. Not going anywhere now." I glanced at my phone on reflex, but the shop hadn't called. I would have heard it ring.

"Well, let me get your salad. You want anything else?" Something that was roasting smelled amazing, and my stomach growled, but I shook my head.

"No. Thank you."

She nodded and headed back to the kitchen.

A short time later another woman came out. She caught my attention more than the waitress had. She was older, with steel gray threaded through her blond curls and kindness in her blue eyes.

"You eat meat, dear?"

I raised my eyebrows but nodded, confused by the question. She set a steaming plate of something roasted in front of me, along with the salad I'd ordered.

Tears sprang to my eyes, and I shook my head in denial.

"I raise the lamb they're roasting tonight. My treat. Mind if I join you?"

"Sure." If she was going to feed me lamb, she could eat with me. I didn't mind.

We ate in silence for a while. I hadn't had a decent meal in… I wasn't even sure. A few days at this point.

"I'm May," she introduced herself.

"Erica." I tried really hard to smile at the woman. I was just so damn tired that I struggled.

"Jeanie said you were having car trouble?"

I nodded.

"And that you're from here originally?"

I nodded again.

"What brought you back this way?"

Shrugging, my gaze trailed over to the jackalope again. "Uh, I was looking for someone like me, but I guess I just ended up busting my car. I should probably go home." I sagged, feeling defeated.

"Like you how?"

There was no way I could answer. I got the same familiar feel from this woman's energy that I had the waitress, but I didn't know them, couldn't share my secrets. It wasn't safe.

"Tell you what. I've got a sheep ranch," she gestured to my nearly clean plate, "and I could use a little extra help right now. It's hard work, but not complicated. It'll give you a little extra money and a place to stay while your vehicle is fixed. There's the use of a farm truck in it and a bunk and food. I know you don't know me, so here's my card. Google the ranch. If you think it's someplace you might feel welcome for a time, give me a call, I'll come pick you up. Until then, I want you to take this and get yourself a hotel for the night. It's a gift. People have helped me in the past, let me help you."

She slid some money across the table.

"Your food and the tip are handled. And there's pie if you want it."

Before I could object, she got up and left. She looked like a farmer, rugged jeans, work boots, light button-down shirt to keep the sun off and a wide brimmed hat to shield her eyes. The kindness she had shown me had reflected in her eyes, and I wanted to trust her.

I stared after her until the waitress came with some of the best apple pie I'd ever had.

"May is good people," Jeanie told me after I'd finished. "She's got good instincts, too. Says you need us."

"Us?"

"I live out there. Head on back over here in the morning for breakfast. Best biscuits and gravy this side of the divide. Also, of the two hotels in walking distance, I would recommend you take the Holiday Inn. The other one is pretty, uh, basic." She grinned and left before I could ask her what divide she was talking about or thank her for the advice.

Feeling a little guilty, but also grateful, I took the money May had left me and headed back out into the cool evening. It was strange. Back in Virginia it would have still been hot, but at this altitude the air had cooled quickly into something almost chilly.

I headed over to the hotel. Hackles rising, I stopped and looked around, but while Laramie wasn't a big city, it was a college town and there were plenty of people out at the moment. I couldn't pick out anything specific that had set me on alert. Frustrated, I hurried to the hotel and went inside.

Turns out Jeanie was right about one thing. The biscuits and gravy were some of the best I'd ever had, and while I'd heard this divide mentioned again, I had no idea what they were talking about.

Still, when May pulled up in her truck an hour after I'd called her, I put it out of my mind. The shop hadn't had good news, and it was going to take a while before I could get my car fixed, even with a little income. Googling the ranch had encouraged me. They had good reviews from both permanent employees and people looking for working getaways, anywhere from a week to a few months at a time. It seemed like a perfect place to stay while I paid for the car. The compensation was adequate, especially with room and board on top of the base wage, and I liked animals well enough.

"Any questions?" May asked once I climbed into her truck.

"Uh, not really. I mean, I'm sure I'll have a ton once we get on the farm. I know a little, but, yeah, not enough to do anything without some instruction."

"That's an attitude we can work with. Now, I realize you're out here looking for something, and we kind of coopted you into this, so if at any time you need to leave or take care of stuff, you just let us know. We'll take it into account, we just need to make sure the animals are cared for."

"Yes, ma'am. I'll pull my weight."

"None of that. I'm May, and I'm sure you will."

We traveled out of Laramie in relative silence. We went west into some high plains and on the very edge, bordering on pine forest, she pulled off onto yet another dirt road. This one was a bit rougher than the others.

"Oh, for heaven's sake," she muttered.

I frowned, following her attention. A couple of pickups blocked a gated drive.

"Pardon, I need to deal with some troublemakers."

The truck slid on the gravel as she slammed on her brakes. She left it running while she hopped out, grabbing a rifle from the rack behind the seats.

I stared as she stalked forward, rifle aimed at two burly men.

I was far enough back that I couldn't hear the words exchanged, but eventually the men got in their trucks and left, though May kept the rifle pointed at them until they were out of sight.

"That happen often?" I asked when she came back, my hands clenched on the 'oh shit' handle on the truck's door.

"Off and on. Got a disagreement with some of the folk around here. They don't like," she glanced at me before shrugging. "Sheep," she finished.

She was going to say something else, but I didn't ask. Nothing in the information I'd read about her ranch suggested anything others might have a problem with, but I was clearly unaware of the local issues.

Nervously, I jumped out and opened the gate for May. I carefully shut it behind me, not wanting to be accidently responsible for animals getting out or anything like that.

May took me on a whirlwind tour before showing me to my bunk. I'd slept decently the night before, so I told her to put me to work.

She smiled and led me out to some of the pens. "It's not glamorous, but right now the biggest need is some scrubbing. Bill and Rocket," she pointed at two beautiful border collies, "will keep you company and make sure the sheep don't get too curious while you work."

"Sounds good. I do have one question though."

"Yes?" She asked patiently.

"What divide?"

May tilted her head.

"You and Jeanie both mentioned the divide."

"Oh!" She laughed. "The continental divide. It's not far from here."

I joined her laughter. "Okay, that makes more sense than any theory I'd come up with so far. Thank you."

"Of course, dear." She gave me a quick tutorial on how to scrub out the stock tanks and feeders and after a quick introduction, I petted the dogs and then got to work.

I was flat on my back in my bunk room, resting after the first day of work. I hurt, but it wasn't a bad pain, and I'd recover quickly enough. Everyone was nice, if a touch reserved, and dinner had been amazing. The others were off doing night chores, but they'd told me I'd done enough for my first day.

Someone knocked on the door to the bunk room before coming in.

"Erica, I wanted to show you something," May said, coming in.

I rolled off the bunk and stood, feeling a touch nervous, though I didn't know why. The older woman led me outside, past the upper sheep pens and out into the rolling pasture that covered over a hundred acres.

It was well past dusk but not quite true dark yet, and the moon had not yet risen. Yet, I had decent night vision, even in human form, and what I saw made me freeze and stare. Figures I'd only seen reflected back to me in still water, or in miniature at the diner, waited in the darkness. Large jackrabbits all sporting horns, just like mine, sat hunched in the dusky light.

Tears welled in my eyes. Surely not?

"Is that what you were looking for?" May asked. I could hear the uncertainty in her voice, and my heart swelled at the chance they had taken, revealing themselves to me. They didn't know for sure that I was what they were, but they'd risked it on May's instincts.

Unable to speak past the lump in my throat, I nodded.

"Well, Erica, why don't you join us. It's not a full moon, but with the werewolves prowling our borders, it's safer to shift in the darker times anyway," May said.

Those men earlier in the day must have been wolves.

I nodded, stripped where I was, and let my animal—my jackalope—emerge, for the first time not afraid of ridicule or of being told I was a freak, or that I didn't exist. I'd found others like me. Finally.

When I woke the next morning, I thought that maybe I had dreamed the night before. Running across the acres of pasture with other shifters like me. Other jackalopes. However, when I went into the dining area to get breakfast, the genuine smiles that greeted me let me know I hadn't dreamed any of it at all. No, I'd finally found my people.

The day progressed and the work went easily with the new lightness in my heart. I made an effort to get to know everyone around their labor, and by the time lunch came, I was feeling more at peace than I had since I was a child.

That peace shattered like it had never existed when I walked into the dining area and saw him. My heart nearly stopped, and I froze, hoping he wouldn't see me.

The man from the coffee shop. The man who had tried to shoot me with a tranq gun. I'd led him here, and now we were all in danger.

I'd have to run again. I'd have to lead him away. Maybe if he caught me, he wouldn't look too closely at the others.

May saw my reaction and her eyebrows rose. The man turned and his eyes narrowed, and his smile turned from friendly to calculating.

I backed out of the dining area.

As soon as I was out of the building, I turned and ran for the trucks. I had to get back to Laramie at least.

The commotion behind me barely registered as I sprinted for the vehicles.

"Erica!" May shouted.

I stumbled, but didn't stop, in full-on flight mode.

The older woman was fit and far more acclimated to the altitude than I was, and she caught up to me.

"Erica, what's wrong?"

"He's…" I gasped, unable to breathe.

"Take a moment. He's not going anywhere. Said he was here to buy some lamb. Take it you know him?"

I collapsed to my knees, sobbing. I'd found what I'd been looking for and now I was going to lose it all again, but they needed to know, to be able to protect themselves.

"He's a hunter," I finally managed to get out. "He must have heard me talking about Wyoming, and he followed me here. I'm so sorry."

"Wait here," May said. "Do not leave."

I was basically unable to refuse her command, as I'd accepted her as my alpha, and I watched as she strode off toward the building, her cell phone in her hand.

Not long after, the men and women who worked here filed out of the main building, all heavily armed, and lined the driveway.

One of the pickup trucks I'd seen before, that I'd thought belonged to the werewolves, came on the property a few minutes after.

I watched in amazement as a couple of men got out, their hands held out to the side in a non-threatening gesture.

May and another woman, Fanny, I remembered her name from introductions yesterday, held the hunter between them. He looked a little shellshocked and didn't put up much of a fight when they handed him off.

The werewolves took the hunter, shoved him in the truck, slammed the doors and drove away. As soon as the wolves were off the property, the majority of the armed people went back inside to hang their rifles. May came back over to me where I continued to crouch on the ground.

"You can get up, Erica. I didn't mean to for you to stay so literally."

"What just happened?" I blurted out as I scrambled to my feet.

"The werewolves are good for some things. None of us want a hunter around, and we protect our own. They see us as prey, so we have to present a large, aggressive presence whenever we encounter the wolves. Even when they're invited."

I stared, amazed.

"You stay with us as long as you want, Erica. You're one of us, and you belong here, and you're welcome any time.

I burst into tears one last time, and May wrapped me in a tight hug.

I stayed for two months before it was time to head home. My car was fixed, and I wanted to get across the country before the snow started flying, though I'd promised to return the following summer. Possibly for good. I hadn't decided yet. Right now, just knowing I wasn't alone was enough.

From the Author

I originally wrote this story for an anthology submission using cryptids to frame feelings of not belonging and being told that you don't exist. There was more to it than that, but it's slipping my mind right now. Anyway, this story made it to the second round but ultimately didn't fit into the collection. I'm glad it made it into this anthology, so now you get to read it.

This story is based on the Wyoming jackalope—clearly—and a story I read about a ranch of LGBTQ+ farmers making a place for themselves in a very conservative area. I really liked the news article and when this anthology call came up, I thought that, and the jackalope, would be a great way to express the themes of the story I wanted to tell.

About the Author

When Julie is not writing, she's often out riding horses or working sheep with her dogs. She is a full-time writer and lives in Colorado with a handful of cats, some sheep, a bunch of border collies, her Arabian endurance horses, and her Irish Sailor. She is the author of many Vampire and Ghost-Hunting Dog stories, the Tales of the Travelers series, and many other young adult books and adult books. Her passions include horses, writing about horses, dogs and writing about dogs. She writes fantasy, sci-fi, horror, and all related genres. She's a member of the Horror Writers Association, and the Science Fiction Writers of America. You can find out more at:
www.writerjacampbell.com

Bellhop Brew

by
W.O. Hemsath

Bellhop Brew

Thursday, June 21st
1928
12:04pm

According to the almanac, the sun would be at its highest latitude in just two minutes. Edith had to work fast. It was the last solstice Jimmy would be at the hotel before heading off to college in the fall. She wouldn't get another chance.

Edith smoothed the white apron over her black uniform dress and straightened her ruffled headband as the elevator came to rest at the fifth floor. After pulling back the accordion grate and exterior door, she pushed her housekeeping cart do wn the hallway toward the honeymoon suite as quickly as decorum would allow.

It would have been a lot easier to brew the potion at home, but this was the most powerful love potion magic could conjure. Nothing about it was easy. It required the hairs of two pure lovers and had to be brewed at the exact moment of the solstice in a place where they had loved. Which of course, with her luck, meant the lovers in the suite had decided to check out late today.

As long as they were actually newlyweds in love though, everything would be jake. The last thing she needed was to wind up with the hairs of two people having an affair.

Again.

Turns out a brew made with those hairs inspired eternal suspicion instead of eternal love. Thankfully, Jimmy hadn't been the first one to see her last winter solstice after she drank that doomed brew. But poor Helen. The maid had up and quit because she couldn't work alongside Edith without being in a constant state of paranoia.

The door to the honeymoon suite stood ajar, and in front of it, a swanky couple nuzzled against each other. The dame fidgeted with her wedding band as if she were still getting used to it. The man caressed her cheek, and she blushed. The way they gazed at each other said they'd rather be checking into the room instead of checking out. A wave of relief washed over Edith. They were definitely newlyweds. And definitely in love.

Even better, the gal had red hair peeking out from under her cloche hat, and the side of the fella's head showed dark brown hair below the brim of his fedora. Finding a hair from each of them would be much easier with such distinct colors.

A strong, keen voice from inside the room made Edith's heart race. "I'll be back to fetch the rest in a moment, but if you'll follow me this way, I'll see you down to the lobby."

Jimmy emerged with his luggage-laden cart, and the couple followed behind him toward the elevator. He looked as spiffy as ever in his pressed bellhop uniform, his cap slanting over his perfect chestnut hair. Edith touched her ruffled headband to make sure it was still on straight and flashed a smile at him as he passed.

He gave a polite nod in her direction, and that was it. That's all it ever was—pleasant smiles and polite nods. He probably didn't even know her name. For two years she'd been stuck on Jimmy, carrying a torch for him as she watched him work twice as hard and with three times the charisma of the other employees. She'd always been too much of a cancelled stamp to go up and introduce herself, but not today. Today she would approach him. Today everything would change.

Today he would fall in love with her.

She pushed her housekeeping cart into the suite, maneuvered around the remaining luggage, and closed the door. Throwing the pile of fresh linens onto the bed, she exposed a set of hidden cleaning supplies on the top of her cart. Lysol, furniture polish, vinegar—or so the bottles said. In reality they were carefully measured potion ingredients.

She pulled a pendant watch necklace from under the neckline of her dress. Five minutes after twelve. She had less than a minute to collect the hairs.

The woman's were easy to find. Multiple ginger strands littered the bed sheets. Edith plucked the longest one and laid it on top of the clean linens. Now to find the fella's.

She ransacked his side of the bed. Nothing on the pillow or under it. Nothing in the sheets. Or the blanket. Nothing on the nightstand either. She ran to the bathroom. More ginger hairs all over the counter, but nothing brown. Nothing that could be his.

It was now 12:06. The sun had reached its highest latitude. In sixty seconds, her window of opportunity would be gone.

Edith hurried back to the bed and rifled through the sheets again. Nothing. A cry of frustration forced its way out as she flung a hair-less pillow against the headboard. If only real magic was as easy as the stage performers made it seem. What she wouldn't give to simply pull the hair she needed from a magic hat.

A hat!

She ran to the pile of remaining luggage, and her heart swelled. There was a hatbox—a plain, boring, masculine-looking hatbox. She tore off the lid, pulled out a light gray fedora and searched the inside band. Bingo! She retrieved a short brown hair and dashed back to the cleaning cart where her mop bucket hung.

Flinging the bucket onto the bed, she poured the pre-measured contents of her bottles into it as fast as she could get their lids off. Spring water drawn by the blue moon's light. Crushed dried roses from a bride in white. The juice of three berries plucked with her own lips. All combined in the minute when the sun's journey tips. And last, the hairs of two lovers whose love was pure, lit with flame that passion may endure. She pulled out a match, lit the hairs on fire, and dropped them into the bucket.

Turn gold, she willed the liquid. *Turn gold.*

But the shriveled hairs just floated on the pale pink surface, the light stench of their burning still lingering in the air.

She checked her watch. 12:07. The minute of the solstice, when the sun's journey tipped from lengthening days to shortening them, was over. She'd missed the chance to make Jimmy fall in love with her.

Resigned to her failure, she sat on the edge of the bed. She still had to clean the whole suite, removing every trace of the lovers who had been there before, so the lovers who came next would feel like the room was made just for them. But she couldn't. The space felt massive, the task too daunting. She closed her eyes and flopped back onto the vast emptiness of the linen-strewn mattress.

"I never pegged you for a dewdropper," a voice said.

Edith sat up faster than a flapper's fringe could shimmy. Jimmy stood in the doorway, watching her rest on the bed she was supposed to be stripping down and remaking. Her cheeks burned hot, and she scrambled to her feet, smoothing out her apron as she stood.

He cocked an eyebrow. "The bed's so messy you have to mop it, huh?"

Edith followed his gaze to the bucket on the bed and wished she had a vanishing spell. There was no way she could make a clean sneak now. She grabbed the bucket of failed potion and concealed it behind her back. "I, um, was just checking to see if the ceiling needed to be wiped down."

He chuckled, and she winced. Wiping down the ceiling? What kind of excuse was that? Figures that the first time she said two words to him, she'd come out sounding like a dumb Dora.

He pulled his empty luggage cart into the suite and began loading up the remaining bags. "Don't worry. Your secret is safe with me. In fact, I might steal it. I usually sneak my naps in the maintenance closet, but I like your idea much better."

She couldn't believe it. He was smiling at her, dimpling at her even. He was talking to her like she wasn't some bug-eyed Betty. He was—

—noticing the open hat box she'd forgotten to close.

Her grip on the bucket handle tightened while she tried to feign surprise. "Oops. I must have knocked into it with my cleaning cart when I came in."

Jimmy shook his head as he lifted the hat back into its box and secured the lid. "Napping on the guest beds? Knocking over luggage? I sure hope you're a better dancer than you are a maid."

Edith cringed as he listed all the reasons he had to squeal on her. It looked like she would lose her chance at love and her job on the same day.

But he had been smiling. And he had said dancer. Why had he said dancer?

In the silence that hung after his comment, Jimmy's playful expression faded to concern. He held his hands up as an apology. "Not that I think you're a bad maid. Everyone takes breaks. And I've run my cart into things plenty of times."

Why did he look so nervous all of a sudden? She was the one who'd been caught, yet there he stood, taking off his uniform cap and running his fingers through his hair.

"I'm sorry. I wasn't trying to insult you, Edith."

She almost dropped the bucket.

"You know my name?" She hated how high-pitched her voice sounded, but she couldn't help it. Jimmy knew her name!

"Of course," he said, rotating his hat in his hands. "You're the choicest bit of calico at this hotel. Which is right intimidating and why it's taken me so long to do this."

"Do what?"

"Ask you to come dancing. That's what I was trying to do before." He continued mussing his hat in his hands. "So, will you? Will you come dancing with me tomorrow night?"

The sun could climb to the highest latitude it wanted—it would still never be as high as Edith's heart soared right then.

"I will," she said, forcing her voice to not squeak. "And I am. I am a much better dancer than I am a maid."

With a grin, Jimmy put his hat back on and straightened himself as tall as he could. "Then I'll meet you in the lobby tomorrow after work. And speaking of work"—he loaded the last suitcase onto his rack—"we both better get back to it."

She stood there, dumbfounded, as he and his dimples slipped back into the hallway with the luggage cart. Then, stifling a giggle, she carried the bucket to the bathroom, poured the pink-tinged liquid into the sink, and watched it swirl down the drain until it vanished.

Who needed magic anyway?

From the Author

In 2019, I saw a call for submissions for an anthology about a legendary fictitious hotel. The anthology wanted stories to showcase five minutes of the hotel's history—no more, no less. Writers could select any five minutes from the day the hotel's foundations were laid to its futuristic discovery by an archeology team from space. While *Bellhop Brew* didn't appear in that anthology, it was definitely inspired by it.

I tend to write contemporary or futuristic stories, so I wanted to challenge myself to write something historical. The roaring twenties seemed fun, and that's what I wanted this story to be—light and fun. Determined to do my historical piece justice, I dove into research, looking up facts such as which names would have been popular for that era, what slang would have been used, what styles of hats would have been worn, and whether things like Lysol even existed yet. I learned a lot during my research, the most important fact being that I prefer writing stories where I can invent whatever I want instead of having to be historically accurate.

As for the plot, planning a story down to the minute got me thinking about when a single specific minute—a pinprick on the calendar—might matter more than the minutes around it. And that's when the idea of a solstice came to mind. Because every story (in my opinion) is better with a little bit of magic or aliens, a witch brewing a potion at the solstice seemed a great five-minute premise to write about.

The biggest critique I've had on this story is that there isn't enough magic in it. But I believe there's more to magic than spells and potions. People can go their whole lives yearning for a romantic relationship but never finding anyone, so when you do find someone who makes your heart flutter and who feels the same when they're around you, it absolutely feels like magic. And I wanted to write a story to celebrate that truth: that there's a little magic in all of us simply because we're human.

I hope you enjoy *Bellhop Brew*. If you want to read any of my other stories, which have everything from androids to space pirates and unexpected fairy visitors to magic coffee shops, visit my author page on Amazon. You can also find other short works (and writing tips) published on my website: whitneyhemsath.wordpress.com or you can connect with me on Facebook (@AuthorWhitneyHemsath) or Twitter (@WhitneyHemsath).

Happy reading, and may your day be positively magical.

About the Author

W.O. Hemsath is the mother of four boys and considers herself blessed to be married to her best friend. She currently lives in Minnesota, but has also lived in Utah, Arizona, California, Argentina, and New Zealand. She loves traveling, cardio dance, watching movies with a bowl of ice cream, and really good back scratches. She has a degree in screenwriting, enjoys teaching at writing conferences, and generally writes stories with a touch of magic, mystery, or aliens. To see what she's written or what she's currently up to, find her online at any of the links below:

Twitter: @WhitneyHemsath
Facebook: @AuthorWhitneyHemsath
Website: whitneyhemsath.wordpress.com

What Price Evermore
by
D.H. Aire

What Price Evermore

*L*ife on the streets wasn't so bad. You wore baggy clothes outdoors to prevent rashes. A bandana was definitely a must. Heard once that was a gang thing, but these days, you needed it to cover your nose and mouth to keep breathing. It's not like I could afford a mask. My taped-up goggles protected my eyes from itching. Oh, when not scrounging for food and drinkable water, I whiled away hours at the library. Place was peaceful and quiet, not like the place I once thought of as home—if you discounted the old librarian.

My hair cropped to near baldness, thin and small as I was, I could crawl into the places where only rats thought to keep me company. That's how I kept myself safe at night, hiding in decrepit buildings on the outskirts of what once was called Baltimore. It didn't hurt that Momma gave me an old kitchen knife the day I turned twelve. Her way of showing she cared. Dad shoved me out the door without a word. I understood. Another baby on the way, and I had reached "my majority" as the government called it.

Truth be told, it was that old librarian who changed my life. I practically begged her to borrow that book, not knowing when next I might be back with winter coming. She stared at me when I demanded a library card.

"Whatever for?"

"So I can check out this book!"

She stared. "Check it out?"

"I know my rights. I read about it. People can borrow books, not just read them here."

"Your rights? Show me your arm."

I drew back. "Why?"

"You can't get a library card unless you were born in this country. I need to scan your ID."

I glanced at the half bare stacks. "Um."

"It's regulations, young man. You want a library card, come back tomorrow. By then, the reader should be working. I'll read your ID for the card then. Meanwhile, I'll keep the book at the desk."

Reluctantly, I handed it to her. "No tricks."

"My word as a librarian."

The next day I came back, worried about her reading my arm, but wanting that card. The old woman actually looked happy to see me. "Come over here, dear."

I pulled back my sleeve and she scanned my barcode. Consulting her screen, she glanced at my face, making a rude noise that sounded like, "Hurrumph." There was a flash.

A moment later she produced my library card and retrieved my book. "You sure you want this one?"

I nodded.

"It's due back in two weeks."

That's when the armored bus pulled up outside, more shadow than visible through the grimy windows. A dozen uniformed guards with machine guns established a perimeter.

Feeling betrayed, I turned to run.

"You've nothing to fear, Child. Everything will be all right."

A man in a rumpled suit came in with a breathing mask on, an armed guard at his side. The librarian pointed. "No guns allowed."

Lowering his mask, the guard smiled. "Not what the sign says."

"Out!"

"Boss?"

"Go."

I half hid behind the reference desk.

"So, this the kid with the library card?" he asked.

The woman nodded. "Yes. Read every other book."

He glanced at it. "*The Collected Works of Edgar Allan Poe.* Interesting. I'm named after him. I'm Edgar Gray—"

"With that Legal Aid place that I bet no one sets foot in." I glared at the librarian.

Scratching his chin. "Perhaps that billboard isn't such a good idea after all."

"I'm a satisfied client," the librarian replied.

"And who knew helping keep the libraries open would have such a benefit?"

I looked around as the old woman smiled.

He sighed. "You want to get your G.E.D.?"

"What's in it for you?" I demanded.

"For me? Perhaps saving my soul." When he saw my confusion, he said, "Believe or not, what's in it for me is the fact you have a library card."

I had no reason to trust him, nor the librarian, now dusting her desk.

"My friends and I are trying to change things."

"Change things? You think I owe the country babies or some other dumb shit?"

He frowned, glancing at the librarian. She nodded, realizing they had misjudged my gender. "No, what I'm offering you is a home and an education, in a specialized area, in exchange for something that will cost you nothing."

"What are you talking about?"

"Hmm, how do I explain this… I'm a lawyer."

"You want my kidney or something?"

"I'm not that kind of lawyer," he sighed. "The Legal Aid Foundation needs all the help we can get. So, Library Card Girl, I'm offering a safe place to live, food, and lots to learn."

"Because I wanted to take out a book?"

"Something like that."

"And if I don't like where you're taking me?"

"You leave." He offered me a mask. "But we could really use your help."

I stared at it. A home? Ha! At least that mask was worth a lot.

A man with a machine gun stood by the bus door as Mister Gray led me up the steps. The driver hastily closed the door behind me. He took off his mask and smiled. "Home, James."

"You know how crazy this is, Edgar?" the driver replied as I clutched the book and mask close.

He nodded. "Professor, we've the space, don't we?"

"That how you're going to explain this to Miss Weiss?"

"That's my problem," he replied, gesturing me to take a seat across the aisle.

I paused, counting six older teens: a couple of boys in ragged jackets, and girls who had doffed baggy coats, wearing short skirts and bikini tops. One girl had a black eye.

They stared warily back at me.

"You found them at libraries?" I asked.

"No, elsewhere," Mister Gray replied. "If you wouldn't mind holding that up?"

Frowning, I held up my library card.

They stared.

Mister Gray smiled, "You want one? See the librarian."

"A Government ID?" one of the boys grinned, rising from his seat.

The others followed. "I was in the moment you offered a safe place to stay!" one of the girls said, entering the aisle.

"Me, I'm in it for the food." A boy laughed, moving past with his own nice new mask. The kids traipsed out to get their library cards.

"IDs?"

Mr. Gray smiled. "Official photo IDs."

I startled awake as the armored bus came to a stop. Mister Gray rose. "Ladies and Gentlemen, the Legal Aid building is in the center of this very well defended block of the Inner Harbor… If you choose to turn down my offer, you might be able to join one of the gangs defending our neighborhood." I glanced back at my new friends, who looked as skeptical about that remark as I was. He put on his mask, gestured for us to do the same.

When I stepped out of the bus, I looked up and stared.

Cylindrical wind turbines spun, hanging off the sides of the old building. "Move along," the nearest guard said through his mask.

I went through the reinforced doors and into the glass enclosure, air blasting outward past me. I removed my mask and joined the others as we finished entering what once had been a landmark. I stared at banks of plants being cultivated by at least a half dozen people, then upwards. The old, faded posters I'd seen across town didn't do this former hotel and plaza justice—not even in the state it was now.

"Edgar!" a woman shouted from the far side of the atrium.

"Uh, excuse, me. Nathan, please, take our guests upstairs to our offices," Mister Gray said.

"Come on, we'll be taking the stairs. The elevators are not going to be repaired anytime soon."

I was not the only one who noticed that where security cameras had been, only wires remained. Nathan nodded to the guards stationed all around us. "We're not big on electronic surveillance."

"Meaning you never know who's watching," one of my new friends muttered.

"EDGAR!" We heard a woman shout distantly.

"Sounds like Mom is pissed."

"That she is—and that's Ms. Weiss to you lot," Nathan replied, leading us into the stairwell past another guard.

Orientation is a funny word for what our first few days were like. We first got a talk on, Mister Gray called it, "respect." "In other words, no one messes with you here."

Our watchdog Nathan added, "That means no, uh, personal exchanges will ever be required of you or tolerated."

Mister Gray coughed, "Exactly, thank you, Nathan. Which means you can never demand any personal, um, favors in turn… The penalty is exile. We run the Foundation on trust. This is your home now. Understood?"

I glanced at my fellow library card holders.

"You mean we've got to be celibate," one of the guys offered.

"It will prevent any misunderstandings," Mister Gray answered.

"You don't want us having babies?" one of the girls said.

"We don't need any complications and, well, the legal consequences for using contraceptives of any kind are severe, so abstinence is the best policy."

"What about our being expected to…provide for our country?" I asked.

"The infant mortality rate is quite high." Mister Gray sighed. "So, the government's position is somewhat understandable. But our abstinence policy meets government guidelines, too."

Miss Susan entered the room.

"One thing more," Mister Gray continued, pausing, seeing the Foundation's other founder. "You are our first, uh, class but tomorrow more people your age will begin arriving. I need you to serve as sort of ambassadors to the others—during what free time you'll have, and there won't be a lot of it. You've pretty much the run of the place, and they will too. See for yourself what I and the others have been telling you… This is truly your home now. But it comes at the cost of learning everything we offer to teach you… Later we'll put that learning to work." He gestured. "Now Nathan will take you to meet your proctor who will set you up on your online education program, so you can begin preparing for your G.E.D…"

I hung back a moment as Nathan led us from orientation. Miss Susan said simply, "Raven's come a calling."

Nathan led us across the floor to a large room with rows of folding tables. There were dozens of old computers with cords and wires yet to be hooked up, then we saw six that were set up, and our waiting folding chairs. "Take a seat. You are about to enter the wonderful world of Free Public Education."

We sat and stared at the image on the screen, the crest of the Presidential Seal. The contraption in front of it had letters on much of it and numbers predominately on the left side.

"You are tasked to complete a minimum of two hours a day toward your online education. I know you'll soon want to do a lot more—if for no other reason than to speed up the process," said our proctor, a bald guy who looked more like a bodyguard than teacher. "I wish you could, but as you'll see the Internet has its limits… Free Education is allotted only so much bandwidth."

We stared at him.

"I take it none of you know how to type."

"Type?" echoed around the room.

"That is a keyboard. You'll begin by pressing the enter key. Press 'A' to begin your education. 'B' to begin your orientation in how to operate your keyboard and program. I know you are more used to Tweeting on screens, but in my day, these now recycled computers changed our world. With our resources as limited as they are I congratulate you on your decision to proceed with your education. It's a HUGE deal."

The screen flashed. *'Would you like to learn to type? Hit enter to begin.'*

I sighed. Hit enter.

'Place your hands like this above the keys.'

"What is this?" one of the guys complained.

The bald guy crossed his arms, "Just play follow the leader…"

We did.

I can't say I was fast at typing, then again, the Internet was rather accommodating in its slowness. It took time for even my choice of multiple choice answers to appear after scrolling to the answer and hitting enter.

The times sentences and paragraphs were even demanded made me question the hours spent on learning to type, which our proctor said was a skill we might appreciate one day. Day two in front of the machines, we read about the laws of the land and our obligations as citizens to make America Great.

I had plenty of time to glance out the window where black sooty smoke from the coal-powered factories wafted past on the wind.

The quizzes on the benefits of Religious Liberty, and the right to follow our conscience with strict adherence, were just the beginning of our mandated educational program. It stressed obeying the rules of the Corporation which would hire us for the rest of our lives and vote on our behalf, while providing us a home and all our basic needs. *The penalty for disobedience is disenfranchisement and loss of the Corporation's housing and the many privileges granted to us as Corporate citizens.'*

I wasn't the only one laughing, which our proctor did not protest in the least.

If I had hoped to learn mathematics, no luck. Apparently, the curricula did not feel we needed it. I knew I'd not learn literature, as that class was being provided after dinner. Professor James taught it. The class was now more than just the six of us. The Public Education room was quickly filling up, as was the open area we slept in. Two full busloads came in the day after we did, more buses with heavily armed escort vehicles, the kind reserved for Corporate support, day after day thereafter.

"What have we gotten ourselves into?" Tommy whispered to me after our proctor had called "time." We saved our progress for the hundredth time that day as the next batch of raggedly dressed kids our age traipsed in for their, oh so popular, two hours of government education.

Shaking my head, I wasn't sure. Nathan called out, "Coming?"

"I've almost finished checking out the fourth floor," Tommy whispered.

I nodded. We'd agreed that first night to take Mister Gray at his word that we had the run of the place. "Good," I muttered.

The one thing our Free Education's curriculum seemed to want us to learn was history. It began with lots of warnings about not believing rumors of what the United States Declaration of Independence or the Constitution promised. We were shown line by line how only certain people were granted rights—just as the barons had in the Magna Carta almost a thousand years ago. The people with full rights were of the heritage and upbringing of the Founding Fathers. The Constitution had never been interpreted other than literally and could not be amended once it had been originally enacted.

After that day's session, Mister Gray met our class afterward and discussed with us the importance of answering the questions the way the Government wanted before Miss Susan, of all people, led a discussion of Mister Gray's diatribe on "Truth versus Truth."

"Lying is the government's stock in trade," Miss Susan said. "Women have the right to vote, not just be expected to be barefoot and pregnant."

"It's not what they claim in the Constitution."

"That point of the Constitution was amended," she replied.

"That's not what that program says—or even what we learned in elementary school."

"My point exactly," she answered.

"When working that program, you answer the way they want you to," Mister Gray added. "You do not question a word, while you are in that room. You'll get your G.E.D. without a problem... But once you've set foot out of this room, you are to question every word the bastards told you. Understood?"

"You saying they can hear us in there?" I asked.

"I am not saying they can't," he replied.

"We don't trust electronics, understood?" Miss Susan said. "Ever."

"Which is why you'll be learning penmanship later today," Mister Gray said.

We stared.

"Welcome to the world of law," he smiled.

"Virginia," said our newest professor, a rather thin, old, silver-haired woman in a frock, after she told us we could put our pens down. I rubbed my cramped hand. "Mister Gray has asked to see you."

"Don't call me that."

"Please don't call me that, Ma'am."

"Uh," I corrected, "please don't call me that, um, Ma'am."

She nodded. "What would you prefer, my dear?"

Scowling. "Just about anything else... Ma'am."

I went up three flights. Mister Gray stood looking out the window, down at the street outside the conference room. The room's closed door had a red panel on it, warning that the room was "connected."

"You wanted to see me?"

He sighed. "James has brought in the next batch of recruits."

"He's not the only one," I replied.

"You and your friends keeping count?"

"It passes the time."

Sighing again, he said, "My colleague Susan is less than pleased at my library card endeavor."

"We noticed… Why are you doing this anyway?"

"It's not like we don't have the space."

"In a week you've brought in over six hundred kids."

"You don't know the half of it… But you'll understand when the time's right. In the meantime, Susan's asked for something, which isn't exactly unreasonable."

"What's she want?" I frowned. Miss Weiss, as she preferred we call her, was not my favorite person around here.

"First, she feels you and your friends need a bath."

"No way."

"After that, she'd like you all to wear the clothes we've issued you… and to convince our other new students to do the same."

I scratched my chin, "We kinda like things just the way they are."

"You do know how powerful you all smell."

I shrugged.

"And you really don't need the kitchen knife."

I shook my head. "Each of us likes to keep our toys handy—mine's a family heirloom."

"Uh-huh." He sighed.

"You don't really expect me to tell the others they stink?"

He shook his head, "We have plenty of filtered rainwater for showers."

I glowered at him.

"And there's one thing more…"

I gave him a long look, wondering if I was about to have reason to use my kitchen knife, fearing, in that moment, everything about this was a lie.

"I need your help in judging if I've made a terrible mistake…"

I eased my fingers from inching any closer to the handle. "Meaning you haven't told Miss Weiss anything about it."

"I knew you were smart."

Nathan brought the latest recruits up, told them they could stake a claim to an area on the next floor. I quietly led three hoodied new recruits back down the stairs as the others were issued sleeping bags and clean clothes, which they all seemed loath to accept.

I took them to what had once been a large storage closet, the door often chained shut. Once I closed the door behind us, Mister Gray said, "Welcome."

One of them held up what should have been a library card, but instead was blank. "We're here…but library cards aren't our thing."

"I understand wanting to stay off the grid."

"But that didn't stop you from sending out your offer."

"I'm happy to help the three of you stay off the grid in exchange for the favor I need."

"Three of us? Who said there were just three of us?"

Eyes widening, I glanced away. "Uh, Mister Gray."

He frowned.

"Uh, are these guys who I think they are?"

Mister Gray merely tilted his head.

"Ahem, scruffy lady, who do you think we are?"

"Uh, 'Them.'"

"What do you think, guys? Isn't it great to be 'Them?'"

"You one of us?" the shortest asked me.

"Friend of the family," I replied, glancing at Mister Gray. "I think everyone here is."

The shortest lowered their hood, revealing short-cropped hair. "You a she?"

I nodded.

"You agree to the job then?" Mister Gray asked.

"Want to talk to Scruffy, here, in private first."

Mister Gray looked at me. "I'll wait in the hall."

I swallowed, nodded, and he left the room. The tallest turned to me as soon as the door was closed.

"Uh, I take it you've a few questions."

"He and this place what they claim it is?"

"You tell me. Whatever your name is?"

"You can call us Jay."

I blinked. "What's he hiring you for, Jay?"

A moment's pause. "Hacking."

I blinked. "Huh, well, then I guess he's on the up and up."

"You're one of the first got a library card?"

"Ah huh," I said, "and we've had the run of the place— mostly. You need a pass for the guards to allow you up to the lawyers and staff floor… But the basement, that's off-limits."

The Jays looked at each other.

"He hit on you?" one asked.

"What? No… He made it clear that no one messes with anyone or they're out on the street."

"You really believe that?"

I nodded. "He says this is home—and it's certainly a better one than I came from. Now answer one for me…just how many kids are getting library cards?"

"Let's just say that your friend there—he's the rather aggressive type. He's got volunteers working at libraries day and night—and kids lined up swearing, of all things, they'll study hard."

I lowered my head, knowing Mister Gray was crazy. "Someone's bound to notice."

"The Elders have been helping with that… But sooner or later someone's going to notice the electric bill."

"Who knew so many kids even knew what a library even was," the tallest said.

I opened the door and there Mister Gray waited.

The Jays pulled back their hoods and nodded to him.

Mister Gray gestured. "My scruffy friend here will be your liaison."

They made no reply as he led us down the stairs, all the way to the basement and past the doubly guarded door.

Lights came on as we entered a corridor, and the guards shut it behind us. "This place's secure, and you've the full suite, in every sense of the word."

"This level all ours?"

"No. As you'll see, we've hidden the suite, but this is the safest place we've got."

Mister Gray led us through swinging double doors. "Inventory was kept down here in the building's former life."

Banks of LED lights came on, and I gaped.

"This is our law library. This is where we do our legal research."

The three lowered their hoods. "You stole these books?"

"Couldn't let them all get burned as kindling now, could we?"

I swallowed.

"Right this way…" He led us deep into the maze of packed bookshelves until he came to one as nondescript as the others and pressed a decorative panel. There was a click and the shelf pulled back into the wall, revealing a hidden tunnel. "Right this way."

Moments later the tunnel opened out into a large open apartment with a tiled pool in the center. Beyond the couches and bunkbeds, I stared at the screens, which looked out through the haze of the city and out at Lake Michigan. Chairs with glowing wires hung from the ceiling facing them. Our hackers threw off their long coats and hopped half naked into the three center most chairs, which spun about, reorienting.

"How long did it take you to smuggle all this in?"

"With the help of some old friends—only a few years," he replied.

The images changed.

"System's secure," one said.

"Building's secure," the second said.

The shortest nodded. "Sending initiation signal."

"Mister Gray?" I whispered.

He smiled. "Now we're getting somewhere."

"What have you done?"

"Let's just say, my young friend, you were inspirational."

The recruitment drive lasted three more weeks, and the number of buses arriving kept coming well into the night. I took those with hoods and blank cards to the basement. I also found myself in charge of their food carts, which I had to shuttle down the stairs, making things difficult. That drew looks, but no one questioned until Miss Susan saw me. "Where exactly are you going with that cart, girl?"

Out of breath, Mister Gray arrived saving me from trying to lie. "Ah, Susan, there you are."

"Where's she going with that?"

"Uh, why don't we show you? And since you're here, Susan. Help us carry these downstairs."

She glowered.

Once at the base of the stairs, we transferred the trays to the waiting cart. "We feeding people in the Law Library, Edgar?"

"Not exactly."

I followed them with the carts.

We entered the tunnel as Miss Susan muttered, "Edgar, what have you done?"

"Let me show you."

She gaped entering the suite, staring beyond it at the ten figures hanging out in the computer control seats. A dozen more watching the monitors, as I found myself doing.

"How's it going?"

"Looks good, Mister Gray."

A countdown was proceeding on one screen. "Five more minutes to what, Edgar?"

"Well, Susan, voter registration for the coming election cycle ends soon," he grinned.

"What?" she cried.

About two hours later, I was upstairs looking out the window as a Corporate caravan arrived. One man exited and then entered the building. Mister Gray came out of the conference room behind me. "We've a guest. Would you be so kind as to bring the bastard up here?"

"Are you all right?"

His smile was pasty. "He's an old friend come a calling."

Miss Susan came down the hall. "This is all on you, Edgar."

"Raven's my problem, not yours…not any longer."

"Make that perfectly clear to him."

I hesitated as she went past and slammed the conference room door. "Mister Gray?"

"His name's John Raven… He's Susan's ex-husband. Go, bring him to me… And this is one time I'm glad you have that knife."

He was dressed in black, an environmental cloak over his shoulders worth more than my father would earn in his lifetime. "So, are you one of his registered voters?"

I swallowed. "Yessir."

He shook his head as we climbed the stairs past the guards stationed at every landing.

"And I thought he was just being frugal not wanting to maintain the old elevators."

"I like the exercise," Mister Gray called down from above, shooing away the guards.

"You would," Raven replied, glancing up at him.

Two more floors, and I saw the two men glare at each other. "Join me in my office?"

The man just stood there. "Edgar, what do you think your fool stunt's really accomplished?"

"Oh, you want to talk here?"

"Might as well… I don't think there's any place private we can really talk."

I took a step back.

Mister Gray gestured. "Stay." I took that to mean he wanted my knife close at hand.

"Edgar, you've embarrassed the government."

"I have?"

"Congress just closed all the libraries you'd fought to keep open. There will be no more photo IDs."

"Not unexpected. I guess I have to settle for five point two million registered voters aligned with Legal Aid."

"All this to get a voter block?"

"Well, we're now opening offices all across the country."

"You think those people out there are going to start coming to you and your friends for help?"

"You'll be surprised, John."

"Susan put you up to this?"

"No, she's pissed at me."

"It's on your head then." Raven smiled. It was feral, and in that moment I was prepared to stab him.

"That what really brought you here?"

"No, I've a message. Don't cross my Corporation like you have the government in your zeal to help people… Goodbye, Edgar."

Raven brushed past me, heading back down the stairs. I glanced back, seeing Edgar shaking with rage. He shook his head. I took my hand off my knife handle.

I hurried back up the stairs as soon as Raven drove off.

"Mister Gray?"

He was sitting outside his room, a book in hand. "Hey, Scruffy."

"What are you doing out here?"

He sighed. "Better light… Thought I'd read some Poe."

"You didn't return it."

"No point now," he sighed. "Think it's time we trade. Start wearing the new clothes."

"You'll burn these."

"Those shoes, too," he nodded. "You'll also bathe and wash that hair. Get them all to, for that matter. It'll be easier on the air filters—and all registered voters have a bathing requirement."

Shaking my head, I said, "You said trade."

He gestured. "You've my permission to take any book from my personal library."

"Your… They're all banned, aren't they?"

"That they are."

"Why? Why am I or any of us here?"

"Legal Aid can't help people without resources. Susan and I grew up with Trust Funds. We put every dime we had into the Foundation and this place to change things. But it wasn't going to be enough. Now we have a national voter base, and we're training future paralegals, who hate the system as much as we do."

Sighing, I nodded.

He rose, held out his right hand. "That too."

"What are you going to do with it?" I drew the knife from behind my back.

"Mount it on the conference room wall."

I handed it to him. "I want that back when you're ready for me to stab that Mister Raven in the back."

He frowned. "As to that, you're going to be rather busy studying. After all, we're going to need a lot of paralegals all too soon. So, leave dealing with Raven to me," he held up the book, "evermore."

From the Author

My story *What Price Evermore* may be too political in the current climate. It touches on book banning, voter rights in the United States, and as any good sci fi story is a cautionary satiric tale about the future...

This story has a very special place in my heart. I'd begun to believe it might never be published, so I'm very pleased that it appears as a doorway into *Particular Passages 3, West Wing*.

About the Author

D.H. Aire often writes a mix of genres. He is an Indy author and has published over 20 books. His love of history and archaeology first found expression in his writing of his epic fantasy/sci-fi Highmage's Plight and Hands of the Highmage Series. His twisted sense of humor comes alive in his Apocalypse Knot, Dare 2 Believe, and Knights Tower Series. He is also a member of SFWA.

Follow him on:
Twitter: @DHAire15
Facebook: Dare 2 Believe
Website: DHAire.net

Jane and Cooper Fight the Devil

by
Michael James

Jane and Cooper Fight the Devil

1. Aunt Lucy Comes to Visit

*J*ane didn't think there was anything more stressful than piano recitals, perhaps not counting the demons that routinely possessed her husband. The day needed to be flawless, or Tammie Benson, that minx, would smear her all over the neighborhood.

Cooper noticed her vacuuming the same spot and gave her a small peck. "Everything is going to be fine, Janey. The place looks immaculate."

She swallowed a sarcastic response. Cooper didn't know how cutthroat things got in the neighborhood when the stay-at-homes got together. They were vultures and hyenas, with nary a gentle soul in the bunch. They'd pick her bones clean and cackle over the corpse.

"It's our first recital, and it took a lot of convincing before they agreed to have it here. This could be a big win for us. I might get Parents Council."

"I know, babe." He stopped and gripped his sides.

"What's wrong?"

"Nothing." He tried to smile, but it was a nervous thing. "My stomach feels off. Maybe I ate something."

"Okay." She eyed him suspiciously. "If anything's wrong, you need to tell me."

"Maybe I'll get a drink. A glass of water might help."

"Sure." She followed him into the kitchen. As soon as they were through the doors, he groaned and bent over to clutch at his sides.

"Coop?"

He looked up and the whites of his eyes had turned a sickly, jaundiced yellow. Small, pockmarked scars crisscrossed his face. She could smell sour candy.

"Oh, come on." Jane sighed and rubbed her temples.

"*Lleh ni tor uoy ees lliw I.*" His voice was chewed rocks and several octaves lower than normal. The lights dimmed.

"Not today. Please, not today."

The thing in her husband hissed at her. "I am legion. I am eternal. I am the Devil."

"Oh, bullshit. You guys always say that. Who is it this time?"

It looked perplexed. "Um. Satan?"

She supposed the demon was used to a more expressive reaction, but after a few dozen of these, she'd gone numb.

The doorbell rang. *Crackers.* She raised her finger at the demon in her husband. "Don't move, understand? I can't deal with this right now."

The demon cackled. "I will feast on your bones. I will eat your skin. I will—"

"Zip it." She poked her head out of the kitchen and yelled for her daughter. "Chloe! Get down here!"

The doorbell rang again. *Crap, crap, crackers and crap.*

"Seriously," she repeated to the demon. "Don't move. Stay in the kitchen and be creepy or whatever."

The demon obliged by levitating and making the cupboard doors open.

"Perfect. You do you. My daughter will be down in a sec. I have to get the door."

She left the startled demon in the kitchen and adjusted her hair. Nothing could interrupt this recital. Nothing.

2. Deviled Eggs

"Tammie, hi. How wonderful to see you." Jane put on her biggest grin and leaned in for a fake air peck.

"Jane, thank you so much for having me," Tammie gushed. Jane could practically smell the insincerity. More parents arrived with their kids. Behind Jane, Chloe clomped down the stairs as only an irritated teenager could.

"What do you want?"

"Can you help your dad in the kitchen? He's on the phone with Aunt Lucy." That was their code word for 'your dad is possessed again'.

Chloe groaned. "It's Josh's turn. I've done the last two."

"Ha, ha," Jane said between clenched teeth. "Just do it honey."

Chloe stomped into the kitchen, slamming the door behind her.

"I'm so impressed you fit us all in." Tammie said. "Especially considering how modest your house is." She flicked a spot of dust from Jane's shoulder.

"Thanks Tammie. Too bad your husband couldn't make it. He seems to spend more and more time away from the family. Oh, hey Jackie!" She waved at another mom and left Tammie gasping. Jane one, Tammie Benson zero. It was on.

She ushered everyone in and then ran to the kitchen see how Chloe was making out.

3. A Bucket Full of Solutions

Chloe had led Cooper down to the basement and tied him up in the possession chair. Soft velvet covered the leather straps so they wouldn't chafe Cooper's wrists, and the chair itself was plush and comfortable. It was as gentle as Jane could make it.

Demon-Coop was in full blown possession mode. The movies were wrong about what real possession looked like. It wasn't scary, it was simply weird. His pupils were bifurcated and slithered like snakes. His hair had grown about six inches and come together to form a hand that gave her the finger. Hair poured from beneath his shirt.

Chloe was following the steps, reading passages from the bible, while sprinkling him with holy water. She was weeping a little.

"What's wrong, honey?" She gave Chloe a hug while Demon-Cooper cackled at them.

"Ah, he told me about Grandpa. I hate that one." Chloe sniffled and wiped her nose.

"Oh sweetie, I'm sorry." One of the demon's preferred torments was to remind them that Cooper's deceased father was in hell, his mouth being used as a semen repository for lesser imps and ghouls. "I know you loved Gampy, but I've told you, he was a shrew of a man, and he deserves this. Did I tell you about the time he called the police on two little Asian kids selling lemonade? He was a racist monster."

"Yeah, I know." Chloe threw a lazy sprinkle of holy water that sizzled when it hit Cooper. "It's hard to hear that one of your relatives is in eternal torment."

"Chloe, you head upstairs, okay? Keep the guests watered and fed. I'll take over." She kissed her daughter's forehead. These little events were stressful, and she tried to limit their exposure.

"Thanks, Mom. I love you, Dad."

The demon responded using the voice of Michael Stipe from the alternative rock-quartet R.E.M. "Your mom hates you and thinks you're a slut. She hopes you die of chlamydia." It flickered the lights and made noises come out of the walls.

"Yeah, okay. Good luck." With a final sniff, Chloe went back upstairs. Jane turned back to the demon.

"It's just you and me now, asshole." She cracked her knuckles. "You've come at a real bad time, and I don't have the patience to let this run its course."

"Jane." The demon now adopted the voice of her uncle, who had died a few years back. "You're a miserable shrew of a wife. You can't even satisfy your husband. I have access to his every thought; he's humping everyone in the neighborhood, including Tammie Benson, and he thinks your deviled eggs taste like beaver piss."

Jane let the demon rattle on. Rain barrels filled with holy water lined the sides of the unfinished basement. Normally she'd only apply sprinkles at a time, but she always wondered how the demon would react to more than a drop. Maybe today was the day to find out.

She pulled the top off one, dipped a cup into the water, and threw it on the demon. The stench of brimstone filled the air and the water sizzled on the demon's skin.

"Aggg, what the hell?" The demon dropped its guard for a moment. "Don't do that. You're only supposed to sprinkle on the holy water. Drops."

"I think I'm going to skip right to a soaking." Jane filled a bucket. The demon licked its lips.

"We can make a deal," it said. "I can make Cooper want to watch Curse of Oak Island with you. I know you've always wanted that. It's easy."

"Get out of him right now." Jane said, brandishing the bucket. The demon swallowed and stuck its chin out.

"Do your worst."

Jane threw the bucket of holy water on it.

4. The HellScream

The demon screamed. It was louder than anything Jane had ever heard, and she dropped to her knees, clutching her ears. Cooper's mouth opened wider and wider and soon there was nothing left of his face, only the blackness of his mouth and the killing pressure of the scream.

It lasted forever and broke time. Random, torturous images flooded her mind. Pulling the wings off a hummingbird. A paper cut between her fingers. A flood of people asking, 'how's it hanging'. Waiting in line at the grocery store, but the person in front didn't use the divider.

The images came rapid fire, and all she could do was curl into herself and hope it would end, but they didn't end, they kept coming and coming and if she had a knife, she would jam it into her ears to stop the sound and the images and *oh crackers*, the images still wouldn't stop and now she was assaulted with the sights of dead owls falling from a darkened sky, and her sister's fingernails being pulled out by a grinning man with no eyes, and someone holding the door open for her but she was like twenty feet away so had to half-run and—

It ended.

Her hair dripped with sweat. The scream must have lasted days. But no, she checked her watch, and it had only been a minute. She smoothed her hair back with hands that shook so badly she almost couldn't get them to function.

Cooper slumped forward, seemingly unconscious, smoke rising from his body. She put her hand under his chin and lifted his head up to check if the demon was still there. Cooper glared at her.

"Your mother sucks a universe of cocks."

Crackers. No way to be sure. Cooper and her mom did not get along, and she'd heard him say worse after a single glass of wine. Regardless, she couldn't spend any more time on this. She needed to get back upstairs for Josh. She hoped the bucket of holy water had unsettled the demon enough that she could loosen the restraints, and she unclipped them from his wrists.

"Cooper, if you're in there, Josh will go on in about five minutes. I love you."

The demon didn't say anything. Jane took a breath and went upstairs.

The scene in the living room was a little chaotic. Her guests were in similar states of unrest, having also heard the HellScream. Tammie Benson, that vulture, leaned against the wall, picking at her nails.

"I adore your musical choices, Jane. What was that last song, Bjork? How quaint."

"If everyone could listen to me for a moment," Jane raised her voice to be heard over the crying. "I'm sorry for the disruption. What you experienced was a HellScream. Some of you will experience strange side effects."

Crying parents clambered forward, reaching out with pleading hands, and spoke over top of each other.

"I can smell time. It smells like cut grass and loneliness."

"Everyone looks like Yule Brenner."

"All my memories have been replaced by the trailer for the movie 'Mannequin' starring Andrew McCarthy."

Jane held up her hands for quiet. "It's going to be okay. The longer I keep talking, the more it will fade, and soon we can get on with the recital. That said, some of you, every single year for the rest of your life at this exact moment, will get your period, regardless of your biological sex or menopausal state. Sorry about that."

She continued to blather while the guests emerged from their fugues, disoriented. To close this off, she brought out the big guns.

"Please turn your attention to the deviled eggs. I said I wasn't going to tell you what I put in them, but the secret ingredient is *soy sauce*. A couple drops into the yolks." The crowd gasped their approval and rushed to the appetizer trays, applauding her daring culinary choices. Tammie Benson, that jackal, scowled. Crisis averted. In moments, everything was back to normal.

"Let's get this recital started," she said, and clapped her hands together.

5. Recitals and Demons and Tammie Benson, Oh My

The recital started with no further complications. The first two kids performed very well, although Tammie Benson's kid screwed up the fourth stanza, playing the piece a bit too *staccato* when the part called for *legato*. Jane applauded anyway, because the kids shouldn't be held accountable for the sins of their horrible mothers, and besides, the staccato interpretation had been inspired.

Finally, it was Josh's turn. Jane couldn't stop smiling. She was so proud of her little man. The way he sat at the piano bench, his back straight, the seriousness of the moment. She wished Cooper could be here.

"Did I miss anything?"

Cooper appeared at her shoulder. He was pale and his clothes were damp, but it was him.

"You're just in time," she whispered. "Are you okay?"

"I'm fine. I wasn't about to let a shitty demon make me miss this moment." He took her hand and squeezed. She could have burst.

Josh had selected a tricky piece, *Sonata in A Minor L.93* by Domenico Scarlatti. Jane held her breath as Josh put fingers to keys and played. Even Tammie Benson seemed impressed and nodded her approval. Jane put her head on Cooper's shoulder, and he kissed her.

"I love you, Coop."

"I love you too, Janey. Sorry I got sick there."

"Not even a thing, babe. We're in this together. Hey, just curious, do you want to watch Curse of Oak Island with me tonight?"

"What?" He frowned at her.

"Nothing. Let's watch."

From the Author

"Jane and Cooper Fight the Devil" was loosely based on my own experiences, not with demonic possession, but with piano recitals. I hate piano recitals so much. I was thinking about what could possibly make them worse and realized that one of your parents getting possessed might do the trick. The story kind of grew from there.

About the Author

Michael James is the author of the series The Hotel at the End of Time. His work has been featured in *Cossmass Infinities* and several anthologies including *Executive Dread* by Jolly Horror Press and *Horror Library Volume 7* by Dark Moon Books. You can connect with him on Twitter @MikeJamesAuthor or keep up to date at:
https://www.michaeljamesauthor.com/

A Mirror in the Dark

by
C.J. Dotson

A Mirror in the Dark

An hour of daylight. That's how long it took for the last of the haunts to dissipate now. At first it had been dawn. Every year, though, more came. As their numbers swelled, their strength grew. The sky burned pink, and Beatha Itheanam swung her silver sword. The sickly glowing forms hung ragged around her. They stared unblinking from pit-like eyes. Gaping mouths, loose and wide, howled.

Her arms burned. The haunts ate more lives every night, and Gairegath's edge alone bit into them. With any blade but the one that foul faerie had given her so many years ago, it was like striking at smoke. The haunts drifted, insubstantial, through any barrier set against them. Their grasping fingers reached through every shield she'd borne. She wore ineffective armor, just for show. The only way to stay safe, the only way to keep breathing, was to fight. All night. Every night. Without a pause, without a break. Alone.

To stop moving would be to die.

At an hour past sunrise the haunts, still wailing their hollow cries, sank down into the earth. One swiped at her as it descended, cold grasp passing her blade and raking through her right leg. Beatha stifled her cry. She never let them hear her scream.

She let out a grunt instead, quickly muffled, and cut at the haunt's wrist. The hand evaporated as the haunt shrieked and finished falling below the ground once more, there to spend the daylight hours waiting its time to return. Half an instant later, the ringing began. As soon as she heard the first bell tone, Beatha straightened her shoulders and brushed a just-graying curl of hair back from her sweaty forehead, then fixed the brave smile on her face. A bare moment after that the shutters and doors on the houses all around her began to open.

Light flashed across her eyes, and she blinked, dazzled for an instant but never losing her smile.

You're getting good at that, a hated voice whispered. Beatha clenched her teeth without shifting her expression and tried to ignore it. The whisperer fell silent just long enough for her to believe that the one barbed comment was all there'd be today. Then the voice added, *All these mirrors all over Opferstadt City, all because some fellow thought that Gairegath shining like a mirror in the dark nights is what makes it work on the haunts. Tsk. They think it keeps them safe, the poor things...*

When the city opened up every morning, the mirrors swung and caught the rising sunlight, throwing wildly dancing beams all over.

Beginning the daily walk back to her mansion she raised her left arm to wave broadly as the cheering began. She rested her dominant hand on the hilt of her sword, as much because it looked right to the city folk as because her arm was weary from fighting.

In spite of the show Beatha put on, her body was heavy with fatigue. Aches and irritation pricked at her, and she let herself be goaded into answering the voice, even knowing that answering it would embolden it for days, perhaps as much as a week. Long ago having perfected the art of speaking to it without moving her lips, she said, "I draw the haunts the way a magnet draws iron. They seek *me*. It's a tragedy if they drift into other places while I'm busy trying to kill them, but..." She trailed away with a sigh. There was no answer from the whispers. "I start every night in the largest park within the city. You know that."

Keeping the haunts away from others made it easier. But she couldn't stay in the parks all night. She had to keep moving.

Every night some haunts found themselves within houses. After sundown some poor fool always died. The victims' neighbors tended to tell themselves that the haunts only got through to those who deserved it. The fortunate living shrugged, or sneered, and moved on. They didn't deserve protecting.

And yet the haunts aren't exact. When they find someone else instead... A life is a life.

"*I* didn't make them like that," Beatha reminded the voice. "And I've never killed anyone."

You killed me.

"You deserved it. And I've paid the price for it. You haven't left me alone since."

You should have known that faeries don't make the same kind of haunts that humans do.

When the fae died, their haunts were not mindless, hungry things. Human eyes lacked the power to perceive them, but they had ways of making themselves known if they had a will to. This one certainly did.

And you haven't paid the half of it, the voice added. *Someday I'm going to find a way to fix that.*

"You've already done worse than—"

A shrill whistle pierced through the bells' melodic notes, interrupting the surreptitious conversation, and for once Beatha didn't jump at the sound. The steam engines had arrived in Opferstadt only a few months before, preceded by the laborers laying their tracks. If Beatha had known then what a racket the new conveyance would cause every day, she would have let the haunts get those workers in the night.

She didn't find the notion of that kind of long travel as novel as the city folk did.

"People everywhere are the same," she muttered with a savagery that didn't reach her face. Beatha was a long-time master of maintaining the proper image. Head high, shoulders back, a smile that was victorious but also a little—only a little— tired. If she didn't have just the right amount of strain showing, after all, the people might think that what she did was easy. Easy wasn't heroic. "They'll turn on each other in a moment even if all they get from it is the chance to *imagine* that they're safe."

The faerie's voice went silent for a long moment, and Beatha focused on giving the people their daily show and getting home. Gracious nods. Confident waves. Firm stride.

Well, better here than in Eiferdorf, the fae mused at last, and Beatha suppressed a shudder at the memory her words conjured. *I bet you'll never forget those cages, no matter* how *long you live.*

Even distracted by the voice of the faerie whispering in her ears, Beatha kept up her charade for the city people without a break or misstep, right up until she stepped off the cobbled street and onto the walk. Beatha turned so her back was to the wall around her property. Facing out towards the city, she swept a bow to the onlookers still cheering and applauding. Her neighbors. Her audience. She straightened, and in a smooth motion unsheathed Gairegath. There was enough distance between her and the folks now, and their attention was on her blade—they couldn't tell the difference when her smile turned to a grimace. She hefted the sword towards them in a salute. It caught a beam of sunlight and cast it back out in a multi-rayed burst. In the bright day, Gairegath blinded.

Very dramatic, the voice laughed. *Right out of a children's picture book.*

Dropping the salute, Beatha turned and strode through the gate. As soon as it clanged shut behind her, she let her smile fall and sheathed the sword again. The wall surrounding her home was thick and tall, the trees just within it taller still, giving her privacy from even the most curious onlooker. Beatha let her shoulders slump. Her body ached, and she could feel the years she'd lost. More than usual. No, it had not been a good night even before the long-dead faerie had begun pestering her, but at least it was summertime and the darkness was short-lived.

The front door of the manor closed behind her, cutting off the sound of the bells and almost quieting the next whistle blast. Beatha leaned back against the wood for one moment, her head tilted back, eyes closed, and then she stripped off her gloves.

Now this doesn't look like a child's idea of a hero, the faerie's voice mocked, *this looks like someone who isn't sure why she keeps up all the charades.*

Beatha never should have stopped ignoring that voice, so she maintained her silence now. She flexed her cold fingers. Summer or not, nothing kept the warmth in when she'd been touched by too many haunts. A hot bath would soothe the aches and the chill even if it would do nothing for the lost years.

Maybe you ought to...who's that? Footsteps approached in the hall.

Beatha stood up straight and opened her eyes, looking to the side where she expected to see Mrs. Hoffman awaiting her orders.

Instead, it was a new woman, her face only vaguely familiar, at least as old as Mrs. Hoffman but plumper and with kindlier eyes. She wore a cook's cap and apron, and, on her hands, she balanced a tray with a teapot and a mug.

"Who're you?" Beatha asked. "And where's my housekeeper?"

"Missus Hoffman sent a runner t'say she's gonna be late again, with that business with her boy," the woman responded. Beatha hadn't heard that particular accent in a good sixty years at least, not since she'd stayed for a time in Sudschrei Bezirk— a long way farther south than Opferstadt. "I'm Estra Weber, best cook south of the Silberbache." Mrs. Weber shifted her grip so that she held the tray one-handed, lifting the mug with the other and passing it over to Beatha.

"I haven't had lemon black tea made this way in years," Beatha exclaimed after the first sip. She shut her eyes and took a longer drink, relishing both the heat spreading through her middle and the fae's temporary silence. "It's my favorite."

Mrs. Weber's eyes wreathed in smile lines as she beamed and answered, "A good cook can tell exactly what sort of tea a person needs."

There was no response from the fae, who seemed to have sunk into a sulk.

While Beatha drank the tea, the cook kept up a cheerful and generally trivial running commentary. Shortly Beatha had let the flavor take her through increasingly distant memories and tuned the other woman out enough that she didn't take much note when Mrs. Weber said, "And I can help with whatever you need while Missus Hoffman is out, of course. I used to polish my share of silverware way back when I was just a scullery maid, an' I'm no expert in chain mail an' all them leather bits an' bobs, but I'm sure polishing them up can't be too difficult. And a sword," she gestured towards Gairegath, "isn't much different than a knife, after all, is it, an' I keep *my* knives gleaming clean."

"Thank you *very* much, Missus Weber, but Lady Itheanam doesn't let anybody else touch her sword. That *should* have been explained to you when you were hired on," Mrs. Hoffman's voice said firmly, and the housekeeper herself came bustling into the front hall from the direction of the servants' entrance. Though she was technically late to begin her day of work at the manor, she was perfectly timely in preventing Mrs. Weber from actually *touching* Gairegath.

Beatha's attention snapped back to the present, and she took a half step away from the cook. "Quite right," she said, handing the empty mug back to the cook with a forced smile.

Mrs. Hoffman shooed the cook back in the direction of the kitchen, then turned to Beatha with an anxious expression. "I'm sorry I was late, Lady Itheanam," she began, "it was—"

"Your son, I know. Don't be sorry," Beatha said briskly.

I would think you'd have more sympathy for Missus Hoffman, the faerie's voice returned then, sharp and malicious.

Beatha covered a grimace by ducking her head as if to focus as she unfastened her bracers and her leather neck guard collar. She removed her belt, then pulled the chain mail shirt off right there in the front hall. Mrs. Hoffman had long ago grown beyond most of her discomfort at the impropriety—she didn't even glance askance at Beatha's choice of wearing trousers rather than a fine dress—and her cheeks barely reddened in a blush as she held out her arms. Beatha piled the lot of it upon her, and Mrs. Hoffman bustled off again to have it all cleaned and checked for any needful mending. Beatha herself took her sword to the small room under the servants' staircase, near the entrance to the kitchen, setting it neatly on its rack within.

I liked it better before, in your first few cities, when you slept with the sword right under your mattress, the voice laughed. *There's never been a more obvious hiding place.*

The hallway was empty, no one heard Beatha as she allowed defensiveness to break her own resolve to ignore the fae. "No one could have gotten to it without waking me."

The problem with sleeping with the sword was that it had triggered the nightmares. They'd never fully dissipated, but she'd discovered that keeping the sword securely locked away somewhere other than her bedchamber had eased them enough that she could still sleep. She closed and locked the door, leaving Gairegath in the dark until she'd need it again.

Her burden laid down for now, Beatha was free at last to make her way to the tub and after that to her bedchamber. A canopied bed and thick curtains on the window let her sleep as deeply as she used to when she could still rest in the night. Or they would have done, if not for the nagging whispers of the long-dead fae, and for nightmares.

Hours later Beatha gave up on her fitful slumber.

You talk in your sleep, you know, the voice said in tones of syrupy solicitation. *You say names, like—*

"Shut your mouth."

I don't even have *a mouth.*

Beatha ignored the voice, took a moment to find her composure again. The carefully selected servants didn't need to think that she was always brave smiles like the rest of the city did, but nevertheless they could not be allowed to see her with tears wetting her cheeks. Always layers, the next only slightly less untrue than the last.

When she was ready, Beatha threw back the curtains on her canopied bed and stood, stretching slowly before she reached for fresh clothes. She selected her garments with exacting care herself, rather than let servants do it. Presentation. One of the first things she'd learned in this game was that if she wanted the wealthy and powerful folks who ran cities to believe that she was a hero, then she had to look the part. Her copper curls had iron streaks through them, and though it had taken nearly a hundred years, her body didn't look like a young woman's anymore. They would be hard to disguise, short of shearing her hair close to her skull, but there were ways to keep her figure at least looking like that of a woman in her early forties for a few more decades. To that end, Beatha put up with a little bit of corseting now, something she'd never done in decades past.

Getting vain, aren't you? the dead faerie's voice taunted, but this barb missed the mark so widely that it didn't sting at all.

Corset, tunic, trousers, belt round the middle, boots up to the mid-calf and snugly laced. Quick glance in the hanging glass to make sure she looked the part. And that was just to go and have dinner in her own manor, surrounded by only her own servants.

Beatha settled herself at the grand table, put a grape in her mouth. She couldn't quite find the pleasure in the meal that she used to. Dissatisfaction, that was it.

Building it all up, playing the new hero in town, come to save them from their sudden troubles, that was always easier…courting the nobility, pretending not to care about them, enticing them to extend themselves again and again, that was always more fun. But this part was mere maintenance. There was nothing left to *gain*.

She picked up a crystal goblet and swirled the wine once, inhaling the aroma before taking a sip.

The town hall bells rang the four o'clock hour at almost the same moment that the steam engine's whistle sounded two short, sharp blasts to warn of its imminent departure. Beatha hated the damn thing. Though it might make it easier to go when the time came.

Look at you, scowling at your fine supper and shuffling your feet, the dead faerie's voice was scornful. *It's painful to watch.*

Beatha's gaze moved to the door that led into her office, and even as she sliced into her ham, she pictured herself instead standing at her desk, bending over the unrolled map she'd laid out there, deciding where to go next.

"I should think you wouldn't mind," Beatha murmured between bites. "If you insist on following me around, I imagine you must prefer it when I spend a few weeks camping in the woods." Her eyes unfocused and she spent the next moment ignoring the fae, picturing herself deep in the trees, enjoying a few weeks of solitude before the haunts caught back up to her.

Lately it was getting harder to find safe places for that. The decades passed, and people whittled away at the forests and wild spaces, leaving her with less and less to go on in between cities.

In an uncanny echo of her own thoughts, the fae's voice whispered, *Your people destroy more of the wild places all the time. Soon the woods will be as dead as I am.*

It wasn't often they agreed, and it didn't change anything between them. The fae had still cursed Beatha, Beatha had still murdered the fae. A moment of accord fixed nothing.

Beatha drained the last of her wine, putting aside worries and distractions both. The day was growing late.

Sometimes the wailing seemed to have words in it. Sometimes the cries sounded like accusation. If she let herself listen to the howls too closely… But no. No, it only *sounded* that way. It wasn't real.

Are you slowing down? the faerie's voice mocked. *Does Gairegath grow heavy, or are you growing old at last? Tired so early in the evening, Beatha Itheanam?*

From within a house nearby, screams. She hated the sound, wished that the haunts would kill as silently as they moved. But their victims always screamed. Some nights the screams drew witnesses, peering from their false safety. This night, however, was barely half over. No one even dared to peek out from between the shutters. Beatha wouldn't have to risk dropping her guard to storm into the home. She could stay where she was. Right in the middle of the wide lane. Not too close to walls. To the dangerous, false sense of security they gave.

The screaming cut off sharply.

You've lived too long. You're losing touch.

Beatha ignored the faerie and the abrupt silence both. She lunged, swept Gairegath in an arc. Drove the haunts a little further back. Spun, slashed behind her. Her breath came hard. Arms and shoulders burned. An ache settled into her back and her knees. They pressed close tonight. Reaching, grasping. The cries rose, overwhelming nighttime noises. When had she last heard crickets, or an owl call? Another life. Her nights were full of moans and bellows. Hollow, burning eyes. Gaping mouths. And always the hands. Swiping, stretching, fingers curling.

"Augh!" Cold pain tore down her back. She spun, sword flashing clumsily. Reflecting the haunt as it struck. Not sickly pale, though, not pit-eyes and loose jaw groaning. Gairegath reflected what had been. Beatha never looked if she could help it. Not since she'd seen a pair of terribly familiar eyes mirrored on the blade. Gairegath bit into the haunt. Took it high, near its neck. It had been a little one, no taller than her hips. Extra careful never to look at those.

Just keep swinging.

Dodging.

Swiping.

Turning, turning, turning.

Her throat was raw. White-knuckled grip on the hilt, fingers starting to hurt. Another frozen piercing through her calf. Strike low. Swing high. Turn. A scream right in her ear. A blow with the blade. Barely protecting her neck. Leather collar would do no good. All for show. Only Gairegath could protect her. Turn. Sweep the blade. Try to breathe slow. Don't check the sky. Not light yet. Tune out the faerie's whispers. No distractions. Strike. Turn. Slash. Turn. Sidestep. Stab. Duck. Turn.

Never stop moving.

When the bells finally rang the hour past dawn, the last of the remaining haunts were a breath slower to fall silent and sink away.

Beatha forced her head high, spine straight, stiff smile. It was all to do again, every morning the same as the last. And as before, it wasn't until Beatha was in the dimly lit front hallway of her own manor that she allowed herself to relax. She closed her eyes for a long moment, her breath shuddering in and out.

You poor, miserable fool, the voice said, and Beatha thought that she heard almost genuine sympathy.

That settled it. It really was time to get going. Even the dead fae knew that the haunts were getting too thick in Opferstadt. She'd spent too long here. It was a mistake she shouldn't have made; she knew the rule. To stop moving would be to die. Another shaky indrawn breath brought with it the smell of lemon black tea, and she opened her eyes.

"I didn't hear you come up," Beatha said to Mrs. Weber. She took the mug the cook offered.

"Well, my dear, I'm not surprised. Those bells every morning do make a racket, not to mention—" A steam engine whistle interrupted her, and though she jumped she also chuckled. "—*that*. They did make the things loud, didn't they?"

Beatha didn't answer, drinking the tea down fast in spite of how it burned the inside of her mouth. Mrs. Weber didn't seem to expect an answer, though, for she never lost her smile and simply lifted the teapot from the tray she balanced on one palm. Beatha let her refill her mug, asking, "Mrs. Hoffman is running late again?"

"Oh, the poor dear, her boy is doing worse yet, I fear," Mrs. Weber answered, the smile slipping into a sad frown. "She sent a runner 'round again, but this time to say she might not be here at all today." The cook clucked and shook her head, then sighed. "Well, it'll mean a delay for lunch, but I'll just have to take care of your gear for you, won't I?"

"I'm sure I have a footman or a stable-boy who can—"

"Nonsense, nonsense! I wouldn't want to put anyone out."

The woman clearly wanted to be helpful. Maybe she even got a bit of a thrill out of handling the famous hero Beatha Itheanam's armor. From the sparkle in the cook's eye as Beatha began removing her leather and mail, she thought that must be it. In fact, the woman went so far as to try to help Beatha out of her mail shirt, something that Mrs. Hoffman had *never* done. She waved the cook off and soon enough she was left in plain clothes holding only Gairegath, which she took to lock away personally, just as she always did.

Weariness dragging her steps, Beatha sought out her rest at last. But once she was in bed, she found herself stiff and wound up. Between buzzing agitation and the faerie's constant recriminations, sleep was long in coming.

"Alright," Beatha panted, falling backwards, "get on out."

The prostitute was slow to push himself up off of her bed, reaching out with one hand to try to stroke her side.

How do you know you've spent too long in one place? the faerie mocked. Beatha gave the man in her bed a hard stare that finally sent him moving at a respectable pace.

Once she was sure he was really getting dressed she threw an arm over her eyes and sighed deeply. Sex wasn't the distraction it had once been, especially with that damn fae murmuring deprecations in her ear the whole time. And, worse, the man was beginning to try to linger afterwards.

Even if she'd wanted him to, the day was nearly over. In the distance the last steam whistle of the evening signaled the final train out before nightfall. A minute or so later she heard the door open, then shut softly, and she stood and crossed to her washbasin. There was time to clean herself up before dressing and donning the armor that the cook had delivered to her door just after she'd awoken from her fitful sleep some hours before.

Minutes later, Beatha descended the stairs and made her way to the little room in which she kept Gairegath.

Oh? the faerie's voice was rich with pleased malice. *What's this?*

"What—" Beatha cut off with an electric jolt. The door was ajar. She wrenched it the rest of the way open and the breath went out of her in a rush.

The sword was gone.

For a moment that seemed to stretch beyond any measurement of time, she stood with one hand on the door and one on the frame, staring into the little room, her eyes fixed on the empty rack.

The sword was *gone.*

Well, you lasted longer than I expected, the malicious whisper broke the grip of shock that held Beatha still. *I thought you'd lose Gairegath somehow* decades *ago.*

"Shut up," Beatha said, but her voice lacked any strength. "What's this…?"

A curl of paper was wrapped around the rack, tied with a frazzled piece of twine. Beatha reached for it, paused, clenched her fist to stop her hand from trembling. Then she snatched it and unrolled the scrap. Handwriting she didn't recognize read, *"You'll be frantic by the time you find this. I'll be brief. I wondered whether to write this at all, but an old woman deserves her little pleasures. You know all about that. Your pleasures are done now, though. The years of living off the deaths of others are over. After you left, after the haunts followed you away and the terror stopped, I traced your path backwards—"*

Beatha jumped as the city bells rang the warning.

A quarter of an hour until sunset, the faerie's warning was gleeful. *You should already be armed and making your way towards the park. Oh…* The glee faded, leaving behind only spite *I'm going to enjoy this.*

But with the sword gone, she couldn't… And she couldn't stop her eyes from traveling back to the note.

"*—I learned your secrets. The fae, the curse, your sword. And I learned why they follow you. The haunts. Your victims.*"

"It's not my fault," Beatha whispered into the empty hallway. "I only wanted to be healed, that faerie bitch tricked me!"

The note was only paper, it couldn't hear her protestations. The dead faerie whispering after her could, though. *I'd be offended if I wasn't having such fun right now.*

"*You look the same as you did at Sudschrei Bezirk. The years haven't been so kind to me.*"

"Kind? I've lost more than anyone could guess!" Beatha hissed, her heart lurching with remembered grief and new indignation. For a moment she couldn't block the memory of the first two haunts. The first two living people the fae thing's curse had drained to fuel her life hadn't been strangers. She'd been a wife and a mother. Once.

"*It's over now.*"

"Over," Beatha whispered the word out loud, voice trembling.

Over, the fae echoed, voice rich with pleasure, *all these years I could have spent in peace and rest, but it's worth it to see you standing slack-jawed and terrified now.*

"It was your own fault!"

And what's happening to you now is yours. Or did you miss that the writer of this note was from another city you left to the hungry dead?

Beatha's eyes jumped back up the page to the words *Sudschrei Bezirk,* then down again to pick up where she'd left off. *"Well, you won't look the same after tonight. The sword is gone. When your victims come for you this time, I hope you understand you brought it on yourself before you're gone too."*

The note ended there. It was unsigned. She turned the paper over. There had to be more. An ultimatum, a demand she could fulfill, a hint, a way *out*.

It was blank.

The voice laughed and laughed as Beatha stared at the empty back of the page.

From outside came the sound of doors shutting and shutters slamming closed all up and down the streets. The noise broke Beatha out of her horrified paralysis. "Missus Hoffman!" she called, trying for a commanding bellow but ending up with a high-pitched shout. There was no answer. "*Missus Hoffman!*"

The fear is stealing your ability to think, isn't it? The faerie gloated, *The cook told you that your housekeeper won't be here today. You're all alone, Beatha Itheanam, and the haunts will rise so soon.*

The cook? The cook! The note could only have been from her, and the obviousness of it struck Beatha like a slap. Trying to control her voice, she hurried towards the kitchen, calling, "Missus Weber?"

The kitchen was empty.

The woman was clever enough to trick you, the voice gloated. *She's clever enough to be long gone by now.*

There was a tingling in Beatha's palms, and panic began to crawl spiderlike up her spine. How long until sundown? Where was Mrs. Weber? *Where was Gairegath?*

She wasted three precious minutes searching the kitchen and the servant's wing. "Where are you? Where did you go? *Where is my SWORD?*"

Estra didn't answer. Of course she didn't. She was gone.

Beatha found herself in the front hall.

Look at you, the faerie sighed with an avid satisfaction. *Bedecked in useless armor. Surrounded by thick, worthless walls. Doomed.*

Beatha's hands shook. In her belly a cold knot of fear twisted and tightened. Every breath she took came shorter and sharper than the last.

The bells rang the five-minute warning. Beatha screamed at the sound, then shoved a fist at her mouth and bit her knuckle. Hard. The faerie's laughter, and the pain and the coppery taste of blood, prodded her into the movement.

She had to flee.

Staying ahead of the haunts would be her only chance. Get out, get away. It always took them time to catch up with her. Just had to keep ahead.

To stop moving would be to die.

Beatha threw open the door and stepped out into the fading light, into Opferstadt. For one moment she hesitated, even now the lure of the familiar trying to hold her still. Then, for the first time since she'd arrived in town nearly a decade before, she ignored the eyes of the few city people hurrying towards their homes. She ran.

In her wake she left fear. The hero of Opferstadt dashed madly through the streets. Beatha Itheanam went armored but without her mirrored sword. She did not smile. Hers was a grimace of terror. The city folk didn't know what was wrong, only that it was grim.

Now them I do feel a bit bad for, the faerie murmured in her ear, *but they'll be better off without you in the end, won't they? When you die, the haunts will finally dissipate for good.*

The sun disappeared below the horizon.

With a howl the first haunt rose up from the intersection ahead of her. Beatha scrambled to a stop, nearly tumbling over herself in her haste. She spun and ran down a side street. As the light reddened and then faded, she fled. But the deeper the night grew, the more haunts rose. Every direction she tried to run, she found herself blocked. Behind her, the way closed off. The haunts drifted in her wake. An ever-thickening crowd.

"Please, no," she whispered. To herself? The haunts?

It was the fae haunt's voice which answered. *Oh, yes.*

The street ahead of her glowed a faint, noxious green with the light of no less than five haunts. Their empty eyes turned towards her, arms rising. They wailed. Beatha kicked in a door and ran through a house, startling shrieks out of the occupants. The shrieks turned into horrified screams as the haunts flooded through after her. They killed indiscriminately. Beatha burst out the back way and vaulted the low wall marking the boundary of the yard. She skidded into a square with a fountain at the center.

"No—I'm sorry—It wasn't my fault," Beatha gasped.

Heedless of her words, dozens of haunts drifted through the square toward her. Beatha turned, but the side street was choked with more moaning, blurred faces. They faded through the walls of the house behind her. Grasping hands reached out from the alleyways.

At last, the faerie whispered. *At last…*

Beatha spun, panting, and spun again. Her eyes widened. There was no way out. Her hand fell automatically to her belt. She hated Gairegath. She needed it.

The haunts fell upon her. The pain overwhelmed. Beatha held out for only an instant. Then she screamed.

"It wasn't my fault!"

Their victims always screamed.

The train was nearly empty. The car in which Estra Weber had seated herself, all the way at the rear by the luggage carriage, was entirely deserted. The few passengers willing to take the late afternoon trains out of the city tended to keep to the front cars, clutching their mirror-totems and huddling together under the bright gas lanterns affixed to the walls. They pulled curtains down over the windows as the sun set and repeated to themselves all of the easy lies that Beatha had fed them when she'd first established herself as the hero of Opferstadt. They whispered that the haunts couldn't catch up to them if they were going as fast as a good horse, and the steam engine went faster than that. They murmured that the haunts didn't infest the uninhabited places so thickly, and the tracks crossed miles and miles of deep woods without passing a single cottage or settlement.

Estra, the best cook south of Silberbache, long ago a resident of Sudschrei Bezirk, knew better. She had spent decades learning the truth, months planning this night. There was only one thing left to do.

She stood carefully as the carriage swayed over the tracks and held the backs of the bench-like seats as she made her way down to where her car connected to the next one. She peered through the little window set into the door rattling in its frame.

There was no one. Estra made her equally careful way back to where she'd been sitting, but instead of taking her seat once more she leaned down and reached beneath it.

What she drew out was long, thin, and wrapped in an old tablecloth. Estra didn't bother to unwrap it. She laid it on the bench cushion and turned to fuss with the window until she managed to open it. Then she lifted the bundle with both hands and unceremoniously tossed it out of the moving train, into the night. The idea of selling it had briefly crossed her mind, but this seemed more fitting.

"May no one ever find it," Estra whispered her wish to the empty train car. "Let no one ever remember her."

From the Author

I initially wrote this story in early 2020 for a heroic-stories themed open call. I aimed to subvert certain hero tropes with this story, and as a result it didn't quite fit with other pieces accepted for that anthology. I didn't want to let it go, though, so I kept it, seeking beta feedback and revising and tweaking a few times. I'm glad this story has found a home, it's one I have really enjoyed working on and sharing with beta readers. I'm excited to share it here, now.

About the Author

C.J. Dotson is a Northeast Ohio native who long contemplated living somewhere other than the rust belt and has finally managed it—C.J. and her family now live in southern Maine, in a house with too many basements and too many irregular corners. She lives with her husband, grade-school-aged son, toddler daughter, her grandmother-in-law, and with her teenage stepson over the school breaks. She loves reading sci-fi, fantasy, and horror, but will read really anything that catches her eye.

In what spare time she has, C.J. likes to paint and draw (mostly with acrylics and charcoal respectively) and she's teaching herself to decorate cakes. C.J. is primarily a writer of novels and short stories, and occasionally flash fiction. She loves to write dark genre fiction.

Find more at cjdotsonauthor.com
Or
Visit her on Twitter at twitter.com/cj_dots

For the Love of Gavin

by
S.A. McKenzie

For the Love of Gavin

Gavin creeps into the darkened kitchen in his socks. The red glow of the microwave oven clock offers just enough illumination to light his way to the coffee machine. He shakes the coffee jar and finds it empty. Gavin sighs. He is going to have to grind some beans. He'll be damned if he'll start his day with instant coffee just because of *them*. Swearing quietly, he adds a measured scoop of beans to the grinder, and, gritting his teeth, switches it on. Outside, the dawn chorus bursts into song.

"He is risen! Praise Gavin! Praise him!" A pair of lovely soprano voices launch into a hymn extolling the virtues of Sumatran coffee beans.

Hunching his shoulders, Gavin turns his back to the window and switches on the electric kettle. He places his coffee mug next to it, handle aligned at exactly ninety degrees to the edge of the counter.

While he waits for the water to boil, he opens the front door. The newspaper has been rescued from its usual landing spot in the flower bed, wiped clean, and placed in the middle of the door mat. Scowling, Gavin picks it up and goes back to the kitchen, turning on the lights as he goes. He adds the hot water to the French press that his daughters gave him for Christmas. While the coffee steeps, he gets out the rest of the breakfast things.

As he makes the toast, Beth wanders in wearing her fluffy pink dressing gown, sleepy-eyed.

"You're up early," she says, pouring herself a cup of coffee.

Gavin spreads Vegemite on his toast with great care, trying to achieve the optimal ratio of brown goo to butter.

"I wanted to see if it would make any difference with…you-know-who." He indicates the east-facing window with his chin. "They're still at it. There ought to be a law against it. Can't you have a word with Shelley?"

Beth yawns and shakes her head. "Shelley says his therapist thinks it's good for him. It's helping him deal with the trauma. Anyway, he's not hurting anyone."

"I wouldn't say that," Gavin says around a mouthful of toast.

Beth folds her arms and frowns at him. "I'm not your handmaiden. Go talk to Dennis yourself." She swallows the rest of her coffee and heads upstairs to wake the girls.

"Actually, according to Dennis, you *are* my dutiful handmaiden," Gavin says, just quietly enough that she won't hear him.

Even after being parked in the garage all night, the inside of the car is hot enough that his shirt sticks to his back. Gavin turns up the air conditioning and backs out of the driveway.

Two young women and a man are already out working in the front garden of the house on the left. They are all dressed in cream-coloured knee-length robes with embroidered borders. When they see Gavin, they press their palms together and make him a deep obeisance. The blonde girl nearest the fence straightens and smiles at him. The robe does nothing to conceal her long tanned legs and her small, pert breasts.

Gavin looks away quickly and turns on the windscreen washer and wipers to clean off the yellow flower petals stuck to the windscreen. When he glances in the rear-view mirror, she is still staring after him, while the other two have turned back to their work.

During his lunch break, Gavin visits the local council office. The receptionist at the front desk is fanning herself with a sheaf of development application forms as he approaches.

"Going to be 43 degrees today in Penrith," she says by way of greeting. "How can I help you?"

Gavin leans on the counter, unsure where to begin. "I have a problem with my neighbour," he says.

"Noise, rubbish, dogs, or illegal parking?" she says, tapping at her keyboard.

"None of those, really. Although they do sing a lot. The thing is, he's started this religion."

The receptionist stops tapping and swivels in her seat to look at him. After a long pause, she says, "Starting a religion is not against council regulations".

"He's holding religious ceremonies on his property."

"Is anyone parking illegally?"

"Well, no, mostly they get the bus, but—".

"Are they making excessive noise?"

"They sing to me when I get up in the morning."

"They're waking you up?"

"No, they wait until I get up."

"And then they sing to you. Loudly?"

"Not terribly loudly. But it's annoying."

She shrugs. "I can fill in a complaint form for you, but I can tell you right now, it's not going to go anywhere. You're going to need more evidence of nuisance behaviour than occasional singing for anyone to bother to investigate."

The blonde girl must have finished her shift for the day. Instead, two dark haired girls are out on the street waiting for him. Even with the windows up he can hear them call out in unison as he turns into the driveway.

"Blessed day! He has returned in all his glory! Praise Gavin!" They toss handfuls of yellow marigold petals in the air to shower down on the car. Gavin parks the car in the garage and ducks out the garage door before it shuts. The girls have gone inside.

Gavin goes out on the street to look at the white picket fence around his front garden. It has been repainted recently. He can still faintly smell the paint. A good job too, not a drop spilled on the pavement. Muttering under his breath, he goes into the house.

"What's this?" Beth says, flipping over one of real estate magazines he'd left on the table.

"I thought it might be time for a change," Gavin says. He keeps his eyes on the courgette he is cutting into long fingers.

Beth snorts. "Are you insane? The market's dropped twenty per cent in the last six months. We wouldn't have a hope of being able to afford a bigger place in the same school zone."

"Not bigger, necessarily. Just—different."

"We're not moving house just because you're not friends with Dennis anymore, Gavin."

After dinner, Gavin takes the full rubbish bag from the kitchen out to the wheelie bin. He lifts the lid on the bin, and then pauses to stick his head inside the bin and take a deep breath. It has been scrubbed clean inside and out, and now smells pleasantly of lemongrass.

The constable at the central police station stops filling in the form on the computer and looks at Gavin.

"Okay. So, this neighbour of yours—Dennis, is it? What would you say has prompted this behaviour?"

"He had an accident. He has some brain damage from it."

The policeman's eyes narrow.

"Let me get this straight. You want us to arrest a disabled man because his friends sometimes throw flowers at you?"

"Well, no, when you put it that way, it sounds bad. Look, it's a religious thing."

"Your religion, or his?"

"His, of course! I just want him to stop it."

The constable stops typing. For the first time Gavin registers the neat black beard and the orange turban.

"You want us to speak to your neighbour because you don't like his religion." It is a flat statement, not a question.

"Look, when you put it that way—"

"We're done here."

Out in the street a warm smoke-tainted wind breathes into his face.

On Saturday, Gavin sits on his patio with a beer in his hand. Next door, his daughters are laughing and splashing. They've gone through the gate in the fence to play in Dennis' pool with his son and daughter, as they've done for years. That's why Gavin and Dennis built the gate in the fence, after all.

He promised Beth that he'd replace a broken bit of guttering this weekend, but he can't make himself move right now. The polished leaves on the trees by the fence reflect darting glints of sunshine back at him. Gavin raises his beer to them in a silent toast. He shuts his eyes and pictures himself back on the cool hillside where he first saw them.

He was sent to Japan to get acquainted with his counterparts in the Hokkaido office. His hosts took him to visit a famous shrine surrounded by beautiful terraced gardens. There were Japanese maples, of course, and blossoming cherries and huge rhododendrons, but it was the magnolias that caught his eye. If there was a god of trees, Gavin thought, then it would take this form. Elegantly arched pale grey trunks and huge glossy deep-green leaves, with bronze undersides. And the flowers—he'd never known you could get magnolias with yellow flowers, flowers the size of dinner plates, all glowing in the soft spring light.

"Golden Moon magnolia," Kenji had said proudly. "Very sacred, very rare. Once, only emperors grew them."

Back in Sydney, Gavin did a little research, and found that Golden Moon magnolias weren't as rare as you might expect. There was a single supplier in Australia who could obtain them—for a price. When the trees arrived, Gavin had looked at their gleaming leaves, and then at the patchy brown grass, tired bottlebrush bushes and the old trampoline. He'd shrugged off any misgivings and dug three deep holes by the fence.

Any worries about whether the trees could survive here soon passed. They grew like weeds, producing multiple shoots that grew into a sprawling thicket. Hundreds of huge golden flowers appeared, blooming gorgeously for a single day, before turning brown and dropping to rot in slimy piles. The trees stretched their gangly limbs across the fence and dangled low over the swimming pool next door, where their habit of dropping rotting flower petals in the water was not greeted with universal delight.

"Before we start," the lawyer says, "It's best to clarify my billing rates up front. Now, a one-hour consultation will be—"

He names a sum that makes Gavin swallow hard. He nods, mutely.

"I just want to find out if I have a case. My next-door neighbour's religious practices are disturbing me."

"You do understand that people are free to worship as they please in this country?"

"Yeah, but are they free to worship…to worship me?"

"I beg your pardon?"

"My next-door neighbour says I'm a god. He keeps worshipping me. I don't like it."

When Gavin gets home, Beth is leaning on the kitchen counter eating a home-made chocolate-raspberry brownie with an ecstatic expression on her face.

"You should try these," she says. "One of the girls who's been helping Dennis brought them round. Go on, have one. They're amazing."

"Barry? Hey, it's Gavin Logan."

"Mate! Haven't heard from you in ages. How's Beth and the twins?"

"Good, good. They'll be starting high school next year."

"Wow. Seems like just yesterday they were only knee-high."

"Actually, I wanted to ask a favour. You remember that time you were telling me how your brother hangs out with those motorcycle guys? That if I ever had someone who needed sorting out to just to let you know?"

"Look, I was pissed as a chook at that party. I don't really remember—"

"I've got a problem with a guy. He won't leave me alone. I just want someone to have a chat with him. You know what I mean?"

"…"

"You did say you owed me one, Barry."

"Yeah, all right. I'll get you a phone number."

That evening, Gavin carries the ladder around to the side of the house with the broken guttering. He climbs up the ladder, then back down again. The guttering has already been repaired. He hears hammering noises from next door, and peeps through a knothole in the fence. Dennis is standing in the backyard leaning on a walking stick and supervising two of his acolytes in the assembly of a small wooden structure. It looks like an open-fronted bird house, mounted on a pole. The acolyte steps back, and Dennis limps forward and carefully pins a laminated picture inside the little house. He puts two sticks of incense in a jar and lights them.

Gavin finds Beth in the laundry, folding clothes.

"Did you by any chance give Dennis a photo of me?" he asks. She purses her lips and shakes her head.

"Not that I can recall. Why?"

"Tell Shelley I detest the scent of patchouli incense," Gavin says, on his way out the door.

The cafe where the guy said to meet is surprisingly upmarket, all black and white tiles and ugly-looking brushed steel chairs. Gavin had expected some seedy pool hall or sticky-carpeted neighbourhood bar. Barry's friend certainly fits the part: big, shaved head, a crooked nose and thick hairy arms bearing an impressive array of tattoos.

"Let me get this straight," he says. "You want me to intimidate someone for you because you don't like his religion? That's messed up, man. You should get some help."

That's just what I was trying to do, Gavin thinks as the gorilla stalks out.

"Barry called," Beth says. "He was worried about you. Seriously, Gavin! If you're not going to talk to Dennis, I think you should see someone."

Gavin remembers visiting Dennis in the hospital. How he lay there on his back looking oddly small and shrunken, until he fixed his bloodshot eyes on Gavin. Dennis had grabbed Gavin's hand and held on with surprising strength. He couldn't speak above a whisper.

You saved me. I can see it in you. The light, it's pouring from you. Thou art God. And then the nurse came in and bustled around fiddling with the beeping monitors and Gavin stood up and babbled *well you best get some rest hope you get better soon bye now.* And fled. Didn't stop until he reached the car park and then stood by his car, taking deep shuddering breaths.

The therapist's office is on the same street as the School of Performing Arts. On his way down the street, Gavin sees a girl coming out of the front entrance of the school. The blonde acolyte. No cream-coloured robe today, just a tight-fitting t-shirt and a pleated red and black tartan skirt. Laughing, she turns to speak to the dark-haired girl behind her. They are both carrying dresses, old fashioned-green velvet with lots of lace and ruffles. Gavin watches them go down the street. *Drama students. Well, bugger me*, he thinks.

The therapist's rooms are a shrine to blandness, clearly designed to cause the least possible offense to anyone, with pale cream walls hung with blurry landscapes and big squishy oatmeal-coloured armchairs.

"So, tell me how the problem started," the therapist says, holding her pen poised above the notepad.

Gavin squirms in the chair. It feels like it is about to swallow him whole.

"There was an…accident."

He'd been finding debris on the ground for weeks. Certainly, Dennis had every right to prune the trees on his side, but some of the branches cut were on Gavin's side. Beth and the girls had gone shopping that Saturday afternoon. A summer storm was brewing. Dark, bruise-purple thunderheads clustered overhead. The air seemed thick and sludgy, making it an effort just to move.

Gavin had looked out of the upstairs bedroom window and noticed movement by the fence. He could see Dennis on a ladder, leaning right over the fence with a pair of long-handled loppers.

He'd gone through the gate before Dennis had seen him.

"What do you think you're doing?"

Startled, Dennis twitched, setting the ladder wobbling.

"Gidday, Gavin. I didn't see you down there." Mildly, as if he wasn't up to anything. He climbed down the ladder and wiped the sweat off his forehead.

"Pretty warm, eh?"

"I would thank you," Gavin said, trying to inject his words with a palpable chill, "to confine your pruning to your property. If you don't mind."

And Dennis just looked at him innocently and said that he'd thought he'd help Gavin out. He rested the loppers on his shoulder, slanting upward, and smiled at Gavin.

The rage was so strong Gavin felt it buzzing in his ears. He wanted to smash Dennis in his smug round face.

And the hand of God reached down and did it for him.

That's what it looked like afterward, those branching lines of lightning burned onto his retinas. Like clawing fingers slashing down, leaving bleeding white wounds in the air and turning all the world a brilliant white.

Dennis was on the ground, unmoving. Gavin fell to his knees. Took Dennis' wrist, fumbled for a pulse. Tried to remember what you do. Was it compression first, then the breathing? He pressed down on Dennis' chest. Tilted his head back. Put his mouth to Dennis' slack wet lips. Breathed out. And another one. Took a breath for himself and yelled for help, for someone, anyone. And the cold rain came down then and pelted them both, huge stinging drops blasting little craters in the dry red soil and sending up puffs of dust with each strike.

There's an amateurish water colour of the Blue Mountains on the wall behind the therapist. Maybe she'd painted it. Gavin wonders what the cream wall would look like with blood on it. A splash of red might liven this place up.

"It was…a bit traumatic," Gavin says, tracing his finger over the rough fabric of the chair arm.

"How was it?" Beth says, as he comes into the kitchen.

"Good," he says. She raises an eyebrow.

"No, really. I think I'm going to take a couple of days off. Work through some stuff, you know?"

"Good for you," she says. "You could use a break."

The truck arrives at 9.30 a.m. The men all have the hardened lobster-coloured skin of people who spend their lives outside.

"Right," their leader says, slapping his leather gloves against his leg. "Where are they?"

"This way," Gavin says, leading them round the back. He points. "The three trees by the fence. I want them gone, stumps and all."

Back in the kitchen, Gavin makes a cup of coffee and turns up the radio to drown out the howl of the chainsaws.

From the Author

For the Love of Gavin came about when I was trying to come up with a story that fit a writing prompt about neighbours. I considered writing a story about the sort of problems that might arise if you lived next door to some sort of minor deity. And then I decided it might be more interesting to write about what might happen if you lived next door to someone who thought that you were the god.

As is the way of stories, when I came back to it after some time, I realised the story was about more than just a conflict between neighbors. To me, For the Love of Gavin is at its heart a story that reflects some aspects of my life as an autistic person. Gavin is a man who is deeply bothered by the behaviour of his neighbor. He tries to get help from both official and unofficial sources, only to be told by everyone, including his wife, that his feelings and the ways in which he experiences the world are invalid. This is not an uncommon experience among neurodiverse people.

This story has become one of my favorites out of all the stories I have written, but it has also been one of my most rejected stories, and I'm glad it has finally found a home.

About the Author

S.A. McKenzie lives at the bottom of the world on one of the better-looking islands of New Zealand, in the earthquake-ravaged ruins of the city of Christchurch. After surviving more than 12,000 aftershocks, they have become adept at estimating the exact magnitude of any quake based on the amount of coffee spilled.

They started writing six years ago and since then their offbeat and blackly humorous science fiction and fantasy stories featuring time travelling rabbits, carnivorous unicorns and man-eating subway trains have been published in more than twenty speculative fiction magazines and anthologies. Currently they are working on a fantasy novel at an extremely slow pace. They can be found wasting time on:

Twitter: @samckenzie2
And online at:
www.hedgehogcircus.com

MVP

by
Amelia Kibbie

MVP

*W*ell, here you are, Mr. Sims." Principal Malcolm spread her arms out. "The most scenic part of our lovely school."

The basement was a vast stretch of concrete, dim, and horrendously damp. The long, low space was crammed with pipes, broken desks, and pathetic cutouts of trees from musicals long forgotten. It stank of mold and mice and something ancient and bowel-like.

Nevin Sims hefted the mop in his hands. "How am I supposed to clean this? There's stuff everywhere!" He kicked at the yellow mop bucket at the bottom of the stairs. A bit of soapy water sloshed out. The area at the bottom of the staircase had a small ring of space providing access to the boiler, but the rest of the basement was crammed.

"You move it all to one side, and then you mop." Principal Malcolm spoke slowly on a sugared knife's edge, as if she were explaining to a toddler. "And then you move it to the *other side*, Sims."

Nevin slammed the mop head down in the bucket. More grayish water slopped onto the dismal concrete floor. "For the last time, I didn't share those pictures!"

"And as I explained to your mother at the parent meeting, since we don't know who did it, you take the punishment." She sniffed and adjusted her glasses. They were as hard and angular as the rest of her face. "Excuse me—consequences. As team captain, you failed to show the leadership necessary to prevent the incident altogether."

"It wasn't that big of a deal!" Nevin shot back.

"Not a big deal? Parker Holland missed a week of school because of this. His mom was afraid he was going to harm himself, and you don't think that's a big deal?"

"They did it to me when I was a freshman." Nevin threw his meaty hands out wide and hunched his broad shoulders, puffed up like an agitated animal in a letterman's jacket. "They do it to everybody!"

"Well, this time someone took pictures. Because of that, you will report here after football practice every night for the next two weeks." Heels clicking, Principal Malcolm ascended to the heavy metal door that opened to the surface world, and slammed it shut. It echoed through the dungeon with an ominous boom. Nevin was abandoned in the blister-colored light of the weak fluorescents.

Cursing, Nevin yanked the mop up from the water and halfheartedly sponged at the grimy floor. What the hell was the point of mopping a room nobody ever went into except when there was a problem with the boiler?

Well, what was the point of dressing the freshmen football players up in cheerleader uniforms? Why make them wear wigs and make up and force them to do cheer routines for the rest of the team? Humiliation. To show them their place in the food chain. And Malcolm meant to do the same to him.

It was bad enough to be down here, but he wished they hadn't told his mother what had happened. She'd cried herself to sleep for three straight nights now. He'd heard her sobbing on the phone to his grandmother. "I don't know what to do with him, Mama!" Her sorrow, her helplessness, put a coal pit in his gut where embers of shame and anger flamed bronze, and grew brighter each day.

"Why did they post the pictures?" He shoved a chair out of the way to mop beneath it. "Who the hell was stupid enough to post the pictures?" Hundreds of shares later, the whole town knew what the football team did to the freshmen recruits.

Nevin wiped sweat from his brow and pulled out his phone. At least he could listen to music—

"Damn it!" Of course there was no reception, data or otherwise. His sweaty fingers fumbled, and his phone bounced out of his hand. It clattered across the floor and under a tall metal bookshelf that sat against one wall near the center of the long room.

He went to break the mop over his knee but stopped. He squeezed the wooden dowel in his powerful hands and forced himself to count to ten. Mom didn't need this. Mom didn't need him in any more trouble, and Mom couldn't pay for another phone.

Nevin knelt down and tried to worm his fingers under the bottom of the bookshelf. As he forced his digits beneath the metal, old paint crumbling off on his palms, an army of white spiders, blind and bone-colored, skittered from beneath. He grunted and yanked his hand away, then shot to his feet to stamp them until there was nothing left.

Breathe deep, down to your toes. Remember what Dr. Evans taught you when Dad left.

When his hands stopped shaking, he squirmed between the side of the metal bookcase and shoved it about three feet along the wall. He squatted down and saw the tip of his phone sticking out. No way he was reaching under again. Nevin pushed the shelf again until his device was free, and then snatched it up to wipe it on his shirt.

He breathed easier. Not broken.

There was a door in the wall that had been hidden behind the bookshelf. A grime-covered brass plate screwed into it read COACH.

"She better not expect me to mop this too," he grumbled, and reached for the knob.

His hot fingers slid over the cool metal. A chill ran up his arm and feathered over his body. It was strange, but the cool sweetness of it eased the angry thump of his heart, dried the sweat that ran from his dark hair and down his cheeks.

Someone had filled in the cracks of the door with some kind of white caulk. Now it crumbled with age when he poked it with his finger.

He tried the doorknob. It was locked.

"Huh." He took a step back but kept his eyes on the door as he slid his phone into the back pocket of his jeans. The musty, moldy stench of the basement crawled up his nostrils and nestled there as he examined the door and the aging placard.

Nevin touched the knob again and marveled at the cool tingle that ran up his arms. He wrapped both hands around the knob, braced his foot against the wall, and pulled.

The door swung open to blackness.

He felt for a switch on the wall and flipped it. A single bulb, protected by a cage-like light fixture, flickered to life.

The room was small, with cinderblock walls. A desk sat against the far wall, next to a large metal cabinet with double doors. The wall on his right was fitted with shelves that held football trophies, dozens of them. Trophies from years he'd been told Ash High hadn't had a football team—1949-1957. The artifacts of glory were coated with dust and strung through with spiderwebs. Smaller awards were arranged around seven massive state championship cups, like worshippers kneeling before their sacred idols.

Old felt pennants rotted where they'd been tacked to a bulletin board over the desk, and the left-hand wall was a gallery of framed photos—a series of football teams in old-timey uniforms. Ash High

Fighting Ravens, every one of them. And in every picture there stood a tall man—a giant, really—towering behind his kneeling players with his hands clasped behind his back and chin uplifted in proud defiance. He had perfectly coiffed silver hair and wore a whistle around his neck over his sweater and tie. His pale gray eyes bored through the dust and years and into Nevin's face.

An unfamiliar, grinding ring echoed through the perfect stillness of the abandoned office. Nevin's dark eyes darted around the dim space.

The sound again.

Upon the desk sat a large gray typewriter, a desktop calendar yellowed as a pirate's map, and a thick black rotary phone.

The phone was ringing.

Nevin picked up the dusty receiver. He lifted it to his ear, and as he did, the spiral cord shed a layer of dust and dead spiders.

"...Hello?" he whispered.

At first, all he heard was static. Then came a high-pitched whining shriek, followed by a few moments of guttural breathing punctuated with some unknown mechanical rumbling. Slowly, these died away.

On the other end, someone cleared their throat.

"Hello there, Champ." The voice sounded far away, but it came closer with each word.

Nevin recoiled from the receiver, as he had when the spiders had poured forth from beneath the cabinet. "Who is this?" That same chill he'd felt on the doorknob radiated from the phone, but this time there was something diseased about it. It crawled along his face instead of cooling his flushed skin.

"Fighting Ravens star quarterback... in the basement mopping the goddamn *floor.*" Nevin was sure now it was a man on the other end. But he was not sure how the man knew his mother called him Champ. "That's a goddamn shame. Those pansy-ass freshmen needed to be put in their place. It's *tradition.*" The words dissolved into what sounded like radio static for a few moments. Nevin couldn't be sure, but between the hisses he thought he heard screaming.

"Who is this?"

"Son," the voice oozed through the receiver again. "You speak when you're spoken to, is that clear?"

"Yes, sir," Nevin heard himself say.

"Good. I like the way you're playing this season, Champ. Keep it up. But don't you get soft on me."

"No, sir."

"That's what I like to hear. Now, on Friday, I want you to throw to that blonde-headed kid. Have him cut to the left every time."

"Throw to Austin Summerfield?" Nevin barked in disbelief. "He sucks. He's got butterfingers."

"Throw it to him. If you can't make the pass, run it. Do as I say, now—is that clear?"

Nevin paused.

"You wanna win, don't you? Hell, it's your senior year, Champ. The state title's on the line."

They were never good enough to take state. They'd be lucky to win half their games.

"Do I make myself *clear*, Champ?" A whining squeal came over the line and made Nevin wince.

"Yes, sir," he said.

Nevin did as the man on the phone said, and they won their next game.

His passes were on fire, and Austin's hands were magic. Nevin's running game was unstoppable. Sidestepping blockers left and right, he ran in three touchdowns, a personal best. Even better, the Washington Panthers' top tackler tripped over some turf and broke his collarbone about five minutes into the first quarter. Nevin's mom screamed herself red in the face as she cheered from the front row of the stands, and Coach Varley was beside himself in the locker room after.

Everyone at school seemed to forget about those pictures of the cross-dressing freshmen that somehow wound up online. Sure, the kids' parents were still upset, the school in hot water, but the general hubbub surrounding the incident evaporated, as if the rumors had been culled away by tales of Nevin Sims, a quarterback unlike any the school had had in years.

The next Monday, school dragged on and on. Even with more girls talking to him, and compliments and high fives from everyone, he could think of nothing but racing downstairs with his mop and bucket once the last bell sounded.

He slopped some water around on the floor for a few minutes, but the door called to him. Nevin had moved the bookcase back over the door after the first phone call, and now he shoved it aside and entered the office. He flipped on the light.

His heart clenched for a moment as his eyes registered a vague shadow form lingering in front of the cabinet next to the desk. It was tall, black, shot through with a strange glow that reminded him of the leftover image of a camera flash. He blinked furiously and took a step back toward safety.

No. Nothing there.

The phone rang.

Nevin crossed the room, gnawing on his lip, and picked up the receiver. "Hello?"

"Well done, Champ, well done." The word *done* crackled, interrupted by static and a far-away yelping sound, followed by more grinding. "It feels good to win, doesn't it?"

"Yes, sir," Nevin licked his lip and tasted blood. "Um, sir? How did you know I'd be—"

"Now this time, son, I want you to just run it. Your coach will tell you to throw, but you just run it, you hear?" When the voice said *coach,* it came out an inhuman growl. "Don't show me any disrespect. I expect loyalty from my men. And you're a man, aren't you?"

"Yes, sir," Nevin's voice was firm and sure, but his insides boiled. "I just, I was wondering, what I should call you?"

"You call me *sir,* Sims! Damn it, did you drink a glass of stupid juice for breakfast?"

He swallowed. "No, sir."

There came a rancid, rotting laugh through the line. Nevin's hand quaked and the receiver vibrated against his ear.

"Just run the ball, Sims. Make me proud."

In the huddle, over the chanting of the zealous crowd, Coach Varley said, "Benton's got a guy who's already had five sacks this season. You guys need to protect Sims, okay, whatever it takes. Sims, you gotta get the ball out of your hands, make sure you aren't a target, because he's gunning for you. Number 40."

Just run the ball, Sims. Make me proud.

"Got it, Coach." He nodded, voice flat, response automatic.

Despite the clammy chill creeping up his neck and into his helmet, Nevin tried to throw. Several incomplete passes later, he spit on the ground and decided to run.

Here came number 40, barreling through the defenders. The world slowed. Nevin could see the player's large brown eyes, bugging wide and showing their whites, the snarl of his grinning mouth revealing the shiny black guard. Nevin clutched the ball against his body and pivoted with the intention to break right.

Number 40's face melted from his sneer of competitive aggression to a slackened look of blank-faced horror. His right knee buckled and dislocated. It folded the opposite way that a leg is supposed to bend. With a piteous shriek, he fell to the turf. No one was anywhere near him, but an old, cold wind blew past Nevin just as it happened. The breeze stank of the basement.

"Run," Nevin whispered, and took off down the field. He ran in the touchdown, and two more after that.

In the locker room during halftime, the team was amped. Coach Varley left them to pound their chests and celebrate and pulled Nevin aside. "Don't get me wrong, I love what you're doing out there," he said, "but those weren't the plays we talked about." He gave Nevin a playful punch on top of his pads. "We already got this season off to a... rough start. I don't want any more problems."

"I want to win," Nevin said, but his words were absorbed by the jubilant roar of his teammates nearby.

"What's that?"

"Yeah, Coach." The noisy locker room also drowned the bitter, ironic twist to his words.

Nevin ran the ball anyway, and it was a shutout.

Mom spent hours on the phone with Grandma that night. He listened through the wall as he pretended to sleep. "People are saying they'll go undefeated! Well, I heard a rumor that there's going to be a recruiter at the next game! Of course, it would have to be a full ride. If his father hadn't abandoned us, well... And I'll tell you this, he doesn't need to see that counselor anymore. I'm sure he's going to be Homecoming King."

Nevin pushed the mop back and forth and ignored the muffled ringing that crept through the door behind the bookcase. When he heard the strange clicking sounds, though, he could not resist.

In the office, the phone rang, over, and over, and over. The typewriter clicked along of its own volition, the metal letters slamming up against the dry ink ribbon. Fear clenched his whole body as the paper roller shot over with a ding.

He inched closer and examined the letter keys as they slammed into the ribbon. P. H. O. N. E.

Nevin picked up the phone. When the pad of his first finger grazed the receiver, the typewriter went dead.

He swallowed the hot gravel in his throat. "Hello?"

A series of whirring clicks, like machinery, infused with static, woven through with sounds like weeping. These auditory scraps solidified. "Nice hustle, Champ."

"P-please," Nevin stuttered at the thought of number 40's leg, crunched in the wrong direction. "Can you please...tell me who—"

"Who I am isn't important." The voice crawled into his head through the hole in his ear. "But you... You're gonna be somebody, Champ. Now, did I hear there was going to be a recruiter at the next game?"

"M-maybe."

"Well, it's time then. I have something for you. Open the desk."

Nevin bent and tugged at the bottom drawer of the desk. It was locked.

"No, the top drawer."

Nevin froze, shivered, and painstakingly glanced behind his shoulder and around the room. Nothing. How did he know?

"Top drawer, son, hurry it up now."

Nevin slid the top drawer open. It came in fits and starts as the metal squealed with disuse. Inside was what looked like a notebook, and a few discarded paper clips.

"That's it. Go ahead, Champ."

As Nevin slid his hand inside, his flesh caught on a strip of sharp metal on the top of the drawer. He raised the torn skin to his lips a moment.

A dry, joyless sound came through the phone receiver, a husk of a laugh, nothing left alive inside. "Now's the time for you to decide. You want that scholarship? To be Homecoming King? Hero of the school? Just pick up the book."

"Sir?" Nevin's fingers ached as they grasped the receiver in a sweaty, shaky grip. "What happened to number 40 last—"

"Or," the voice cut in, "do you want to be remembered as the quarterback who got in trouble for making the freshmen dress up in cheerleader costumes?" He paused. "Which do you think your mother would choose?"

Nevin hesitated for a few more seconds, and then reached into the drawer again to pick up the notebook. Blood from the cut on the back of his knuckle smeared against the ancient cardboard cover and over the name scratched on it with black ballpoint pen: COACH ABNER.

It was a black and white composition notebook with curled edges. Nevin set it gingerly on the desk next to the unnatural typewriter and used his free hand to open it.

It was a playbook. The first few pages had diagrams for some pretty standard plays. But as he continued, Nevin was struck by the sudden genius of the strategy, the clever variations on the old standards. The plays were interrupted after a time by drawings of other things. The first few just looked like places where the author had violently scratched something out, making a black smudge. After a while the sketches began to take on a shape, a humanoid outline of something with owlish eyes and outstretched limbs, primeval and unsettling.

"Take it," the voice, Abner, purred over the phone. "I know you'll make me proud. Go get 'em, Champ."

Nevin replaced the receiver as though he moved through water. Then, he felt around the back of the desk and pulled the phone cord.

The cracked rubber cord came off in his hand, completely rotted through. It disintegrated at his touch.

"Well, well, well, Mr. Nevin Sims. I didn't expect to ever see you walk through the library doors of your own free will." Miss Nathaniel removed the bejeweled reading glasses from her lined face and let them hang around her neck. She regarded him over a thick Victorian novel.

He cleared his throat, a nervous, awkward grunt. "I can't find the custodian," he said. "I need somebody's key to, uh, let me into the basement."

Her mahogany eyebrow shot high and incredulous, painted to match the hair she shamelessly dyed the same color. "The basement? Whatever for?"

He shifted to his other foot and stuffed his hands into the pockets of his letter jacket. "Um, my consequences. The mopping."

All through the halls she carved him up with a steely side-eyed glare and jingled her keys to punctuate her distrust. At last, they reached the basement door.

"Miz Nathaniel?" he mumbled as she turned the key. "How long have you worked here?"

"Since 1983." He could smell cough drops on her breath.

"Oh."

She picked up on the crestfallen shrug of his shoulders. "Why?"

"Did you know Coach Abner?"

She put her hand on her plump chest a moment, then took a breath and returned her posture to the usual ramrod. It was the closest thing to a sincere emotion he'd ever seen her display. "Well, I suppose with the internet these days you can't keep anything secret. God knows we tried." She let slip a tired, sad laugh. "You have to give us some credit. We've kept it silent for over sixty years. Of course, all that happened before my time." She bored into his gaze until he looked away. "I think it's better for the truth to come out eventually. A school built on a foundation of lies will not stand forever."

"...Okay," he said, as sweat prickled his brow.

She looked at the door. "And you're supposed to be mopping?"

He nodded. "The, uh, the mop and stuff's already down there."

"I see." She turned the key in the lock and swung the old door open. He jogged halfway down the stairs before she called his name. "Don't touch anything down there," she said, backlit by healthy hallway fluorescents. "Best not to move any furniture. Some of it's falling apart. Just do your penance and move along, Sims."

He nodded.

Her shadow glared at him a moment before she swung the door shut. It clanged with significance.

"Dude." Austin sidled up to Nevin's locker as Nevin fumbled with his combination, befuddled with Monday morning. "Coach was pissed at you after the game."

"Yeah, I know."

"Yeah, but, like, what if he kicks you off the team?" Austin shrugged his backpack higher on his massive shoulders with one hand and ruffled his long blonde hair with the other.

"He's not gonna do that, dumbass." Nevin pounded on the locker. "We won. We destroyed Mt. Grange. Besides, I don't care. I'm gonna get recruited. The guy from Duke already called my mom."

"Those plays were…" Austin shook his golden head. "I've never seen anything like…"

"That's because you're dumber than a box of rocks. That's why you're not the quarterback." Nevin finally wrestled his locker open.

"Dude, something's wrong with you." Austin gave Nevin's shoulder an angry shove. "You never come out and do anything anymore. I texted you like fifty times last weekend."

"Whatever." Nevin pulled his math book out of his locker and opened his bag. Out of the corner of his eye, he saw Parker Holland scurry by, so far over on the other side of the hallway that his shoulder rubbed the lockers on the opposite side. The freshman kept his eyes down. Nevin sneered in his pathetic direction.

Suddenly, Austin grabbed Nevin's book bag and shook it. The contents spilled out—a dirty tee-shirt, some ratty notebooks, a binder, a bag of chips, and the playbook from the basement. Before Nevin could react, Austin scooped it up and flipped through it. When Nevin lunged for it, Austin pulled it out of reach. "Is this where you get the plays?" He stopped at the picture of the owl-eyed thing. "What the hell is this, Nevin? It looks—"

His words choked off. Right there, in front of dozens of students passing to their next class, Austin's body rose up several feet into the air. He gurgled and stiffened as his limbs seized and his eyes rolled back to blood-threaded white. The swoosh of air, the stench of the basement, and then Austin's prostrate form slammed into the opposite wall of the hallway before he crumpled to the ground. The playbook landed just at Nevin's feet.

A couple of hours later, the paramedics had taken Austin away to treat his alleged grand mal seizure, and Nevin walked the hallways of his school where the crowds parted for him, where hands leapt to faces in an attempt to hide frantic whispering, where eyes widened or dropped to the ground in fear and reverence. Nevin's mind flooded with his own importance, and his brain swelled with the sensation of power, of notoriety. His heart, however, withered against his ribs, shriveled at the thought of Austin's white eyes rolling up into his brain, the crack of bone as he crashed into the wall.

Nevin returned to his locker and opened it.

Inside was a fat three-ring binder, covered in tattered old cloth and smeared with dust. A yellow post-it note affixed to the cover said *Nevin—the truth will set you free… Miss Nathaniel.*

He slid it into his backpack along with the playbook and went to football practice.

That night, Mom got on the phone with Grandma to brag about their meeting with the recruiter. Nevin went into his tiny bedroom and shut the door. He put in his headphones so he couldn't hear her pride seeping through the wall.

Cross-legged on his narrow bed, he put the old cloth binder in his lap and opened it.

The pages of the tome were mostly newspaper articles, clipped carefully and pasted onto card stock. There he was. Coach Abner, his picture attached to an article from the local paper welcoming the new high school football coach to the district.

Next to the first article was a post-it note, from Miss Nathaniel again. *These clippings were compiled by my predecessor, Priscilla Bouzek. When I took over, she gave it to me & told me to keep it locked up…*

According to the introductory article, Coach Thomas Abner was from Iowa, played football there, and fought the Nazis in Europe when his country called for aid. Honorably discharged, he came home for his teaching degree and coaching license.

Nevin flipped further. The Fighting Ravens' 1949-1950 season was mediocre at best. But when the '50-'51 season started, they were unstoppable. State titles, shutout games, players recruited to colleges, and numerous letters to the editor that praised the ingenious coaching of Mr. Thomas Abner. State title seven years in a row.

Nevin was not the best reader, but he picked up on patterns with ease. In every write up of every game, it seemed like a player on the opposite team was injured. Sometimes severely. And in September of 1954, a player died. Broken neck. What a horrible accident, the article said.

More accolades, until they abruptly ended.

A small clipping from the police blotter. "Officers were called to Ash High Tuesday night at 6:00 pm to investigate a possible assault. No arrests were made."

Next to this was a handwritten note, the words crudely shaped and often misspelled.

Miss Priscilla, I got your note—you are right he did this to me. I forgot to mop his office and went down. The door wasn't locked, and I thought I heard someone yelling, so I went in. There were candles in there and the lights were off, though I can't say why. He turned on me and his eyes were red. I swear to God. He hollered at me to get out, and it wasn't his voice it was someone else. Then he attacked me and broke my arm and smashed up my nose, and he would have killed me if he hadn't slipped on the wet floor. But the cops don't believe me. Only you believe me.

Then: BELOVED LOCAL COACH MISSING.

Articles documenting the search. All in vain. Up and vanished.

At the very end, Nevin found a typewritten document, full of boxes and numbers, but with a narrative below. It was smudged and purplish-looking--obviously a copy of some kind. More squinting revealed it was a police report from the day Coach Abner disappeared. Someone named James Finn reported another assault at Ash High. Nevin's eyes dripped down the page.

Coach Abner asked me to come to his office after practice. We talked for a while about my throwing arm. Then he pulls out a knife and tells me, "Get on your knees, Freshman." I tried to run, and he grabbed my shirt. And he tried to stab me, but somehow I got away. I remember hitting him below the belt. I ran upstairs and out the doors and straight home. I thought I heard him screaming behind me—no, no, no, no, over and over.

At the bottom of the report was a handwritten note in a box set aside for Officer's Remarks. Someone had written, *Witness is a freshman at Ash High. As a kid, known for being a tattletale. Wants attention now that Coach Abner is missing—last to see him alive. My opinion: no reason to follow up.*

The last page was tissue-thin and typewritten. It was undated.

A few weeks after Coach Abner disappeared, all of his trophies and belongings were placed in his office, which was locked and sealed. We are now forbidden to speak of him. This is the truth to the best of my ability to relate it. Sincerely, Priscilla Bouzek, Ash High Librarian.

Nevin was halfway down the basement steps, his feet hesitant yet tugged insistently by some invisible thread through his chest, when his cell phone went off. Nevin shook himself free with a jolt and jogged back up the steps to the door of the basement. He leaned out to get reception. It was after football practice—the only sound in the vast, silent school the whir of a far-off custodian's floor polisher.

"Mom?"

"Hi, sweetheart! Are you on your way home?"

His grip tightened on the old door handle, the metal sliding between his clammy fingers. "Uh, almost. I have to mop the basement."

"I thought you said you'd be finished by homecoming."

"I, uh, I like to help the custodians." He stole a few furtive glances down the darkened hallway. Outside, the wind picked up, and leaves scattered against the windows, explosions of heady color, brilliant in death.

"Honey, that is so sweet of you. Okay, I'll put dinner back in the oven for a while. I wanted to let you know that if you get the scholarship, Grandma says she can pay for your books."

"How?" He ducked back into the cellar doorway. The rotted basement smell came to his nostrils again, like dust and grime and old things, yes, but also like spoiled eggs now. "Grandma doesn't have any money. She's living on social security."

"Well, we have some family heirlooms. Jewelry, things like that," Mom said. "We can put them to good use this way. Look, we can talk more later. Love you."

"Love you, Mom." He said it quietly to avoid a pinch of desperation in his voice bouncing between the cell towers. He hung up and looked down the flight of stained concrete steps.

Just walk away, he thought. *Just leave. Just go home. You don't have to go down there ever again.*

He opened his backpack and pulled out the stained playbook.

The thought flitted over the surface of his brain like a wisp of smoke. *I could burn it.*

Something shoved him from behind. He stumbled into the staircase and managed to catch himself against the wall just as the basement door slammed shut behind him with a thunderous crash. The subterranean, charnel stench swirled around him as he stumbled to the bottom of the stairs and huddled against a rusted file cabinet.

The phone in the office was ringing. The sound should have been muffled through the door and the bookcase covering it, but he could hear it clearly, as if the phone were right beside him. Each ring was louder, louder, louder, grinding, grinding, screaming, grinding. Nevin cursed and put his hands over his ears. It made no difference. The sound of the phone wrapped around his head, an audial noose, tightening, squeezing—

He lurched over to the bookshelf and reached out to shove it to the side. It jumped out of his way on its own with a metallic scream. He stumbled and fell into the door and clawed at it. Collapsing inside, he screamed as the ringing jackhammered through his head. Nevin crawled on his knees to the desk and snagged the curly phone cord. The receiver dropped into his hands. Panting, Nevin raised the heavy black plastic to his face.

A rumbling un-sound chanted over the disconnected wires. It seeped into his ear, and morphed between shrieking, grinding, and heavy breathing. "Please," he whispered, "Oh please, please stop…"

The un-sound melted with a trail of insect-like chittering in its wake that died away until all he could hear was the breathing. Then, "Burn it? I'll burn *you*, boy. I'll burn you. Do you hear me?"

Hot tears stung his eyes. He blinked and they cascaded down his cheeks. "Yes, sir."

"Stop crying, you goddamn baby. It's like you've forgotten all I've done for you," the voice said, low, but snarling with blood-curdling rage. "All those touchdowns. The recruiter. Did you forget where all this success came from?"

"…N-no, sir."

"Do you want it to go away? For everyone to see who you really are—a mediocre quarterback with no brains? A kid so rotten his dad left him? You wanna break your mother's heart?"

"No sir." Nevin used the desk for support and climbed to his feet.

"Champ." The voice cooled, pooling through the receiver, slow like honey now. "You know nothing's free in this world, right? Everything has a price, son. Everything."

Nevin's eyes flicked over to the large metal cabinet by the desk. It had started life a hideous avocado green, and the layer of dust and cobwebs did nothing to improve its surface. Was that a bloody thumbprint on the handle?

"Well, now it's time to pay. It's time for the master to eat," Coach Abner said. "And you better feed him, Nevin, if you know what's good for you."

Nevin took a shuddering breath.

"Bring down one of those little pansy-ass freshmen." A rumble of bestial hunger echoed behind his words. "Time to cull the herd."

"Yo, Parker." Nevin's stomach lurched as the boy's name formed on his lips.

The slender freshman cowered at the sound of Nevin's voice, then turned and squared his shoulders in an attempt to appear threatening to his potential predator. "You're not supposed to talk to me outside of practice and games." The quaver in Parker's voice betrayed his arrogant posture.

"Yeah, I know." Nevin scratched the back of his neck. "But, um, I want to show you something."

"Whatever. I've heard that one before." Parker turned back to his locker and fiddled with the combination. It was after practice, and the building was practically empty. "Y'know," Parker snapped, "my cousin in Denver saw that picture. Not friends with anybody from around here except me, and it showed up on his feed. That's how many times it's been shared."

"Look, just come with me for a sec."

"Yeah, right, Sims." Parker shoved a book in his locker and shut it, and then zipped up his bag.

"It's a surprise," Nevin scrambled, trying to keep his voice cool, brotherly. "It's really awesome. It's, um, it's my way of saying I'm sorry."

Parker turned, eyes incredulous beneath his dishwater brows.

"I'm sorry," Nevin repeated, and realized it was true. "I really am. Seriously, no joke." He stuck out his hand for Parker to shake.

Parker's hand inched forward and clasped Nevin's for a brief squeeze. "Okay. Thanks." A smile climbed Parker's innocent lips. It was a blade in Nevin's gut, that smile.

Nevin tried to ignore the itch of tears in his eyes. "So, yeah, um, you wanna— "

"Okay," Parker said, shouldering his backpack.

Nevin led him to the basement door. "It's down here."

"Huh." Parker laughed as Nevin revealed the staircase. "Cellar door."

Nevin paused. "What?"

Parker offered him another crushingly trusting smile. "Cellar door. Remember when Miss Nathaniel came into English to teach us some stuff about poetry? She said that J. R. R. Tolkien, the guy who wrote *Lord of the Rings,* said that 'cellar door' was the most beautiful set of words in the English language."

"That's cool," Nevin lied, and ushered Parker down the stairs to the subterranean level.

"This is gross." Parker stopped short and surveyed the dilapidated furniture and dungeon-like walls. Nevin put a hand on Parker's back and guided him forward through the gloaming light of the struggling fluorescents to the office door.

"Coach," Parker read on the plaque. "Whose office is this? Whoa, check it out!" He bounced over to the shelves of dusty trophies. "I didn't know we won this many state titles! How come it's not on those banners in the gym?"

Parker pointed out various trophies and plaques as Nevin went to the large metal cabinet by Coach Abner's desk. He put his hands around the two handles and opened it. The hinges complied with a series of unhappy squeals.

The shelf at the top, at chin level, held a strange assortment of items--feathers, rocks, petrified candles, a chalice of some kind, and a human skull. Within the circle of these relics was a knife made of black stone; something out of a museum, inlaid with red gemstones.

These things Nevin saw first, since they were at eye level. Instinctively, he knew what it was, though he did not consciously know the word—altar.

It took a moment for his eyes to register what was in the rest of the cabinet, beneath the altar shelf. The skeleton of a man was crammed into the space beneath the shelf, folded in on himself. Ragged pieces of cloth clung to the ribcage and shoulders, but the leather thong that held the whistle around his neck had not entirely disintegrated. The remains teemed with spiders, bone-white arachnids with tiny pinprick red eyes.

"What—" Parker turned around and caught a glimpse over Nevin's shoulder. "Jesus Christ, is that a body?" Nevin did not move. "Sims, what the hell?"

The room's temperature plunged into frigidity the second that Nevin's fingertips caressed the handle of the knife. He turned to his victim and lunged forward. Nevin snagged Parker by the shirt collar and used his bulk to throw the other boy to the floor in front of the cabinet. A deep red glow emanated from the lower cubby, and the remains of Coach Abner were gone—at the back of the cabinet now was nothing but a swirling red and black vortex. The stench of sulfur poured forth along with animal hoots, growls, human screams and weeping, mechanical grinding, and the roar of flames.

Black smoky tentacles emerged from the vortex and snaked along the cracked tile floor toward Parker's prostrate body. He saw them and screamed. Parker tried to rise, but Nevin grabbed him by the hair and dragged him to his knees. He raised the knife.

"Go ahead," came Coach Abner's voice from somewhere in the cabinet. "Do it. Do what I failed to do. Feed the master, and the world is yours."

Beneath the demonic cacophony pouring from the cabinet-portal, a frantic, childlike voice filtered through to Nevin's ears, like slices of sunlight that shone stubbornly through deep storm clouds. "Nevin, please let go! I'll do whatever you want—please—oh my God *what is that thing?*"

"Feed him. Feed the master. FEED HIM!" Coach Abner roared over the savage cries of Hell that rolled over Nevin in horrific sonic waves.

"Nevin, no," Parker wept, and tugged at the hand that was locked in his hair. "Please, Nevin, I want to go home! I want my mom!"

Home. Parker's mom. Mom.

Nevin dropped the knife and clutched Parker's arm. He shoved him against the office door, away from the cabinet. Parker huddled against it, sobbing, unable to tear his gaze away.

Nevin looked down at him, tears in his eyes, and smiled. "I really am sorry," he said. "For all of it." He choked. The black smoke tentacles wormed themselves around his waist, neck, legs, and arms and he welcomed them, opening his palms to the sky. "Tell my mom—"

A roar split the atmosphere and a blast of sulfuric heat rolled out of the portal. Parker shrieked, clawed the door open, and ran faster than he'd ever run in his fifteen years of existence.

Miss Nathaniel used her key to open the basement. "Cellar door," she said under her breath, and took the steps carefully. "Cellar door. Cellar door. Cellar door."

Her heart clanged against the bottom of her chest when she saw the door and its plaque. COACH.

She opened the office and exhaled a shuddering breath. Although she was not a praying woman, she prayed now, prayed against the otherworldly whispers she could hear in the corners, the despair in the walls.

Miss Nathaniel cleared her throat. "Coach Abner. I came to return this." She tossed the playbook she'd taken from Nevin's locker into the room. It landed directly in the center, a few feet from the desk chair.

"I brought this for you, too." She lifted two mason jars full of gasoline from her bag, one in each hand. Indignation and grief coursed through her, and she flung them into the room. They smashed against the desk and the cabinet. Fuel splashed everywhere.

The librarian lit a match.

"I don't care if the whole school goes down with you," she said.

From the Author

I initially wrote "MVP" to submit to a horror anthology about spooky basements. I grew up in a home with an unfinished basement that could be a little spooky, but since our house was so small we had no choice but to use it frequently. No, for me, the basement of my middle school was way spookier. Built in the 1920s, it was the stereotypical red brick school, and had seen better days by the time I attended in the '90s. It was also full to capacity, so the administration had to utilize parts of the basement that probably were never intended to be educational spaces.

I remember the frigid concrete floors of the art room, having math class in the room next to the boiler with insects crawling around in the corners, and being forced to change out for gym in an ancient, moldy, subterranean locker room where you didn't let your bare skin touch anything.

These experiences, plus my continued presence in schools as an educator, inspired "MVP." I suppose it's no surprise that so many of my stories take place in schools, considering this is my sixteenth year in public education. This job has also afforded me numerous glimpses into the toxic masculinity of the sports world, and of course many of the characters are based (loosely or not so loosely) on students and staff that I have worked with in the past.

If you like stories where otherworldly events take place in a school setting, check out the wonderful anthology *We Cryptids*, where you can read my story, "Three Collapses," and discover how Mothman interrupts a school board meeting.

About the Author

Amelia Kibbie is an author, freelance writer, and secondary educator. Her debut novel *Legendary* was published in 2019 by Running Wild Press. Amelia's short stories have appeared in several anthologies, including the pro-human sci-fi collection *Humans Wanted, We Cryptids, Witches, Warriors, and Wyverns* and *Enter the Rebirth.* The literary journals *Saw Palm, Quantum Fairy Tales, Wizards in Space,* and *Intellectual Refuge* have featured her work.

She is active in her small Iowa town, serving on the local Historic Preservation Commission and Arts Council. She was named the local Poet Laureate in 2020 for a two-year term. Her next project is to renovate the turn-of-the-century church she just purchased into a home, with the help of her husband, daughter, and four cats. Find out more at:

ameliakibbie.com
and
https://www.facebook.com/ameliakibbie

Amelia tweets @AmeliaKibbie
and can be found on instagram @hollycat83

After The Wish

by
Carolyn Kay

After The Wish

assubal picked at the grain in a scratch on the mahogany bar in Rezalli's Pub. It wasn't so much a scratch now as a long, deep scar. He'd been picking at it off and on for the past ten thousand years. He looked at his reflection in the gilded mirror behind the top shelf liquor. What he could see of his green skin and blue-black horns hadn't changed much in all that time—maybe a few more lines around his yellow eyes, and the shadows of a deeper sadness below his sharp cheekbones.

The dim pub was cozy without being crowded and had always been a place of solace for him. There were a few other patrons, otherworldly beings like him, chatting quietly in overstuffed burgundy booths and at the solid oak tables scattered through the room. Music played in the background, but it was so quiet he couldn't exactly tell what it was, just that something soothing was playing.

"Want another Widow-Maker?" Ezafon, the elven barkeep asked. Ezafon hadn't changed much either. His hair had gone more blue than silver, and his ears were longer than when he'd started as a young elf of only two hundred, but their kind aged almost as slowly as genies.

"Yeah. Make it a triple," Aassubal replied. He really wanted to forget this last job. Sally's ocean blue eyes floated to the forefront of his memory. He angrily swiped them away, inadvertently gouging another scar in the bar.

Ezafon set a thick, black iron cup on the bar. It hit with a dull thud, and noxious yellow foam boiled over the edges, hissing, then disappearing with a pop when it hit the top of the bar without leaving so much as a condensation mark. He pointed at the new scratch in the bar. "Hey now, you're going to have to conjure Rezalli a new bar top if you keep that up." The elf paused, tilting his head as he considered Aassubal. "I know you're always a bit down after a gig, but what happened this time that's got you so agitated?"

Aas knew it was an empty threat. Rezalli had long ago spelled the mahogany to protect it from everything. Or almost anything. A couple of free wishes, and Rezalli's fondness for a few 'signs of use' kept Aassubal out of the doghouse. "You know me an' kids, Ez. They always tear a little piece of my heart out with the last wish." Aassubal put his fist over the first of his hearts, right where a human's would be. "But this last one, Sally. She tore the whole damn thing out."

Ezafon nodded his head sideways at a long-haired man in white robes at the end of the bar and gave Aassubal a knowing look.

Aassubal, had been so preoccupied when he came in, he hadn't seen the demi-god. "Pardon my language, Jes. I didn't see you there." He gave a slight nod to the figure, who held up a forgiving hand, but said nothing, never turning his gaze from the TV above the bar showing the news. Aas made a mental note to toss a coin in the swear jar at end of the bar when he left and returned his attention back to the barkeep. "Anyway, this one, Sally. What a sweet girl. Totally down on her luck like most of them, but not a single wish for herself. I don't get it. The world the way it is, half of it burning down, the other half drowning. She could have been like any of the hundreds before her and wished for safety, or riches, or hell—sorry Jes—even food." He paused for a moment and materialized two coins in the air over the swear jar. They rang like silver bells as they dropped into the container.

Jes smiled, got up from his seat and approached. He put his hand on Aas's shoulder and said, "It's alright. I've been there. Swear as much as you want tonight, it's on me." He snapped his fingers and the old pickle jar filled with gold coins and the sound of an angelic choir echoed briefly through the bar. "You did well on this one. I don't think she'll forget you." And then he disappeared. Very few demi-gods could disapparate without a waver in the magic field around Rezalli's. It always impressed Aas.

"Yeah, so what'd she wish for?" Ezafon asked, clearly unfazed by the demi-god's exit.

"She wanted her little brother to make a difference in the world, and to make sure he'd live long enough to do so." Aas felt a tear form in the corner of his eye.

"And?" Ezafon asked when Aas didn't elaborate.

"And yeah, the little brother practically saves the world, single-handedly. So, I showed her that, and fixed it so he'd survive long enough to do it." He sniffed, then took a long draw on the Widow-Maker. It burned like the sun going down, drying his tears and scorching everything else. It felt good. Better than the pain constricting all four hearts. He tried to continue but couldn't speak past the smoke in his throat. Ez handed him a frosted glass of milk. He downed the whole thing in one swallow. Ice followed fire, and his emotions cooled with his throat. "Thanks." Ez nodded. "Kicker is, I showed her her fate too, on the house, before I granted her wishes, and she still went through with it."

"Let me guess, she dies." Ez said, obviously thinking he'd heard this one before.

"Yeah, but not the way you'd think. I'll bet you think she dies taking a bullet, or jumping in front a knife aimed for him, or something?"

Ez shrugged and nodded. "Maybe poison meant for him?"

"Nah. She lives to a ripe old age—nearly a hundred if the vision's right. But she dies alone, forgotten by those she helped. Forgotten by the savior of the world, her own brother. They won't even mark her grave." Aassubal chokes up with a noxious mix of rage and sadness, unable to continue. He might have to have a chat with Jes. See if the sage could put in a good word with the old man in the Astrals—see that she gets some kind of benies when she makes it up there.

"Well, that sucks," Ez says. "All that, and she didn't use any wishes at all for herself?"

Aas shook his head. "Nope. Makes me wonder if she's not part jinn. Not many humans left who are that selfless. Hell, never were, actually. The occasional rock star, a saint or two, maybe." He shrugged and belched a bit of smoke. "Pardon." He paused for a moment, thinking. "It's a rare soul who can hold phenomenal cosmic power in their hands and not even give themselves a dime with it. But she did. And then, without even a 'thank you,' she skipped off into the smoke-filled sunset as if nothing'd happened." He slumped, resting his forehead on his arms.

"It's ironic, really. She sacrificed her own comforts and

happiness for her brother, and he'll forget her, just like she'll forget me." He sighed. "I should know better, after all these years. We jinn are tools, nothing more. We're the interface between humans and the universe, granting them their most ardent wishes. Who thinks of thanking the hammer when it's no longer of use? I just wish one of them, sometime, would say 'thank you.'"

A warm hand rubbed his back, and a deep alto voice said, "Chin up old friend, they forget all of us. It's just part of the job. You think people thank Jes much when things are going their way?" Bealzimore, a soul-gathering demon—one of the good ones—knocked back the remainder of the Widow-Maker. She shook her blue, horned head, belched fire, and slammed the iron cup on the bar. "Damn Ez, you make the best drinks." She flicked two coins into the swear jar and turned back to Aassubal. "You know damn well they don't. That's why He's in here, sipping rum and Cokes every Tuesday. Humans are a selfish, thankless species, and yet, here we are."

She sat down next to Aas and for a moment looked sadly at a worn, stuffed rabbit that had appeared out of nowhere. She caught Aas looking at her and snapped her fingers, causing the old toy to disappear.

Aas smiled at Bealzimore. She always found a way to lift his spirits, even if it was in a back-handed sort of way most of the time. It was true—all of it. Ez did make the best drinks, Jes was in here every Tuesday (once he thought about it) and the lack of gratitude was in the contract he'd signed. Part of the small print at the bottom he hadn't bothered to read all those thousands of years back. Phenomenal cosmic power, blah, blah, blah, everyone moves on like you were never there. He shrugged to himself and ordered a round for the bar. Tomorrow was another day.

From the Author

If you're on social media for any length of time, you'll come across memes of people befriending demons; whether their own or because they mistakenly summoned them. That got me thinking about whether or not demons and their ilk were really as bad as they're portrayed in most fiction.

To explore that, I wrote a story set in a post-apocalyptic world in which it was up to a varied group of fae and demons to collect souls and ferry them to the afterlife. My main character, Bealzimore, was a heavy-metal, kitten-loving demon tasked with the tough cases—souls in danger of being consumed; kids who didn't know they were dead—the heart-rending stuff. The story got an Honorable Mention in the Writers of the Future contest, but in the end, I think it was a little too preachy for publication.

A bit later, after a conversation with my husband that ultimately ended up on the subject of genies and how no one actually thanks them for granting wishes, "After the Wish" was born. It's set in the same post-apocalyptic world, and I couldn't resist putting Bealzimore in it, even if it's just a cameo. One of these days I'll write another story with Aassubal and Bealz. I think they'd make a pretty good team.

If you liked this story, you might also like my Steampunk Fantasy series, Galessel's Tale.

My Bibliography and website:
https://www.carolynkayauthor.com/

About the Author

From an early age, Carolyn Kay's been steeped in the worlds of fantasy and science fiction. She watched Star Wars at the drive-in and viewed Star Trek (the original series and Next Gen) religiously with her parents (yes, she's that old). Legos and Star Wars figures were her favorite toys, and Madeline L'Engle and Tolkien graced her bookshelves at a young age. So, it's no surprise that she writes stories in a variety of genres, or that her first novel was an Avengers-Star Wars crossover fanfic.

Carolyn melded two of her favorite genres, steampunk and fantasy, together into a series titled Galessel's Tale, set in a world co-created with her husband and award-winning illustrator, Chaz Kemp. She's also authored several short stories and a sci-fi novelette.

A government drone, she carves out time to write in between the day job, belly dancing, gardening, photography, and herding two very independent felines.

You can find her at carolynkayauthor.com and on most social media platforms under the username, Bewitchinghips.

Confessions of a Brownie
by
J. L. Royce

Confessions of a Brownie

I, Nigellus Severus, born in the province of Thracia in the third year of the reign of Gordian III, write this chronicle in confession of my sins, grievous and many. Having survived some two thousand years to this, the twenty-fourth century of the Common Era, I look back upon a life spent cowering in the shadows of human civilization: an outcast, a freak.

I am Nigellus Severus, and these are my sins.

What am I? That question remains unanswered despite my best efforts. If you know the language of my birthplace, then you may assume from my name that I am small and dark: small, yet unlike a dwarf; rather, formed in miniature, and imperfect. (My mother wished to call me 'Flaccus', for my ears were comically large even at birth. She related this whenever she was sober enough to articulate her unrelenting hatred and mistrust of her only son.) How is it that my spark of life seems inextinguishable? I broach that question whenever I encounter a human intelligent and compassionate enough to converse with me.

I was sickly at birth; they would have exposed me to die, had my father not clung pathetically to his hope for a male heir. Misshapen and repugnant, I disgraced them. The crude gossip of consort with an animal or a demon followed Mother to an early grave.

Ah, Mother: thus I confess my Original Sin: I was born.

In the fourteenth century of Europe, I found myself in the Low Countries, fleeing the onslaught of the pestilence known as the 'blue sickness' (later called the Black Death). It swept the known world in a whirlwind of death, from the Far East through the old Roman world of my birth, striking Europe through her ports on the Mediterranean, then north again and east to finally smite Russia.

I'd fled before it, hidden in caravans of merchants, supply wagons of armies, coaches of princes. (My unusual constitution offered me protection against the ravages of this disease, but I had no wish to test my luck by remaining within the afflicted areas.) As I could not risk the cities, I sheltered amongst the farmers and herdsmen.

Imagine a village—no, just a half-dozen squalid huts—huddled near the seaport. I had taken shelter in a lean-to serving one such hovel as a barn, housing an emaciated cow. I had worked its teat with my gnarled hands, greedily drained it in my hunger, and fell into a sated sleep, curled in the straw.

Dawn brought her to my attention. She glided through the near-darkness effortlessly, with pail and stool, and sat before the cow. The watery light was barely sufficient to reveal her form. She hummed as she worked, in a style I had last heard in the province of Aelia Capitolina, and thus I knew her to be a Jewess, or at least familiar with their culture.

"Poor thing," she murmured to the pathetic beast, "are you drying up? I'll try to find you better feed."

She started and sat erect. "Who's there?"

The shelter had lightened enough that I could make out her fine features as she stared about the corners. There was no hope for it, yet I was reluctant to reveal my wizened visage and shriveled form. My Flemish was passable, but I thought of a way to mollify her.

"I am but a weary traveler; I will be on my way if you would depart and leave me to slip out." I had announced myself in the corrupted Hebrew-German found in Christian Europe.

At my words, her expression softened. "Are you of the People? It is not our custom to turn away the traveler."

A foolish custom, I thought: my strategy had entangled me further.

"You would do well to avoid all but your family, these days," I warned. "The sickness walks the land, and respects neither custom nor kindness."

"Ignorance is no protection from evil. I would hear of your travels, sir, and prepare myself for what comes."

This one's wits were too sharp by half!

"All I know is that which I hear," she continued, "for I am blind from birth."

I was not one to indulge in *schadenfreude* (though soon I would embrace it), yet I confess a certain relief upon hearing of her disability. I stepped out of my hiding place and stood a few paces out of her reach, testing her claim.

"Then I accept your hospitality and trust I shall not bore you with my conversation. Although not a Jew, I have lived amicably with your people in several locales and may offer news of their fortunes."

"I am Avigail, daughter of Moshe and Rebecca." She stared through me, smiled, and made a little curtsey worthy of the finest lady.

My birth name is archaic and generally suspect. "You may call me 'Brownie'. Are your parents about?"

"My father is in the countryside, doing his skilled labor—repairs of tools and shelters, in the main. My mother passed away, several years ago."

Better and better! I glanced about, and seeing no one to detect me, let Avigail lead me out to the hovel attached to her home. A cat darted past our feet and into the surrounding undergrowth.

I have dwelt in palaces and huts, in underground cities and vessels plying the stars. I was imprisoned in laboratories and dungeons, even a zoo, once: studied and abused. The modest home of Avigail and Moshe was as welcoming as any I had found in many centuries of wandering.

Avigail spoke. "Your voice manly; yet you are…low." She giggled at herself. "Pardon; I mean to say, you cannot be very tall."

Perceptive, this one. "Indeed; for I am stunted. Though mature, I am but the height of a child."

"Oh." Perhaps she imagined a handsome, strapping squire lounging in her silage. I pushed aside my spiteful reaction.

To be unique in anything—appearance or intelligence— is to be unwanted and unappreciated.

She recovered her manners. "Please, sit by the fire. I have gruel still warm, over there. The cow produced little milk for it, I'm afraid."

I felt a touch guilty. "Keep your milk." The pot with its coagulating mash was warm on the hearth.

"Save some for my father." I served out portions in two bowls that were to hand.

She seated herself on a stool close by and accepted the proffered bowl.

"What is your destination? My hunger is for news and knowledge."

"I am making my way to Russia, as I've heard it is untouched by the pestilence; and, I have never visited it."

"You flee this scourge; is it so deadly, then?"

What could I say? *Entire villages, decimated. Cities ringed by mounds of the unburied dead. The worst of humanity exposed, as parents abandon children, priests their flocks…*

"It is serious. You would do well to keep watch, lest it steal into your home and rob you of your life."

"I hear it is ill vapors," she opined. "The physicians protect themselves with herbs and flower garlands."

Such gestures meant little to the beast that roamed the land, but I had no wish to dispel all hope.

"I have a theory…" It was not strictly my invention, more a notion. "Life is a struggle; whether in the forest or the sea, the strong devour the weak."

She leaned forward, lips parted. Her teeth were still unbroken and whole; her hair, lustrous and long.

"While in the East, I spent time with an Arab philosopher, who created discs of the purest glass, shaped to make things appear larger…"

I realized the futility of my declamation, given her blindness, and began again. "Imagine…beans. You can touch them, feel their shape, their consistency. And seeds smaller than that; and even smaller, pollen grains. What this wise man did was to devise a way to make the tiniest speck of pollen feel as large as a…a gourd."

Her blind eyes went wide. "So, then you might touch it, feel the texture of this tiny thing?"

"Yes—but for sight. And what he found was a smaller world in every pollen grain, and in a drop of water tiny creatures too small to be seen or felt. The fluid of blood, too, throngs with life, multitudes dwelling inside every living being. They live and die within us. And the leaf of a plant—therein lies more tiny rooms than the grandest of castles."

I was caught up in my imagination. "Who knows what transpires in these invisible worlds?"

"And you believe that some tiny invaders are responsible for our ills?"

She was bright! "I think it possible that, not out of malice but simply the will to survive, invaders might inhabit and affect us—we, who are like worlds to them."

Avigail sat back and clapped her hands in delight. "I knew you would take me away to some foreign land, full of strange beasts and warring tribes. But you reveal wonders within, and all around us!"

"It is not for your amusement," I warned. "The origin of the pestilence is some creature traveling with rats, fleas, and yes, people. It is important to avoid the infected—keep your home clean, kill the rats, and avoid touching the sick."

The girl stood, holding out her hand. "Your bowl?"

I drained the last of the watery mess, thanked her, and passed it over. She readily navigated her world—a common room and two sleeping pads, one with a tattered hanging in front of it. Avigail wiped the bowls and placed them aside, then rejoined me at the fireside and pleaded for tales from my travels.

Avigail's reactions guided my selection from my centuries of wandering, and hours passed until I demanded a respite. I needed to reconnoiter, and she had chores to perform before her father's return. She gave me leave to occupy the animal shelter, for which I was grateful, though I would rather have had the fire's company— and hers.

Again, I awoke in the watery dawn, a little more comfortable thanks to the rough weave mat Avigail had lent. A slight pressure along my legs told me of a presence; in a dim fantasy, it was the girl, beside me. I raised my head, looked into a pair of pale green eyes, unblinking.

You're ugly; you smell bad. The voice was a low purr.

"But I'm warm. Well, keep your fleas to yourself." I pushed the cat away from me.

At my words it hissed, ears flattened.

"Yes, I understand you, cat." (It was just another personal aberration. Perhaps those demented enough to believe in 'familiars' share my nature. But I have no supernatural talent; just a unique brain.)

The brindled gray crouched just out of reach, regarding me. *I'm cleaner than you*, it yowled. *And healthier. And younger.*

"Far younger. Avoid the fleas, if you'd stay alive. Kill the rats near your mistress but avoid the slow ones—they are sick."

I sat up, reluctantly, clutching the crude blanket. "Have you a name?"

The animal stroked its face with a dampened paw. Then it straightened, wrapping its tail about its forepaws.

Grace-by-sunlight. Kittens-aplenty. Death-by-moonlight—

"Moonlight; that will do. Tell me: is the girl kind to you?"

She is tolerable, the cat purred. *Softer than you.*

"Too true. And her father?"

Smells of death, Moonlight growled. *Soon to be not-here.*

With that, the creature hunkered down into the straw.

"What? When?"

Last night, he returned. Moonlight closed his eyes and ignored me. A cat has little interest in human affairs.

Avigail knelt beside the cot nearest the fire. A figure twitched under a blanket, groaning.

"How is he?" I asked.

The girl started, half-rising. "Oh—Brownie—you gave me a shock. A farmer from up the road brought him home. He found Father at the side of the lane, too weak to walk."

Her face was gaunt in the flickering firelight.

"Have you slept?"

"No; I've kept watch. He burns with fever, yet has no drainage—"

I stepped closer and cautiously peered around her. He appeared unresponsive, and unlikely to comprehend me even if he awakened.

"You should rest," I said. "I'll keep watch."

Avigail was ready to object but slumped and nodded. "I will milk the cow before I sleep."

She would sleep better knowing she'd finished her chores.

"Do you have other family to call?"

"None."

I touched her father's forehead with the back of my hand.

"Can you bring a bowl of water and a cloth? I will try to relieve his fever."

She frowned. "Does not the fever help to burn away ill humors?"

"He is too hot; his body is burning up."

Avigail nodded and went to fetch the water. I pulled aside the blanket and raised his shirt. As I feared, the swellings were visible at the groin. Baring his chest, I saw them at the armpits as well. His thin arms bore a scattering of black marks where the farmer's fingers had lifted him. There was no doubt in my mind: it was the pestilence.

I had little hope for the father but decided I would attempt to save his daughter.

I searched their home for supplies, yielding a woman's kerchief. Folded into two layers, it would suffice as a mask for her. I chanced upon a cache of cloth squares. Several stacked together and tied with the lacings from the old man's shoes gave me a mask. Although I had not yet sickened, I wished to take no chances.

Avigail reappeared with the milk pail and water bucket. She covered the milk and set it aside.

"Sit down and hold still," I said.

She flinched as I placed the triangle over her lower face but permitted me to tie it snug behind her head. "This mask will help protect you."

Avigail touched her face, frowned, and ran her fingers along the edge.

"I know this!" she cried. "Have you been through my things?"

I ignored her protest. "Wash your hands every time you touch your father—not dipping into the bucket but pouring out a little water. And change your bedding before you lie down. I'll help you."

"What about a mask, for yourself?"

I passed her one of the cloth squares I had found. "These will do."

She fingered the cloth, and her mouth went round. "These are my...bleeding cloths!"

I took it away from her. "No matter—I left some."

"Why are you doing all this?" Avigail asked.

"Because it may save you."

"And Father?"

I hesitated. "You can't help him if you sicken."

Avigail nodded; she had lived in darkness her entire life, and yet bore no malice towards the uncaring world.

"Let's get your bedding outside—I'd help but would rather remain unnoticed."

"Of course."

We carried the mats and blankets from her corner, and she fetched a broom with which to beat them. When finished, I helped her restore her bed.

Avigail gestured at her father. "Should we…"

"No; let him rest." *He'll likely die soon anyway, and we'll want to burn everything,* was my unspoken thought.

She paused. "Thank you, for staying, for your help. When you feel the need to go, you shouldn't stay. I can't…"

"Thank you for sheltering a trespasser."

"Will you watch Father, while I rest?"

"Of course."

Avigail retreated behind her thin curtain and stripped off her clothes, tossing them out of her curtained corner. Sightless, she had no notion of privacy beyond what she had been told, and I shamelessly watched her groom herself through the sheer hanging. She was common, yet extraordinary. My longing for her only redoubled my determination that she should survive the sickness.

At last, she lay down, clad in a simple shift, her long hair loose and combed. Perhaps my sigh was in the universal language, for a sibilant voice purred in the darkening chamber.

You want her. Moonlight was a deeper shadow in the failing firelight.

I tossed more kindling on the coals, then larger deadfall. The cat watched in respectful satisfaction, eyes glowing, as the fire resurged.

Avigail's breathing had deepened immediately into an exhausted sleep.

"My lust is no concern of yours," I muttered to the cat.

Take her, then. The cat settled into a self-satisfied repose.

The labored breathing and intermittent groans of the old man filled the small room. He was a half-century old—an infant compared to me. I watched him for hours, cooling his forehead with the damp cloth, but his fever did not break. Beneath his labored breathing, I could hear the girl in her abyssal sleep. The specter of her suffering the same fate haunted me. The longer she was exposed to the dying man, the more likely she would fall ill. How many human lives had I seen come and go? It would be a matter of a minute or two to end his suffering—and perhaps save Avigail. To force his soiled shirt into his mouth, cover his face…then convince Avigail to leave, with me…

I drifted off to sleep, crouched in the corner by the old man's cot, wondering how far my lust might carry me—one sin, or two?

I awoke to a clamor outside, and a heavy fist on the flimsy door.

"Open!" A gruff voice demanded in Flemish.

The door groaned and flew open, the latch shorn away. Two soldiers entered, glaring around the dim interior. They saw the old man on the mat, and one called to the door.

"He's here, priest! There lies the plague-bearer!"

I hid behind a folded screen in my corner and watched. A stooped figure entered and reluctantly approached the sick man.

"Who is it? Brownie—is that you?" Avigail appeared, wrapped in her blanket. The soldiers looked puzzled, waiting for direction from the priest.

"A Jewess," he explained.

The older soldier confronted her. "*Jodin?*"

Avigail, staring in blind confusion, nodded.

The priest glanced over at her. "Your *Pater Noster*—say it."

She struggled to understand his thick dialect. "I do not know…"

He nodded. "Take her," he directed the soldiers. "This sickness is the Jews' work."

The priest said a brief prayer over her father. Crossing himself, he rose and confronted her.

"Good people have fallen ill, all tracked to *that*." He gestured towards her father.

The priest made for the door. "Bring her."

"What about the old man?" the younger soldier asked.

"Leave him."

The uniformed men grabbed her arms. Avigail stumbled along until the men roughly lifted her from the ground.

"Brownie!" she cried, in her half-Hebrew dialect. "Help me, please!"

The priest raised the cross at his neck. "She calls for her demon, her familiar!"

I crouched in the darkness, awaiting the inevitable search and discovery.

"A gray beast, I saw," said the senior soldier.

"Capture it, for examination," the priest ordered, "or slay it if it threatens."

The party departed, Avigail's sobs fading as they made their way down the lane.

I abandoned the father; one of his buboes had burst, draining pus into his clothes and bedding. I could stay and be discovered by looting neighbors or returning soldiers, or leave and pursue Avigail's captors. The longer I waited the worse my chances.

I gathered a few useful items—a crude knife, an old cloak, and several candle stubs—and slipped around to the animal stall. There I drank what little milk the cow carried, warm from the teat, knowing another meal might be a long time coming.

I headed towards Bruges and its port and caught up with her captors. Crouching in hedges and ditches, I followed the Flemish soldiers with their cart of prisoners to their destination.

The militia barracks lay on the outskirts of Bruges. It was but a half-day journey, so the afternoon was only half gone. Zee Bruges, the port, had brought wealth—and, more recently, the pestilence—from Italy. In my headlong flight through Europe, I had unwittingly followed the pestilence by ship to this land.

I sheltered outside the fortress, watching and waiting for the opportunity to pass the gate undetected. In the early evening, a hayrack trundled up. After inspection, it lingered unattended as the driver shared news with the guards. As they listened to his tales of death, I darted over and hopped aboard, secreting myself within the hay bales. There I sweated, stifling sneezes, until the driver thrashed the mule into motion and brought me into the fortress.

Clusters of one and two-story structures surrounded a square, with the church in the center. The cart was driven back to the stables and stopped. I fled into the depths of a warren of stalls and bins before the driver could dismount and unload his cargo. There I waited until the cart was emptied and driven off.

I scanned the court in the twilight. Three pyres, with posts and ropes ready, were piled high with dry wood: intended for the prisoners. Nearby stood the gaol, a small stone building set against the fortified wall and apart from the rest of the structures. Two guards lounged before its iron-barred door.

I crept through shadows to peer into a barred window, where I glimpsed Avigail and two others. Around the corner, a larger window opened onto the gaol's hallway. My wizened form worked to my advantage, as I squeezed between its wide-set bars and dropped into a corridor outside the cells. At their cell, I studied the door. I knew the door could be lifted out of its hinges—by one far stronger than myself or the prisoners. Instead, I set to work on the lock, using the knife and a bailing hook I had stolen.

The door creaked in protest as I drew it open and slipped inside. One prisoner lay at the far wall, breathing with difficulty: perhaps the deadly affliction of the lungs. I wondered if the fool of a priest would realize that he had doomed the church and barracks by bringing her within the walls.

Avigail huddled with a third woman in the opposite corner, both asleep.

"Avigail!" I whispered, touching her shoulder. Her blind eyes flew open, and her arms pinwheeled in terror.

"Quiet!" I cautioned.

"Brownie!" She clung to me, our first and only embrace. "But—you are so small!"

It was not the time for lies or explanations. I disengaged myself and hushed her, having no desire to meet her sleeping cellmate.

"We have no time to waste! When I go back out, I'll create a distraction."

I worked feverishly at the lock on her gauntlet with my makeshift tools, at last forcing it open.

"Come—" I took her hand "—I'll show you where to hide."

"My father—" Avigail began, when the prisoner slumped beside her woke.

The woman's eyes went wide with fear at the sight of me. "The demon is here!"

Fortunately, her voice came out a muted croak.

Avigail tried to calm her. "He is a friend, mother Mary—a stranger."

"Friend with the Devil!" Mary set up a wail of terror.

I placed a hand over her blistered lips. The murmured conversation of the guards ceased; the outer door opened with a clatter of keys and a creak.

"Now!" I urged. Avigail gripped Mary's shoulder, urging her to flee. The old woman shrank away, still screeching.

"Go!" Avigail shook me off. "I cannot fend for myself, and they will capture us both if you try to lead me. I'll quiet her."

I cursed and swung the cell door shut upon us. I pulled myself up to their window and clambered through, with some difficulty.

Mary found her voice and gave a full-throated scream. "The Devil is among us—looks, he flies out the window!"

My only luck was that both guards abandoned their post to investigate the clamor. I slipped off to a corner near the gate. I crouched, waiting for an opportunity to return and lead Avigail to freedom. But that moment was not to come.

The guards were more conscientious than I had hoped. Mary's shrieks abruptly ceased. Minutes stretched and still they failed to appear. Then one of the guards emerged and trotted off to the church. He returned with the priest.

Is cowardice a sin, or merely a moral failing? I watched in growing fear as the guards led the prisoners to their respective pyres. The sickest, practically carried out, was coughing uncontrollably, her phlegm spraying the soldiers. They roughly lifted her in place and secured her arms above her head. Mary was babbling again about the flying imp, the Devil's spawn, the blind girl's lover, and more nonsense. Avigail was silent, her head bowed but turning side to side, listening, searching…

A crowd had gathered and chattered eagerly. A half-hour later the priest returned and knelt at each victim's feet, praying and assuring them that confession would open the gates of heaven to their otherwise damned souls. None could make a coherent response. I knew that Avigail had little Flemish and less Latin with which to understand the priest's pleading.

At last, the time came. The sun had risen over the fortifications; the square was full of milling, impatient spectators. The priest raised his arms and crossed himself. Most of the onlookers joined him as he intoned, "…*ora pro nobis peccatoribus, nunc, et in hora mortis nostrae. Amen.*"

Did the onlookers realize how close their hour of death might be, with the pestilence at their door?

One by one, the priest implored each prisoner to confess and receive mercy—God's, if not Man's. The coughing plague victim had not the breath to reply; Mary had not the wits. He turned to Avigail.

"And you, child of Abraham, unchristened murderer of our Savior!" The crowd muttered deprecations. "Do you repent your consort with the Devil?"

Avigail shuddered. "I've done nothing," she sobbed in her stumbling Flemish, "I must help my father!"

"The plague-bearer!" thundered the priest. "Spreading death through Christendom!"

"No—he's a good man. We're innocent!" With that, she bent her head and prayed. I recognized the cadence if not all the words of the Torah.

The priest held his crucifix high as he withdrew from her. Three soldiers came forth, bearing torches, and lit the pyres.

"Kneel!" thundered the priest to the throng. Those too slow or disinterested to comply were motivated by soldiers with staves. He raised his arms again.

"*O gloriosa stella maris, a peste succurre nobis…*"

Peste—I would live to watch it walk through humanity again and again, for centuries. I would learn a bit more, but that day I had no hope to offer.

The afflicted woman barely stirred as merciful death embraced her. Mary screamed, begging for mercy, then for death, then incoherently, as the flames hungrily devoured her dress, then her flesh. Avigail's thin shift caught ablaze, and the fire-swept wind tore it away. The crowd moaned as her naked flesh dissolved in the flames.

Avigail died in silence, as she had lived in darkness; but I was sure she was murmuring, *Brownie…*

I crept away from that cursed place, coward that I am, as night fell and the smoldering pyres were cleared away. I made my way back to Avigail's simple home, to find it ravaged and looted.

The house had been pilfered, her father was gone, no doubt dead and carted off to an anonymous grave. I gathered a few items in a sack to prepare for my flight. I made my way into the hedge without a plan. I heard a feeble cry.

Cold…

Moonlight had been gutted and tossed aside to die. I emptied my sack and gathered the cat into the rough cloth, bundling up its torn body.

Time for another life, it purred.

"I have but one life—I think—and it stretches longer than my heart can bear."

Girl?

"Dead—murdered."

Moonlight closed his eyes. *You?*

"I'll go away—wait out the madness, somewhere. I cannot forsake human company, much as I would like, for they may hold answers."

Why care? Hunt; make kittens; rest; watch. That is all.

"That is all," I repeated. I had tried to live as he suggested, for human lifetimes, but the mystery of my life was like an insatiable appetite.

Warm, Moonlight purred.

Humans shriek and curse their fate, and weep when they pass. Animals are more sanguine; why, I know not. I thought I might help Moonlight pass, but he died as softly as he had prowled the night in life.

The ground was soft. I clawed a hole in the undergrowth where he could rest.

Have you guessed all of my sins? The tale is not yet done.

I'd planned to slip away on a trading vessel, perhaps farther north to a colder, more desolate clime; so I made my way to the docks of Zee Bruges.

I hid near a quay, biding my time. A rat scurried forward—drawn by the scent of the cat's blood on my sack. I kicked it away, only to have another take its place. These death-trading travelers emerged from the shadows to sniff and scramble towards me.

I emptied the sack, then stunned the nearest rat with a blow from my staff. I tossed the limp body into the sack.

There would be retribution on Earth, at my hand.

I caught the sickest vermin readily, choosing only the afflicted. Then I was back on the road, making my way back to where Avigail had died.

Each cart queued before the gates received a rat or two; the rest went down the town well. My sin of wrath warmed me through the chilly night, as the girl might well have done.

The pestilence burned on. I watched humanity shrivel in its flames, as Avigail had, in anguish and ignorance.

I, Nigellus Severus, thus bring to a close this chapter of my confessions. We seek answers, you and I, yet find none.

From the Author

Written in 1872 by Dinah Maria Mulock Craik (aka Miss Mulock), *Adventures of a Brownie* is a charming collection of tales about a foot-tall fellow who lives in a coal bin and chats with the family cat. A Henry Altemus edition (the illustrated Vademecum series, probably 1899 by the numbering) was presented to my father by his teacher 'for headmarks' in elementary school, and thus came to me.

At some point a notion settled in the back of my mind and hibernated there: the story of a strange, stunted, creature, living in the shadows as an outcast, an immortal witness to the human condition, feared and envied. What would such a person see and suffer through, in the long centuries from Pax Romana until humanity left the stage? How would it change a person, to witness the same mistakes made, again and again?

Hope you enjoy "Confessions of a Brownie." ...jlr

About the Author

J. L. Royce is a published author of science fiction, the macabre, and whatever else strikes him. He lives in the northern reaches of the American Midwest. His work appears in *Allegory*, *Fifth Di*, *Ghostlight*, *Love Letters to Poe*, *Lovecraftiana*, *Mysterion*, *parABnormal*, *Sci Phi*, *Strange Aeon*, *Utopia*, *Wyldblood*, etc. He is a member of HWA and GLAHW.

Some of his anthologized stories may be found at:
www.jlroyce.com

Follow him on Twitter: @authorJLRoyce.

Where his Soul Was Drowned

by
Kitty Sarkozy

Where his Soul Was Drowned

We've all had the feeling of being watched when we're alone. We've all gotten up in the middle of the night to use the bathroom and, in those few seconds before the light comes on, had this feeling that someone is already in there, that creepy tingle up the spine when looking in a mirror and not being 100% sure that the person looking back is just a reflection. You move your hand, your image moves in exactly the same way, maybe you make a funny face, then you feel stupid and childish for even wondering, so you turn away, ignoring the little smile you see from the corner of your eye.

I have been there, right down to the silly embarrassment of testing my reflection, until the day I found out my fears were not so silly, and a reflection is not always the truth. Mirrors show up in myths all over the world. You know that breaking a mirror will give you seven years of bad luck. You might have heard that spirits can enter your home through a mirror, or that staring too long at your reflection can allow it to steal your soul. Some families, like mine, cover all reflective surfaces after a death. Maybe a mirror can predict the future or let you peek into distant lives.

If you ever see something in a mirror that is not true, is not an exact reflection of the real world around you, you should be afraid. Think about the last time you looked in the mirror: are you sure the reflection was accurate? Are you sure nothing was in the wrong place, no little thing missing from the reflection? Is that you looking back into your eyes?

I can move between this world and the world on the other side of the glass. It is a very rare talent, so rare that few people even know it can be done. There are words for it in most cultures, but since Lewis Carroll, most would call me an "Alice". Just so you know I am not British and would look silly in her cute blue dress. I am the sort of person who gets stopped by strangers who find me familiar and is often told I have "that kind of face".

I have known about my ability to walk between worlds for a while. How I fell in for the first time and got back out is a long story, which I'm going to skip for now. The talent might be genetic. I think it comes from my father's family, but correlation isn't causation so don't quote me. Some humans who are predisposed to this might live their whole life without ever touching the other side of the glass, without ever knowing another reality exists. Others fall in and never find their way home. There are some who lose part of themselves to the glass. Don't for a moment think the ways belong to or were created by humans. We get lucky or unlucky, we fall into other worlds by accident. I've been researching for years and been through one time, each way. I'm as close as anyone on this side of the looking glass might be to an expert, and I don't have a clue how it all works.

Other things know a lot more than me.

Such as the vampire killing innocent people in my town.

Do you remember back before vampires were sparkly, sexy, and shirtless? Back when they were soulless monsters who were to be feared, not tragic romantic heroes to be pitied and longed for? You know that a vampire casts no reflection, right?

I know of a few things that don't show up in mirrors. Vampires are the only type I know that started out human, technically. They are often attractive, they are never heroes, and no matter how hard you try, you can't fix them with your love.

Here's an old story you might know. Once upon a time an extremely attractive young man fell in love with his reflection. He would kneel at the edge of a clear calm pond and stare at his perfect face for hours. The more he looked, the more beautiful his reflection appeared, and the farther away it felt. He longed for the boy in the lake and couldn't bear to be apart from him. One day while gazing upon his true love, the boy leaned too close and drowned.

This story of the boy Narcissus is a pretty good explanation for how vampires come into being. There's nothing wrong with liking how you look or gazing into the mirror. However, every time you do there is a chance that something on the other side will take notice. The more often and longer you look, the greater your chances of being seen, until your reflection is looking at you more than you are looking at it. It pulls at you, taking little bits of your soul into itself, patiently feeding on you every day. Once the creature has a taste for you, it's like that Depeche Mode song, it just can't get enough, and then you literally go out of your head, slipping and sliding into a different place. Your soul is drowned in the mirror, trapped in something like a freezing, pitch-dark lake. Your body, no longer casting a reflection, walks away, a soulless thing that knows everything you know. Hungry.

These soulless things are vampires. Drawn to passion and warmth, they aren't pleased to find only emptiness inside of them where love, joy, hopes and sorrows dwelt. They have no pity, no compassion. You can't ask them for mercy; they have none to give.

They feed on emotions. I suppose, in theory, they could feed on love, lust or desire. Maybe some of the older ones do. But think about hunger. Imagine you haven't eaten all day. Your stomach is growling. Your blood sugar is low. Are you more likely get drive-thu or go to the grocery to shop and then cook? Or would you go outside, dig a hole and plant seeds? Love is a seed. It takes time, patience, and care. If vampire wanted to feed on love, he would have to already be well fed to start with and possess the time and resources needed to develop and nurture relationships.

Whereas sorrow, fear, and pain are fast food. It is possible to take a person from perfectly happy to total terror or agony in a just a few seconds. It finds a victim, causes horrible fear and pain, feeds as long as it can, and leaves behind a broken, bloody corpse. I am pretty sure they don't actually drink blood, but there are so many things I don't know, so don't take my word for it.

I do know how to kill one, which is why I am sitting in front of this mirror, staring into its shadowy depths, looking for a drowned soul.

Somewhere in these shadows he is lost. I hold a picture of the body the vampire is walking around in. Attached to the picture I have some of his hair, something written in his own hand, and a few other odds and ends I got from his room. In the picture he is young and attractive, with short blond hair, bright blue eyes, and a charming, white-toothed smile. He sits on a porch swing with a dog beside him.

I found this same dog dead in the backyard of the house, neck broken. Inside I found both his mother and little brother dead, their faces covered in blood and twisted in terror. I wonder if it was one of them who took this picture.

The police scanner chatters softly in the background. They haven't found these first bodies yet. I'm listening for any other violent deaths to be reported. It would save time to have a starting point once I'm able to track it.

I need to trap his soul so he can help me find the body. Unfortunately, it's more like a dowsing rod than GPS. I can use it to figure out the straight direction he is from me, but nothing more. Not how close he is, not which streets are the best way to get there. Just compass direction. The bodies I found were cold and stiff to the touch. They had been dead for a while. Half a day? Odds are also good he hasn't gone far. Vampires tend to stay close to where they lived, or where their soul was drowned.

Which is why I took the mirror from his room with me. I couldn't scry it there; the police could show up at any time. Not to mention, I have no interest in hanging out at a house reeking of blood and fear. The cops will not notice a small wall mirror missing from the boy's room. If all goes well, by the time they find him he will be a corpse too.

I hold a glass bottle, painted silver inside. I hold both the bottle and the picture up to the mirror calling to him. His name was Daniel. Maybe he went by Dan or Danny. I call all three names in turn, sitting there long enough that my shoulders ache and my feet fall asleep. I can't stop pulling now. I feel him out there, moving ever closer to the reminders of the life he once had.

I try to picture how his home looked on a beautiful summer day. I recall the family portrait I saw in the living room, focusing on his mother's smile and his little brother's freckles. I try to imagine them having dinner. Going to a park. If he was a person I knew, calling his drowned soul would be easier, but I have to just make the best of it, keeping the images vague.

My arms start to shake from the tension of holding them out so long. I can't keep this up forever. If I don't find his soul in the glass soon, I am going to have to stop, rest a while and then try again. At least three hours will be lost. Three hours of innocent people being in danger.

Please don't think I have some sort of hero complex. I understand that people are in danger of one sort of thing or another all the time, and that normally isn't my problem. I'm not the type who risks my own life as a hobby. I would rather call 911 and let the professionals handle it.

But in this case, I'm the only one who has any chance of dealing with this. I had to enter a house, look at dead bodies, steal some personal possessions from a guy I've never met. Now I have to trap his soul in a mirror bottle and then hunt his body.

I know people who would be better suited to this task, who have done this sort of thing before. But they are either on the other side of the country or the other side of the glass. Dr. Ramsey was able to tell me what to do, but he can't help me.

My mind wandering, I almost didn't feel the little tug, like a fish on the line: Danny's drowned soul nibbling at the bait. I was calling Danny with his possessions, thoughts of his family. He felt my call and became curious.

I pull at him, clearing my thoughts of anything but Danny. I take a few guesses at the joys Danny might have experienced. I think about the feel of sun on flesh, the taste of a good cheeseburger, the sound of music. I think about how it feels to smile, and the smell of fresh cookies. I think about first love, winning a game, opening a birthday present. I sigh, imagining the comfort of sleeping late in a warm bed.

Then he is there, in the glass, where my reflection was a fraction of a second before. I let out a little scream and almost jump away. He looks very much like the boy in the picture, but with subtle differences. His face is smeared with blood, a few tear-streaked lines down his cheeks. His eyes are full of pain the boy in the picture had not yet experienced. He reaches out to me, dried blood under ragged fingernails. His mouth moves, but I can't hear him. I know he is afraid, confused.

I dropped the picture, quickly reaching both hands towards him. This might be my only shot. I held the mouth of the bottle against the glass with one hand while my other hand sank to the elbow in the mirror. The inside of the mirror was freezing cold, so cold my brain read it as burning. I nearly pulled my hand back out of panic before grabbing the drowned boy by the shoulder, closing my hand and then reaching down his back and chest with my fingers, and then again and again. I was trying to ball him up small and tight, like folding socks. After doing this a few times I moved my hand toward the bottle containing a single strand of his blond hair from the brush in his room, soil from his yard, and a little food from his fridge. Home.

I put my hand, still scrunching, against where the bottle touched the mirror, willing him into it. It seemed to take forever, my fingers completely numb from the cold, to get him into the bottle, but it couldn't have been more than a few minutes before I was putting my empty hand over the opening and pulling them both away from the mirror.

I capped the silver bottle and then put it down into a Crown Royal bag, pulling the drawstring tight. When I held the bag by the cords it spun for only a moment before starting to pendulum, pointing towards my window. I was tired, sore, and hungry, but there was no time to waste. I got a few things from a beat-bronze chest in my room and headed down the stairs.

I had a vampire to find.

Using the sway of the bottle, it took me a few hours to find the right part of town. It was in the east side of the city, which was heavily populated and full of restaurants, cafes, cute shops, and nightclubs. I circled around the area in my car, the bag always swinging towards the nightlife area known as "The Village". As far as I could tell, he wasn't on the move. The thing about sunlight being deadly to his kind isn't true, but it is based on truth. They hunt best at night and are not as powerful during the day. He shouldn't be out walking the streets.

I parked in the empty lot of a Mexican place that I'd eaten at once or twice, and then started following the bottle. I had to turn around more than a few times, but finally found where he was: a busy local coffee shop. The vampire sat in a big green armchair against the back wall, slowly sipping something from a white mug and stared off into space. Vampires eat and drink just like humans.

If I didn't already know who I was looking for I never would have suspected this guy of being a soulless monster. It looked like a regular high school or young college guy. Its clothes were rumpled but not blood splattered, hair was messy in a stylish sort of way. It looked just as likely to have been out all night partying or up all night studying.

I looked away from it before it could feel my gaze, hoping that it didn't feel any pull towards Danny's soul. This was not a good place to reintroduce them. I went to the bar and ordered a double espresso mocha. I needed it.

I sat down in the sitting area along the opposite wall from the vampire. Its eyes flicked up to me for just a second and then away. It wasn't interested in me, being well fed and day-dazed. I picked up a book from a loaner shelf and sat pretending to read. The sitting area wasn't full; only 3 people, other than the vampire and myself, in the mismatched, secondhand chairs. I saw that I had inadvertently picked up something by Pynchon, but since I couldn't afford a stifling conversation with people who appreciate his work, I swapped it out for something more unassuming.

After a while, it finished its drink and closed its eyes, appearing to doze off. The vampire might have really been asleep. They must sleep if they eat, right? It makes sense. It was about an hour, and another coffee for me, before he awoke. The sun was no longer leaving beams of light along the floor, though it was still a few hours until sunset.

The sitting area was a lot fuller now. People were sitting at the tables with their laptops open, or in the other comfy chairs with a book or playing with a cell phone. The vampire scanned the crowd quickly, looking hungry and impatient. There was little chance he would attack anyone here. It was a soulless monster, not a mindless beast. They know better than to attack people in a crowded place.

It stood up and left the coffee shop, agitated.

After a moment I put down the book I had not really been reading and followed it out the door. The vampire walked farther into the center of The Village, staying in the shade of the buildings as much as it could. It got farther away from me as we walked. With its lead and longer legs, I would have had to jog to keep up, and that might tip it off. A few blocks down it turned into an alley.

As soon as it turned, I started running. I couldn't lose it now. I prayed the alley was a dead end. If so, this was about to be over. If not, I might lose it and have to go back to using the bottle to track him.

By the time I reached the alley, I was at a full run, or at least as close to that as I ever got. Running is not something I make a hobby of. Mainly I run when chased. I scanned the alley for it. I was looking towards the left when I was roughly grabbed and pulled into a recessed doorway. We were both in shadow, but I didn't need to see it to know this was Danny's shell holding me. This close I could feel the hunger and hate coming off it.

I was so stupid! I should have started walking once I entered the alley. I should have realized an alley would be a great place for an ambush. How wonderfully polite it must think me, running right into a trap mere seconds after it was set.

One of its hands was around my neck holding me to the door, the other held my right arm behind my back. He was squeezing my throat hard enough that I couldn't draw adequate air into my lungs, but not so hard that I was going to pass out quickly. It hurt. The vampire was strong, not superhuman or anything, just a large healthy, athletic guy in his prime. I couldn't fight it off physically, I knew that. But even so it was hard not to drop the fuzzy purple bag and start trying to pull his fingers away from my neck.

"You were at the coffee shop; I know you were watching me. Now you followed me here. I am rather attractive but isn't stalking a little much, miss?" he said, moving his face closer to mine, until our noses were almost touching. "You should have just taken a picture".

Even in my panic, I had to wonder if losing your soul might make you lose your sense of humor, because that was a joke a six-year-old would laugh at.

It pressed Danny's body against mine, nuzzling my neck.

"You smell good. You smell scared," it said.

I was terrified. I had never been so frightened on this side of the glass. I couldn't scream, I couldn't move. I had seen what it had done to Danny's mother and little brother. People it had a connection to. People it still had memories of. What sort of things was it going to do to a stranger?

I could feel its hunger, pulling at my fear, gobbling it up to fill the emptiness where Danny was supposed to be.

With its mouth against my ear, it started telling me how it was going to devour me. Its breath was hot and wet. Rotten. Its voice was playful, delighted to marinate me in fear and despair.

"After I'm done with you, I'm going to find everyone you care about. Or better yet maybe we can find them together, yes? And you watch them suffer until you are begging me to devour you," it said with a pleased chuckle.

At least it was having fun. Distracted.

Bending my fingers down, I began working one into the opening of the drawstring. Then two, pushing it open enough to grab ahold of the neck of the bottle. Pulling it out of the bag.

This isn't how I wanted things to go.

I dropped the bottle, trying to put what little force I could behind it.

The bottle shattered as it hit the ground at my feet, cold mist boiling up.

The vampire let go of me right away, and I fell to the ground breathless, eyes watering.

It tried to run but wasn't fast enough. Nothing could be fast enough. I made the bottle as much like home as I could to lure Danny.

But it wasn't home. Danny's home was currently legging in back out of the alley.

The mist condensed into a tight ball and shot down after it.

The vampire crumpled to the pavement.

I struggled to my feet, lungs aching. Dizzy and exhausted, I wobbled to the body. I knelt down and checked for a pulse. It was present and strong. I wanted to scream, I was so frustrated. That isn't how this was supposed to go! I was trying to figure out a way to kill him that would look like self-defense. Given that my neck was bruised with the shape of his hand and that once his family was found everyone would know he was an unhinged murderer, self-defense would be believable, if I did it right.

"Hey! What's going on, are they ok?" I heard from the sidewalk.

Damn. Too late.

"I don't know. This guy attacked me, then passed out or something! I don't know what's happening," I said, putting all the fear into my voice, sounding younger, confused, helpless.

Danny opened his eyes and looked up at me. I watched him change as his soul and body caught up with each other. Danny's time drowning in the dark, freezing liminal space was enough to give him some serious issues. Then he got to see how his family died. I don't know exactly what it did, or how long it took to kill them, but I saw the aftermath and knew Danny had entered a nightmare that he might never return from.

Danny began to scream.

Everything after was lights and movement, people rushing to me, questions, then cops, more questions, paramedics. I sat on a gurney, as the EMT checked my injuries and watched as the cops wrestled Danny crying, screaming, laughing into their car.

From the Author

Long ago I wrote an entire YA novel about a high school girl named Marney who goes through the looking glass into another world where she learns about herself and her family. A few weeks later I started trying to edit it, that wasn't fun at all so I decided to write a short story that takes place in the same reality instead. The novel and this story draw on some of my biggest fears. Who is looking back at you from the mirror? Are you 100% sure it's a reflection and nothing else? And why do people change suddenly? We hear stories all the time about a perfectly normal, kind person who all of a sudden does something horrific. In my own life, I have had people do things that were so out of character that it's hard to believe this is the same person, which got me thinking, that maybe it isn't.

About the Author

Kitty Sarkozy is a speculative fiction writer, actor and robot girlfriend. She is an Associate Editor and narrator for Pseudopod (https://pseudopod.org/) an award-winning weekly horror podcast in the Escape Artists network. Several large cats allow her to live with them in Marietta GA, where she cultivates extensive gardens into a perfect, tranquil place to hide bodies. For a list of her publications, acting credits or to engage her services on your next project go to kittysarkozy.com or follow her on twitter @KittySarkozy.

Teresa's Guitar

by
Erik A. Johnson

Teresa's Guitar

S cott shifted the green cloth music bag to the other shoulder and, with three fingers, lifted his black guitar case. Calculus homework and Saturday morning soccer practice filled his thoughts. He stopped at the light pole and punched the 'walk' button with his thumb. The street was busy, so he'd have a long wait for the light.

A nearby police car with silent flashing lights caught his attention. A policeman opened the trunk and dropped a black classical guitar case into it. In an instant, Scott recognized what it was. The solid sound it made hitting the trunk floor was proof it wasn't a cheap cardboard case. A second policeman opened the left back door and had his arm on the neck of a crying girl. Handcuffs held her hands behind her back, and he nudged her inside. A silver headband held her long black hair in place.

"I didn't do anything," she wailed. "The guitar was in the bushes. I don't steal."

"Yeah, sure you found it." The policeman closed the car door.

The police cruiser left with no siren wailing or red and blue lights flashing. Tires crunched on gravel as the car pulled onto the street.

What was in that guitar case? Treasures come in plain packages. A concert model or even an expensive student guitar would fit in that case.

He grasped his own treasure, a Cordera 7, safe in a padded case. It came from a music store going out of business and was hanging in the final clearance rack, broken enough to cost the same as a set of new guitar strings. Using a guitar repair book found at the thrift store, he fixed it. The Cordera came alive and beautiful music flowed. His thoughts returned to the guitar dropped into the police car trunk. Something in that case might be better than a Cordera.

Scott hustled across the street and walked at a leisurely pace to the donut shop. He enjoyed a chocolate shake with a side of French fries every Thursday afternoon after his guitar lesson. He munched a crisp fry with the other hand holding open *A Classical Guitar Journey*. Brushing back a dangling blond forelock, he poured over a Giuliani waltz. A simple piece, but his anguished playing exasperated his guitar teacher. After supper he'd try the frustrating little waltz again. Scribbled lesson notes he had made on the page should solve the problem. He closed the well-used book, and his thoughts returned to the mystery guitar. A leg bump to his guitar case made sure it was still there.

Simple, go to the police station and ask if the guitar was stolen. When police can't find the owner, it goes to the monthly police auction. He'd be at the auction with hard earned savings in his pocket, hoping the guitar was still unclaimed. Total disaster if the guitar would have been returned to the rightful owner.

Black hair with a silver headband. Who was she? Did the girl steal the guitar? Scott tried to picture her face but had only a quick glimpse. The silver headband might be a clue. Girls at school wear silver headbands every day, so the key was that guitar. Which girl plays a guitar? He closed his eyes to picture girls in the halls carrying guitar cases, but his mind drew a blank. With one last slurp, he finished the malt, so time to go home. Three Calculus homework problems to do, and he'd finish them well before dinner. Mom would work until eight tonight, so he and his sister Sarah would have a late dinner ready for her. Tonight would be ground beef casserole and boiled carrots. As he stepped out of the malt shop a face filled his thoughts—Teresa Alvarez.

He stopped and closed his eyes to focus on the image of her face. It was her silver headband that had caught sunlight streaming in from the history class window, and it distracted him. He didn't know her, just saw her in classes and in the halls. Teresa always smiled and laughed. The crying girl in a police car had to be someone else.

His pace quickened as he took the quiet side street to his apartment building. No need to obsess about a guitar, the answer would come Saturday morning at the police station.

Scott lifted his bicycle wheel into the aluminum bike rack at the police station main door. He entered the quiet lobby and stepped up to the tall counter. "Hi, Mrs. Wilson, could you tell me something about an incident Wednesday? A girl was arrested for stealing a guitar."

She smiled and pulled up the police log on her computer screen.

"Here it is, Scott. We captured a robbery suspect and recovered stolen merchandise."

"Who was it?" he asked.

"Can't tell you that. It isn't on Public Record yet, so ask me Monday."

"Where's the guitar?"

More taps on the keyboard. "We returned it to the owner, the Guitar Shoppe on First Street."

"Thanks. I know where that is."

Scott didn't learn who the guitar girl was, but he had an irresistible pull to find out, a pull as strong as wanting his hands on the mystery guitar. He lifted the bike from the rack and stared at the handlebars. A piece of the puzzle had fallen into place, and a familiar place would have the answers. He'd take a short cut through the lumber yard to get to First Street.

The Guitar Shoppe, on the oldest street in town, nestled between Gloria's Antique Emporium and The Imperial Russian Tea House. The shop had long been his refuge on cold afternoons after school. He'd thumb through the trays of guitar music and, every once in a while, find a piece that intrigued him. The music was often too difficult for his meager talents, but on occasion a score went into his growing library for the day when he'd be able to play it.

Scott pushed opened the green front door and heard the brass bell jingle. He walked past hanging guitars, inviting sheet music trays, and stood at the low wood rail that separated the store from the workshop. Albert Daras built his magnificent guitars there. He stood silent so as not to break Mr. Daras' concentration.

Albert didn't look up. "Afternoon, Scott. What brings you by? Haven't seen you for over a week."

Scott bit his lip to prevent blurting out he had been playing soccer instead of practicing guitar. "Been busy with schoolwork."

Mr. Daras gave him a skeptical look before returning to his work.

"I have a question, sir."

"I told you not to call me that." Albert frowned. "How is your Cordera and your lessons?"

"The Cordera is perfect, and the lessons are okay. Can't complain."

"That sad look on your face is worse than the time you lost your gloves. Are you still lusting after a rosewood Concert Master?" he chuckled, putting a cap on a glue bottle.

Scott grinned. "Well, a little, but tell me about that guitar that got stolen. You know, the one the other day."

Albert cleaned his glasses with a red handkerchief while walking to the railing. "Sorry to disappoint you, but it was a student model. I had promised it to someone before the theft, and he picks it up tomorrow."

173

Scott's face fell. "I thought maybe I could start a new repair project."

Albert put his arm around Scott's shoulder. "You could have repaired it, but it would never be as nice as your Cordera. What you need to fix up is a concert master guitar." He paused, lit his pipe, and took a puff. "Like the one on your bench. It came in yesterday."

"Work on a real concert master? I'm not ready for that."

"Sure you are. I know what you can do. Besides, I need an apprentice." He crossed his arms and stared into Scott's eyes. "Although that might cut into flirting with the girls and playing soccer."

A thousand people would kill to be Albert Daras' apprentice. Doing little things for him, sharpening chisels, gluing guitar parts together, and never complaining was nothing. Becoming an apprentice to a master luthier? He couldn't come up with an answer.

"See you Monday afternoon," Albert said, walking back to his workbench.

Scott answered without thinking. "I'll be here."

Albert sat and balanced a chisel in his hand. "The student guitar now has a new case, and the old one is by the music stands. It's yours if you want it. I can't use it."

Scott stepped outside and looked down at the empty guitar case dangling in his fingers. Decals of places visited by the previous owner covered the top. He wondered what to do with it, but it would be stupid to turn down something offered for free.

Teresa was sitting with giggling girls across the cafeteria. She was beyond beautiful and had sparkling brown eyes. She loved to chat with everyone, but Scott never had the nerve to talk with her. He didn't have the nerve to talk with Jennifer Brenner or Mary Beth Tyler, either. Mary Beth would come into his thoughts at the oddest times. Teresa wasn't in jail, so she hadn't stolen the guitar. That had to be it. She wouldn't be laughing if she was out of jail on bail. The hair was the same, but her headband was a deep red. Who was the girl in the police car? He still didn't know.

The ringing bell ended lunch break and thoughts turned to calculus. He took his usual seat in the back of the classroom and fiddled with his folded homework paper. The teacher stood with hands clasped behind his back, waiting for the bell to begin the class period. Hands dropped as the ringing bell fell silent, and he spun to face the white board. Time dragged as if pulled by a turtle, but finally calculus class wrapped up, and students gathered their papers to fill backpacks.

Scott hesitated and then sat next to Teresa as she dropped a pencil into her purse. She looked over in surprise.

"I thought you might want this." Scott blurted and turned his eyes away while handing her a red folder. A single large black musical note he had drawn filled the cover.

Teresa opened the folder and pulled out *A Classical Guitar Journey*. She thumbed through the pages. "Wow, this is great. Thank you." She paused and her eyes narrowed. "Why are you doing this?"

He wiped sweaty hands on his legs. "An extra copy. Maybe you could sort of use it and play some pieces." He wrung his hands. "Waltzes are toward the back."

She stopped at a page and studied a line of music. "Yes, I love the music, but without a guitar, it'll be a while before I can use it." She stood, clasping the book tight to her chest, and gave him a warm smile.

Scott sat staring at scribbled numbers and symbols in his notebook and tried to figure out what to do next. He sighed and left the classroom. Students eager to start the last Friday class filled the hallway. He wove through the crowd still wondering about the stolen guitar. She had accepted the book, and he still didn't know.

It had been a long, awkward day, and he was ready to forget the disaster of giving his best guitar book to Teresa. Scott slid a textbook into his locker, and his friend Dirk opened the locker next to his.

"Hey, man. What're you doing tomorrow? Eddie got his dad's car, and we're going to the new *Galaxy Warrior* movie. After that we'll hit the pizza place. Join us?"

Scott closed the door and snapped the lock shut. "Thanks, but I'll be at the guitar shop. After that I have to drop off something and then go to the bookstore to order a guitar book. Saturday night looks good."

"Great. Come over to my place after supper, and we'll play the new Dungeon Crawler computer game."

Scott had never walked in the part of town across the railroad tracks. What would people say about a blond guy in a Chicano neighborhood slinging a guitar case? He looked again at the small piece of paper with the penciled name and address. A thin, black 583 on the white porch column was the right house number. The small house had maroon curtains hanging in the two front windows. It needed paint, but the yard was tidy. Dead wires sticking out of a hole were for a missing doorbell. Scott knocked. A balding short man with a paunch opened the door.

"Does Teresa Alvarez live here?" Scott asked.

"This is the Alvarez residence," the man answered. "What do you want?" A touch of hostility filled his voice.

"I brought this. It's for her."

The man looked down at the guitar case and then into Scott's eyes. "What is it?"

Scott stammered, "It's something special."

The man lifted the guitar case. "I'll see that she gets it. Who should I say was calling?"

"She'll know." Scott's voice dropped off, and the man closed the door.

The bell announcing Monday's first class hadn't yet rung, and Teresa bumped into Scott in the hallway.

Her brown eyes sparkled. "Hi, did you solve the Calculus problem?"

His mouth moved a few times before awkward words spilled out. "I think I did. It's like the example on the opposite page."

"That's right. I forgot about the example. Thanks."

Teresa smiled and Scott returned a smile. She disappeared into English class and left him standing in the middle of the hall.

Giving Teresa the Cordera was beyond insanity. She probably didn't have money for a decent guitar, so she could have tried to steal one. Giving her the Cordera was the right thing to do. Besides, finding another classical guitar lover, a girl no less, was beyond amazing. Two seconds had passed since Teresa left and already he missed her. Scott wanted to look into her eyes again.

He had dragged the dull sounding plywood top guitar, his first guitar, from the basement to continue his lessons. Each note he struck reminded him of why it had been in the basement, and why he loved the Cordera. If nothing else, the cheap guitar fit the decal covered case. A concert master would fit in the case, too, but that would be like putting a bumper sticker on a red Ferrari. Sometimes people bring Mr. Daras a decent guitar as a trade-in, one that had sat unplayed for years in a closet. Maybe one day he could buy a concert model cheap and fix it up, like he did with the Cordera. Someday, somehow it could happen.

Scott slapped his forehead for not telling Teresa's father who had brought the guitar, but it was too late for that. She better like it. He cleared his thoughts and sat at his favorite table in the cafeteria back corner and opened the crisp new *A Classical Guitar Journey*. He braced it against his backpack and lifted a fork full of salad.

"You're the one."

He looked up at Teresa, who was standing across the table with tight lips, piercing eyes, and fists on her hips.

"Excuse me?"

"You gave me a guitar, didn't you?"

"Well, I suppose I did." He closed the book.

"Why? You owe me nothing."

"No, I don't, but you don't own a guitar. You said so when I gave you my book. Besides, I'm getting another guitar."

"What do you want from me?" she scowled.

"I don't want anything. The guitar was a gift. If you don't want it just give it back."

Her face froze for a moment, and then she sat across from him folding her arms on the table. Her eyes softened, but she still stared straight at him. "I'm sorry, really. Thank you so much. Yes, I practice every day and use the book you gave me. Nobody does nice things for me, like a gift guitar."

"Glad you like the Cordera. It wasn't worth anything when I got it, but I fixed it up. I fix things."

She uncrossed her arms. "You can fix a guitar?"

"I help Mr. Daras at the Guitar Emporium, and he's teaching me how to build guitars. I'll never have money to go to college, and I'd rather build guitars for a living than flipping hamburgers for the rest of my life."

She raised an eyebrow. "I thought you were a video game freak."

"Not exactly. The guitar is my passion and video games are a hobby. A guitar responds to what you ask of it. You can't force out any music or become a master by picking it up every once in a while. It can return love. A game can't do that."

"I never thought of a guitar that way." She twisted her lips for a moment. "So did you come up with that saying?"

Scott laughed. "Mr. Daras told me. He tells me a lot of things about guitars."

"He's teaching you a lot of other things, too."

Scott blinked. He must have said something stupid again.

She smiled. "So, what are you working on?"

"The little waltz on page 24 is giving me fits. It looks easy, but I have a problem getting from here to this note." He turned the book and held it open while pointing at the music and keeping it out of the mashed potatoes.

"This is awkward." She came around the table and sat close to his left arm. "Much better. So, is this the place?" Her warm leg pressed next to his, and she leaned into his shoulder to put her finger on the page.

Her pleated blue dress crinkled as she moved, and a trace of roses in her hair reminded him of his grandmother's garden.

"That's the place." He forgot to be shy, and they talked about the little waltz, guitars, and composers.

Soon lunch was over, and time to go to their respective classes.

Scott stopped in the middle of the hallway and slapped a palm to his forehead. Meeting her after school tomorrow to practice in the Imperial Russian Tea House back room? Insane. A date. A real date? Is guitar practice with a girl a real date? Nope. What will she say when she sees the cheap guitar and realizes I gave away my prize? What now? He dropped back to the wall and closed his eyes.

Scott shuffled into the Guitar Shoppe without a greeting and slumped into the creaking wood chair by the toasty warm wood stove. He didn't bother to take off his snow cap and gloves.

"Is this another visit by the Harbinger of Impending Doom?" Albert Daras asked, with a slight smirk. He hoisted a guitar to a wall hook. "You either lost your guitar, or it's true love."

"Probably both." Scott grunted and slammed fists against his forehead.

"Want to talk about it?"

"I suppose so." He pulled off his gloves. "Whatever came over me? I wanted to find out who owned that stolen guitar and gave a girl my guitar lesson book to find out. That didn't work, and when she said she loved music and didn't have a guitar, I gave her the Cordera. I can't believe I did something so stupid."

"Well, Scott, that was extreme, but a nice gesture."

"That isn't even the worst part. In fifteen minutes, I meet her next door to practice guitar together in the back room."

"Playing guitar with a beautiful girl? Never happened to me, but when I was your age, I dreamed about such things." Albert sat next to him and laced fingers together.

"You don't understand. This is a total catastrophe and I'm doomed. When she sees my cheap guitar, she'll know I gave her my treasure. I'm doomed."

"That's about as bad as it can get." Albert stood and smiled.

"Nothing could be worse," Scott tilted his head back and stared at the gray tin panel ceiling.

"Drastic problems call for drastic measures." Albert lowered his voice. "And I might be able to help. The Altimira Concert Supreme won't have to go on the wall for sale just yet, so please use it."

"I can?" Scott's face lit up. "You mean borrow a real guitar?"

"Don't slobber on the top like you found the crown jewels of England, and I don't want to see even the slightest scratch."

"Oh, I won't hurt it. I'll treat it like my baby...if I had a baby. You know what I mean." His voice dropped off as Albert brought it out from the work bench and laid it on his lap. Scott ran his hand along the silver frets he had replaced only a week ago. He lifted it into place and played the first notes of the Vivaldi prelude he loved.

Everything was perfect. Strings were perfect, and the sound was perfect. With such a warm resonance in the lower notes, the Cordera faded from memory. He paused and lifted his left fingers from the strings. It seemed immoral to love two guitars at the same time, but he didn't have a Cordera anymore. Now it was Teresa's to love.

A strange new thought filled his mind. Cordera guitars aren't rare, and he could find another one. His hand hovered above the strings. He couldn't find another Teresa.

"Where have you been going after school every day?" Dirk asked, pulling a notebook from his wall locker.

"Guitar practice," came the evasive answer.

Dirk snickered. "Nobody loves a guitar that much. I'll bet you're seeing a girl and are hiding it from me. Has to be Jennifer Brenner. How'd you pull that off?"

"No way. She's beyond awesome and has to beat guys away with a stick. I'd never get within a million miles of her."

"Now we're getting somewhere," Dirk said, shoving a finger to Scott's chest. "Out with it. You found something more important than pizza, didn't you? I'll bet you have a girlfriend."

"Not exactly, but if I tell you, you'll have to keep your big mouth shut." Scott pushed his finger to Dirk's chest. "If you don't, you'll wish a zombie was chewing on your arm and not me coming after you."

"Well, if it's that serious, my lips are sealed."

Scott twisted his head around to make sure nobody was listening. "It's Teresa Alvarez, and we've been dating."

Dirk fell back in shock. "No way."

"Yes, Way."

"Oh man, you don't want to mess that up. She's a far better catch than even cheerleader Jennifer."

Scott smiled as Dirk left and then reached into his locker. A big hairy arm with a snake tattoo on it slammed the door hard against his wrist.

"Keep your hands off my sister, A-hole!" Rudy Alvarez screamed and grabbed Scott by the throat. "You tried to buy her with a guitar. I'm going to break you in half."

Rudy pushed him into the lockers and cocked his fist back ready to strike. Before he moved his hand, Teresa stepped between them.

"Stay out of my life! This has nothing to do with you," she shouted.

Rudy slapped her spinning into the lockers and down to the floor. Scott swung his arm back to hit him, but Rudy's heavy blow to the chest sent him crumbling him to the floor. He pushed up on his elbows and Rudy kicked his ribs, slamming his head against a locker.

"Are you crazy?" Two guys rushed over and pulled back a raging Rudy. One of them said, "You hit your own sister. What the hell's wrong with you? Bad, man, really bad."

Scott struggled to sit, gasping for breath.

Teresa's nose bled from hitting the floor, and she reached for her backpack.

A voice from the gathering crowd shouted to get the security guard and the school nurse. Scott reached out to Teresa as his breathing came back. She huddled against the lockers with knees tucked and held a bloody lace trimmed handkerchief to her nose.

"I'm so sorry," he said putting his hand on her shoulder.

"Don't be. Papa told Rudy a hundred times not to hit me, and he'll pay. My family doesn't live like this." She left with a clutter of girls as Dirk helped an unsteady Scott to his feet.

Scott sat in the cafeteria back row, cradling his sore right arm in his lap as Teresa set down her lunch tray and pulled out the chair next to him. He looked over and forced a smile.

"How's the cheek?" She touched his black and blue bump. "He hit you real hard, and that was three days ago. I'm glad you're back in school."

"I'm fine," he answered, "as long as I don't breathe, laugh, walk, or raise my arm." He stopped at the look of concern in her eyes. "Don't worry, I'm fine and will be back on the guitar in a couple of days. Tell me a good joke, and I promise to laugh."

Teresa's smile turned warm, and she put her shoulder against his. When their arms touched Scott saw extra makeup covering the bump on her face.

"How's the nose?" he asked.

She touched her cheek and he saw hurt in her eyes as she looked down. "School food smells the same, so I suppose my nose is okay," she said, trying to sound funny, but he knew the shame of her brother striking her was a deeper hurt.

He pushed his mashed potatoes around in circles with a fork. "There's something I'd like to know, but you don't have to tell me if you don't want to. You really don't."

"Tell you what?" she asked with suspicion.

"Well, was it you I saw in a police car for stealing a guitar?"

She turned away, and her shoulders moved as she cried. He cursed himself for asking a cruel question.

"It was me," came the soft answer.

"You don't have to say a word, and…"

"They arrested me but let me go when we got to the police station. Chico Silva had stolen the guitar and money from the guitar store cash register. He got caught with the money while hiding in an alley and confessed. I found the guitar in the bushes and couldn't resist picking it up. I wanted to hold it in my hands for a few minutes before the owner came. I get good tips working at the Imperial Russian Tea House, but it would take a long time to earn enough to buy a decent guitar. The police came as I sat on the stone wall with the guitar in my lap. That's all."

His mind went blank, and he put his hand on hers while staring into her eyes.

"Papa wants to meet you."

"We already met," he answered.

"No, I mean really meet you. I want you to have dinner with us Friday. Mama wants to meet you, too."

He sat back and thought for a moment. "Will Rudy be there?"

"No. Papa threw him out of the house for hitting me and put all of his stuff in a pile by the mailbox. He's living with Angelo or Tony somewhere. He also got kicked out of school for a month for starting a fight."

"Well, I suppose, if I'm not doing anything," Scott said.

"You aren't doing anything. See you at seven."

Scott enjoyed the summer break and uninterrupted days working with Albert Daras. You have to be gentle with a guitar and let it sing, Mr. Daras had said. He said a lot of other things, too, and Scott finally realized it was about more than guitars. In a month he would be a high school senior, the last school year, and then, nine months later, he'd be out on his own. The Guitar Emporium had been a refuge, but now it was his rock and a place to plant his feet and someday spring away.

Albert hovered over Scott's shoulder. "Gentle. Use your fingers and without force. If a guitar fights you while being born, it will show pain every time someone plays it."

Scott set the intricate rosette into the shallow trench around the guitar top sound hole. He ran his thumb along the rosette edges and eased it into place with no gaps or bumps showing.

"Perfect fit," Albert said, straightening up. "Your first guitar will be superb. I'm sure of it."

Scott stood and wiped hands on his brown apron. "Life takes a funny turn when you aren't looking. Six months ago, I was alone and had a Cordera. Now I have a girlfriend and no Cordera. Nothing works out like you think it will." He sighed. "And she plays a whole lot better than I can."

"Things work out in funny ways, like you said." Albert tipped his glasses back with a finger. "You could practice more."

"I'd have to practice day and night for a year to catch up with her."

"Practicing doesn't always guarantee success, but to help you on your way, the Altimira that you restored is yours."

"What? You can't do that," Scott blurted and dropped the clamp. "It's a top-of-the-line concert master and worth a small fortune."

"Wasn't worth anything when you first laid your hands on it. It's only worth a fortune because you made it so."

"But… You can't do that," Scott blurted.

"Yes, I can." Albert ran a finger along the fingerboard. "I have twelve guitars on the wall for sale and ten commissions to build concert masters. I expect more orders, and I have enough wood in the storeroom to build a hundred more. I'm sure I can spare one or two guitars."

Scott frowned. "Is this another life lesson?"

"Probably."

"Maybe I should pay more attention to things." Scott twisted his face in confusion. "So, what happens next?"

Albert smiled and crossed his arms. "You and Teresa will figure it out."

From the Author

I have more classical guitars than I need and might want to have one more. My library of guitar music books would shame a library, too. So, to help fight off the urge for that guitar, I wrote a story about how a kid got his dream guitar and something far more important.

Enjoy!

About the Author

Erik Johnson writes Sci-fi and Fantasy novels and short stories of all sorts. Getting several short stories into printed anthologies showed that publishing can be done. Prior to answering the Muse's call to write, he had an engineering career. Projects all over the world gave exposure to a lot of strange and interesting things that are fodder for said novels. On occasion he can be found at costume cons resplendent in one of many Star Trek uniforms as well as at writing cons and workshops in more modest garb.

Rhamendren, Land of Silence

by
Lynne Phillips

Rhamendren, Land of Silence

*T*he wind snatched at the layers of furs encasing Rhadern, the Beast Master. It blasted his body, tearing at his exposed skin, sharp, bitterly cold shards of ice cutting those parts the wind uncovered.

The Rhamendren beast moved restlessly as the Beast Master's sinuous arms struggled to control it. His short legs straddled the beast, clasping its flank. The beast strained against the harness, rolling its eyes in panic. Grey hair buffered by the gale and ears pinned back in fear, the beast's deep-set eyes scoured the skies for danger.

Shards of ice peppered Rhadern's face, and a haze of snow hampered his sight. He sniffed the air, his large nostrils opening and closing to warm it before it hit his lungs. His eyes scanned the skies, seeking the cause of the beast's distress. The icy gale relentlessly blasted them with its silent fury as the beast and master sought a potential threat.

"Warning. Warning. Starship Galaxy malfunction. Starship Galaxy malfunction," a strident robotic voice recited. Gripped by some unidentified force, catapulted through time and space, the starship flew unmanned, the twelve seasoned astronauts oblivious to the warning. They were still unconscious when it crashed into a mound of soft snow.

Rhadern watched a flash of light streak across the sky and a dark object plummet into the snow on the edge of Lake Rhadeen. Stroking the beast's neck, he telepathically reassured it.

Be still my friend.

As their minds met, the beast quelled its fear. With great strides, it descended the mountain to the lake. Lake Rhadeen, frozen during the prolonged severe winter, shimmered in the moonlight, dark shadows from overhanging trees adding to the ethereal effect. The Beast Master marvelled at its splendour, his mind momentarily distracted.

The beast, now calm, stepped onto the lake's solid surface, his eyes fixed on a dark outline and a row of diffused lights flickering on the far side of the lake. Still hindered by the wind's icy blast, Rhadern couldn't identify the object. Remembering tales of intruders who came from the sky and attacked the beasts, he wondered if they had returned. The last intruders had almost annihilated the beast clan.

Running his fingers through the beast's tangled mane, the Beast Master transmitted his thoughts.

Nym, you have a long memory. Are they intruders?

Perplexed, its sight hindered by the snow, the beast shook its shaggy mane.

Master, I do not know. I need a closer look.

The drop to the ground was high for Rhadern's short legs, but the beast fell to its knees, allowing him to scramble off.

The beast's bony horn penetrated the lake's frozen layer, and it swam across the lake, towards the unknown shape. Giant cracks appeared in the undulating ice as the beast's strong tail propelled it through the water. As rapidly as it cracked, the smooth surface restored after the beast passed.

Lost in thought, Rhadern waited for the beast to return.

Commander Scott Macarthur, nicknamed Mac, was the first to recover. Shaking his head to clear his thoughts, he felt for injuries. A bump near his left temple and a sore elbow seemed to be his only injuries. His skull ached and his brain felt confused.

"Crew, report your status." His raspy voice sounded loud in his ears.

A few groans and denials sounded loud in the eerie silence as some crew responded.

Sebastian, the medic, opened his eyes and lurched to his feet. Several others rose, clutching each other for support.

Carter and Sorenson remained sprawled on the floor.

Reggie Sorenson had a deep laceration to his head, but his eyes reacted to a flashlight. Jed Carter's head was bent at an unnatural angle. Sebastian shook his head before checking the others. Most only had bruises and minor cuts, but they all looked disoriented.

"Anyone else got an intense headache and bursts of light behind their eye?" he asked. A chorus of yeses sent him looking for painkillers.

Henry Finch, the zoologist, limped to the infirmary. Retrieving a body bag, he placed Carter inside. Peter, the Navigator, helped him carry the body to the cryovac bin.

A staunch Catholic, Henry crossed himself before they sealed it. They had no time for more sentiment; the survivors had priority.

Lots of hot coffee and a hearty meal helped them revive enough to assess the situation.

The beast's horn shattered the icy surface. It clambered out and shook its long shaggy coat as the lake restored its surface in his wake. Rhadern waited for the beast to settle before he sent his first thought.

Nym, what was it?

Master, it's a metal ship, similar to the one that came several winters ago.

Nym, keep watch in case they are a threat.

Yes, Master.

A group of long-haired juvenile beasts raced past. With a swift motion, the Beast Master lassoed one and clambered onto its back. The youngster's long loping strides relaxed Rhadern as it carried him back to the warmth of his cave.

Nym skirted around the edge of Lake Rhadeen, past his own nest. Three rhadlings opened their mouths, demanding food. In the distance, Nym saw his mate returning to the nest dragging a fat hairy boar. Satisfied its thick layer of blubber would satisfy three hungry baby beasts, he kept moving. He hunkered down next to the dark object, slowing his heart rate to protect him from the cold. Only his alert eyes, watching intently, revealed he was anything but a pile of grey fur, quickly covered by a layer of snow.

The starship teetered precariously until more snow built up around its exterior, making it stable. The lights and the monitor screens flickered, the quiet hum of the air filter a background sound. Mac waited for the crew to assemble in his office.

"I'm not sure what happened. Pete is calculating where we might be, and Sandy messaged NASA. Any other suggestions?" Mac valued input from every member of the crew; in the past, their combined teamwork had helped them in tight spots. He had faith this mission would be the same.

Rupert, the engineer, cleared his throat, taciturn and serious. "I'll check if the starship can fly in case we need to leave in a hurry," he said.

"Thanks, Rupert, there could be damage. Adam, do an inventory of our supplies," Mac said, before turning to the communications officer, the only female on board.

"Sandy, check the external monitors. Let's see what we've got ourselves into."

A layer of white ice coated the glass until the demister cleared the screen.

"Only snow and ice, sir, and damn cold; the thermostat says minus eighty degrees Celsius," Sandy said, turning on overhead screens so everyone could watch.

The landscape, with a thick blanket of white, was a surreal, wintery scene. Falling snow blurred the setting until dark shapes appeared together to the right of the screen, several hundred metres away.

Zooming in, Sandy shouted, "Shit! They must be at least four metres tall! What are they?"

"They look like some sort of beasts. They're looking at us." The zoom revealed a dozen large, horned, hairy creatures with shaggy coats. Their deep-set eyes locked onto the starship.

"Creepy. They make the hairs on my neck stand up," Sandy said.

As fast as they appeared, the shapes turned and disappeared, leaving the landscape devoid of everything except a desolate wintery scene of an icy lake and falling snow.

"Sandy, replay that."

She reran the last few minutes twice, but it all happened so fast it was hard to determine what the creatures were.

"Anyone interested in checking out the inhabitants?" Mac said, making eye contact with each astronaut. He trusted them all, having flown with them several times. This mission was an ultimate destination. They knew before they left Earth the possibility of returning was slight. Nobody on board had families to return to; they considered each other family. Each in their own way a misfit, they were passionately loyal to the team.

"I'll go, if someone will cover me," Henry, the zoologist, volunteered, always hoping to discover some new species.

Pete the Navigator raised his hand. "Count me in if I can take Simon's experimental zapper. Our standard ray guns would be ineffective against something that big if it attacked."

Simon, nicknamed the Mad Scientist, was always trying to improve on their equipment. He had been working on a super laser. "Sure, why not? I'm keen to know if it works," he said.

With extra insulated thermal suits and special filters on their helmets to warm the air before it hit their lungs, Henry and Pete pulled on snowshoes and prepared to leave.

The starship's exit door resisted the snow heaped high against its outside. Simon fiddled with the controls. The door sprang open, and an icy blast of air rushed into the starship. He closed it again.

"Go through the escape hatch. We can't leave that door open for long, or we'll all freeze," he suggested.

Visors down, Pete and Henry stepped into the escape hatch, the door closing behind them with a whoosh.

"Are you ready?" Simon called. Pete and Henry gave thumbs up as Simon released the hatch and it thrust them outside into a hostile blast. Before they could move ahead, the wind flattened them against the starship. They took several tentative paces.

"Are you ready, Henry?" Pete asked.

Henry fiddled with the coms switch on his helmet, before indicating he wasn't hearing anything.

Pete could see Henry's lips moving, but he wasn't getting any coms either. He threw up his hands and mouthed, "What the fuck?" Henry shrugged, and they both staggered forward.

"Pete, Henry, you okay?" Sandy said but didn't receive an acknowledgment.

"Mac, they're not responding," she said.

"It must be a glitch. Can you fix that, Sandy? I'm not happy if we can't monitor what they say and talk to them," he replied.

Pete and Henry trudged towards the area where the dark shapes were last seen. The deep snow hindered their progress. When they reached the frozen lake, Pete checked the ice would take their weight before he beckoned Henry forward.

They proceeded cautiously until two half-grown beasts moved into range.

Keen to look at the creature up close, Pete set the zapper on low impact and fired. One creature collapsed, dazed, but not killed. The other raced away. Wanting to examine it before it recovered and fled, Henry and Pete moved over to the disoriented animal.

Nym watched with interest, not moving, not feeling any threat, until two half-grown rhadlings skittered onto the ice in front of the intruders. He waited to see the intruder's reaction; not prepared to intervene unless there was trouble. One of the intruders flung a beam of light and a youngster fell, unmoving.

Nym dived under the ice and circled them.

The ice cracked and buckled as the beast passed underneath Pete and Henry, the undulating ice throwing them off balance. They looked around, bewildered, as they tried to steady themselves.

"Call them back," Mac ordered. "There's something under the ice."

"Return to the starship. Abort mission. There's something under the ice. Return to base!" Sandy said, but Henry and Pete didn't respond.

"Look, there it goes again," she yelled, as the ice behind Pete cracked and distorted. "Some sort of creature is approaching them beneath the ice."

The heaving ice was enough warning for Henry and Pete to abandon their interest in the unconscious creature. They both turned and headed back to the starship. Henry led, with Pete only six paces behind. Pete stopped, adjusted the super zapper to full impact, sweeping it around in an arc. Not seeing any threat, only the undulating ice, he relaxed and followed in Henry's footsteps.

The beast burst through the ice behind Pete, his enormous body dwarfing the two astronauts. Sensing its presence, Pete turned, swinging the zapper, aiming it at the beast's body, but before he could fire, the beast opened his massive jaws wide. His long yellow teeth closed on Pete, plucking him off the ice, crunching bones and equipment before sinking below the surface.

The lake resumed its glassy veneer.

Henry felt the air recede. He glanced back to check on his friend, but saw only a bleak white landscape; no Pete. His eyes scanned the area again. Pete had disappeared. With no weapon to defend himself, Henry scrambled to the starship. Heart racing, he stumbled and fell multiple times before he reached the hatch.

Several hands sprang to the hatch and pulled him inside, everyone talking at once.

"Are you hurt, Henry?"

"Why weren't your coms turned on?"

"How come you didn't turn back on Sandy's command?"

Henry looked perplexed. "I didn't hear any orders. I couldn't hear anything, not even Pete speaking. There is no sound outside."

"That's impossible; you must have heard that wind blasting in your earpieces." Mac said.

"No, even though the wind tore at our clothes and whipped around, it made no noise. I saw the ice buckling and cracking, but all I could hear was an oppressive silence. It was eerie."

He looked at the stunned faces around him.

"What happened to Pete? I couldn't see him after the ice buckled, and we turned." His troubled eyes searched the crew for answers.

A few crew members shuffled their feet. No-one made eye contact until Mac touched his arm. "Sorry Henry, one of the giant hairy things ate him."

Seeing Henry's stricken face, Sebastian stepped forward to check his vitals while Sandy rewound the recording.

"All signs normal except for an increased heart rate," Sebastian reported. "How do you feel, Henry?"

"I've felt better." He shrugged off any sympathy.

"Film's ready, sir."

Henry's face blanched, his heart hammered in his chest, and the hairs on his arms rose as he watched the beast's gigantic teeth chomp down. Pete's body danced like a marionette as he frantically tried to zap his attacker. The last image was matted, silvery fur sinking below the ice, leaving Henry alone, struggling back to the starship.

Emerging on the other side of the lake, Nym clambered out, shaking his shaggy coat, dispelling water from the outside layer, the thick undercoat maintaining his body heat.

The largest of the snow-covered caves, overarched by a huge rock formation, loomed ahead. The entrance to the cave was dark and smelled of damp fur and stale air. As he advanced further in, it opened up into a large warm cavern, well ventilated by a series of air tubes to the outside.

Rhadern sat on a seat made from the bones of a rare rhawhale. Giant ribs, draped with furs, encircled him. The beast hung its head in submission before his master. Their minds connected.

Nym, what troubles you?

Master, I ate an intruder. I thought they killed a juvenile. It was only stunned. It escaped unharmed.

The Beast Master's brow furrowed.

That was foolish, Nym. Now the intruders will retaliate. The Beast Mater waved his hand in dismissal.

Distressed to disappoint his master, and fearing his family was in danger, Nym lumbered away to protect his nest and brood of rhadlings.

The Beast Master closed his eyes and summoned the oldest and wisest beast. Mage, the teller of tales, carried the history of the clan in his memory.

Head held proud, but hobbling with painful joints, the ancient beast approached Rhadern. He bowed to the Beast Master and fused their thoughts.

Master, you wish for my counsel?

Mage, I have need of your wisdom and memory. We have new intruders.

Master, the last intruders came and began killing us. Your father saved us from extinction.

Nym, my companion, killed one.

Master, that is unfortunate, they will see us as the enemy and hunt us.

Everyone sat around, chatting, waiting for Mac to speak.

"We're not going anywhere for a while. Let's check out this place. Prepare the spacebots. Reggie, you and Will take one. Sebastian and Adam follow them but be careful. We only want photos. Keep away from any natives. Cover each other's arses; we don't want to lose anyone else," he said.

The lightweight spacebots, equipped with weapons and surveillance equipment, comfortably held two people. Sebastian signalled to Reggie they were ready. Reggie released the lever that shot both spacebots out of the starship. They flew over the frozen ground, hovering just high enough to avoid the taller clumps of ice and snow.

"I hope we don't encounter any of those gigantic beasts," Sebastian remarked to Adam, who peered out the domed top. Receiving no answer, Sebastian touched Adam's arm to get his attention.

Adam jumped. "Fuck!" he said, "You startled me."

"I guess we're all on edge," Sebastian said. They both laughed, relieving the tension, and settled back to watch the unfolding vacant, white landscape.

Reggie and Will's spacebot tailed them as they skimmed the surface. At one point, they drew level, waved, overtook them and zoomed across the shiny lake. A pallid sun hung in the sky, emitting little clarity, just a soft silvery glow like a wintry moon back on Earth. The view changed; stunted trees littered the landscape, a pile of logs and branches looked like a large nest.

"If that's a bird's nest, we're in trouble," Sebastian said. There was no sign of any birds. Icicles hung from trees, crystal prisms sparkled in the pale light. Adam slowed the spacebot to marvel at the sight. Reggie and Will continued to move across the frozen lake.

Something flickered in Adam's peripheral vision. The forked tail of a gigantic, hairy beast disappeared into a hole in the lake. He scanned three hundred and sixty degrees. There was no sign of the spacebot, which was travelling metres to their left only two minutes earlier, and without coms, he couldn't confirm their situation. He signalled a turning motion with his hands and Sebastian raced back to the safety of the starship.

The spacebot clamped onto the starship, and Adam and Sebastian climbed out to the distraught faces of the rest of the crew.

Sandy set the camera on replay. Everyone watched as the film revealed Reggie and Will's fate. One minute they were skimming across the surface of the lake when the ice warped and cracked. A massive horned creature emerged, its red eyes blazing, as it snatched the spacebot in its massive jaws, long teeth chomping, ripping it to pieces. Bits of metal flung in all directions, just a glimpse of Reggie and Will's stricken faces before they disappeared down the beast's throat. The beast dived back underneath the ice. A last flick of its enormous tail and the lake froze solid again.

Nobody said anything. Stunned faces failed to make eye contact.

Mage returned to the Beast Master and bowed low, fusing their thoughts.

Master the intruders emerged in two flying machines. They were close to Zerin's nest. She destroyed one, and the other retreated. The eggs are safe.

Rhadern contemplated the situation.

I think I should try to communicate with the intruders. This situation needs to be explained before they retaliate.

Master, remember the last intruders killed your mother. Perhaps it is better to annihilate them first. There aren't many. We could take them.

No, Mage, we need to learn the intruder's intentions. Send a message to the beasts to avoid contact.

Rupert approached Mac. "Good news," he said. "I've been working on the boosters. If this ice and snow melts, we can take off."

"Hopefully this place isn't perpetual ice and snow, and the snow will melt. Do we have enough supplies, Adam?"

"Plenty of dehydrated supplies, and we can melt snow for water. We should be okay."

"What about the inhabitants?' Mac said.

"Let's avoid the lake if possible. So far, they've all emerged through the ice."

"That makes sense."

"Perhaps it's time we were more proactive and thought like hunters. They have no hesitation in eating us. They might be an excellent food source if our supplies run out," Sebastian suggested.

"I'd rather not attack, unless we are desperate, Sebastian. Sandy, concentrate on helping us discover more about this place," Mac said. "Turn on the long-distance scanners. What else is out there?"

Seeing pieces of Will and Reggie's space bot strewn across the lake, the crew stared mutely, each person lost in their own thoughts. The cameras zoomed farther out, rotated a full circle and revealed a group, a family. Two large grey-furred beasts perched on a nest surrounded by three smaller, without horns. The little ones resembled yaks with their long hairy coats, although they sat upright on their haunches. Red eyes locked onto the camera, seeming to follow its rotation.

"I guess that solves the question about the nests," Adam said. "They must have incredible eyesight. I wonder what other senses they have."

Sandy scanned to the base of a mountain that touched the lake. A herd of twenty hairy creatures ran across the screen. All the same size, several metres high, they moved on sturdy legs, their long, silvery hair flowing behind them. Their forked tails swayed rhythmically as they disappeared from sight.

The camera panned further. Two fat, four-legged, hairy pig-like creatures rooted around in the snow looking for food, but they were kilometres away and differed from the beasts seen earlier.

"Scan back to the family," Mac said.

Sandy zoomed back, but the nest was empty in its wintery landscape of ice and snow.

"Simon. I'd like you to try contacting a beast. Is the translating machine you've been working on ready?"

"It's ready Mac, but if Henry is correct and there's no sound, it won't work."

Simon set the machine on several radio wave lengths and multiple frequencies. After twenty-four hours with no reaction, he turned it off.

"Sorry Sir, no response.'

"Try again from outside the ship tomorrow."

"Sure, but I think we'll get the same result."

Rhadern summoned Nym.

Friend

Master

I want to check out these intruders.

He looped reins around Nym's neck and climbed onto the beast's back. Nym carried him out of the warm cave into the silent land. A group of rhadlings romped in the snow next to their nest, oblivious to the cold. A herd of juvenile beasts raced past, scattering the babies. Rhadern glared at the herd and merged his thoughts with them.

Make yourself useful. Go hunt rhaheen piglets.

Sorry, Master, going now.

The juveniles raced off.

Rhadern rode Nym hard, venting his anger, reining the beast within sight of the starship, and climbed down.

Rest, Nym, I am going to try communicating with the intruders.

At the edge of the lake, he closed his eyes, sending a telepathic signal. The silence strengthened his resolve. It allowed his thoughts to travel towards the intruders. Oblivious of the cold, he remained in a trance for several hours before he collapsed exhausted on the ground.

Master! Did you establish contact?

No, Nym, I don't think it's possible. I'm tired. Take me back to the cave.

"Mac, I think it's worth trying to make contact from the top of the mountain. We might get better reception," Simon said.

"Take Rupert, Henry, and Ivan, see what you can learn about this place."

The larger domed autobot zoomed towards the mountain, avoiding the taller mounds of snow.

At the base of the mountain, a dark shape appeared on their screen. It looked like a pile of rusted metal, the first unnatural thing they'd seen. Rupert manoeuvred the autobot closer. "What is it?" he said.

"It looks like a space capsule from the early space exploration last century," Simon said.

"It looks like the ones they sent chimps up in. Let's check it out." They trudged over to it, eager to discover something that could have originated on Earth.

The words 'Arthur and Martha' etched across the rusting space capsule intrigued them. Simon recorded the find on the autobot's cameras and they continued flying to the top of the mountain.

"That was strange," Ivan said. "If I remember my history, they called all the early chimps sent into space Arthur, but I've never heard of Martha."

The trip was futile; there was no response from the transmitter. After six hours, they turned back. Exhausted, their eyes strained from continually scanning the white landscape, they looked forward to a hot meal.

The wind increased its fervour, buffeting the autobot. Rupert tried to keep it level as the gale intensified. It flipped the autobot onto its back. Simon's head smashed against the dome, knocking him unconscious. Ivan and Henry clung to the rails as the autobot flipped and spun in the storm's fury. The autobot lifted high into the air; it twisted and spun until a downdraft caused it to drop. Henry's head hit the wall, killing him. The autobot was out of control as it spiralled, tossing the astronauts around. Plummeting again, it speared into the ground, crushing Rupert and Ivan on impact. Simon remained unconsciousness as the wind abated and the shattered autobot gathered snow.

Sandy had been monitoring the autobot's trip.

"Mac, you'd better see this. The autobot is out of control. The wind is over two hundred knots. They have no chance."

Ashen faces watched the autobot nosedive into the ground. Sebastian raced to the spacebot. The spacebot shot out into the cold. The wind rocked the little vessel, tossing it like a leaf in a gale. Everyone on board held their breath. They gasped. Several times, they held their breath as Sebastian fought to keep the spacebot moving towards the crashed autobot. The wind abated slightly, and Sebastian reached the base of the mountain. Back in the starship, the crew monitoring his efforts cheered.

Snow had half buried the autobot. Sebastian used a laser, melting it enough to open the hatch. Wrenching the door open, his heart sank. His friend Henry's skull was crushed; Rupert and Ivan a crumpled heap in the corner.

Simon lay sprawled on the floor, his breath shallow, his heartbeat slowed by the cold. He was badly bruised and still unconscious, but there was nothing Sebastian could do for him until he got him back in the starship.

Realising the retrieval of the bodies would have to wait until the storm abated, Sebastian pulled Simon into the spacebot and shot back to base, where eager hands pulled him into the starship. For two days, Simon lay in a coma. Sebastian applied heat packs and a shot of adrenaline.

"That's all I can do," he said. "Now it's up to Simon to see if his body is strong enough to recover." On the third day, Simon opened his eyes. "Welcome back. How are you feeling?" Sebastian asked.

"I'm still alive, but what about the others?" His first concern was for his friends. The faces of the other astronauts told him the answer.

A watery sun appeared on the fourth day, the storm having dissipated. Sebastian and Sandy took the other autobot to retrieve their friend's bodies and remove the cameras and other equipment. Buried in a heap of snow, only the glass dome of the autobot remained uncovered. The laser was too slow. Sebastian produced a flame thrower which melted the snow around the entrance so Sandy and Sebastian could begin their grim task of retrieving their friend's bodies.

It was a sombre trip back to base. The troubled look on Sandy's face mirrored Sebastian's as he gazed out through the Autobot's domed top.

Back in the starship, they viewed the footage and listened to the recordings.

"Do you think it's a space capsule that was carrying chimps?'

"Looks like it."

"I remember they sent a lot of Arthurs into space, but I don't remember them sending a pair of chimps."

"They don't tell the public everything you know."

"True. No-one except NASA knows about our mission."

Rhadern could see Nym's distress.

Nym, why are you troubled, my friend?

Master, the gale destroyed some nests, and we could not protect all the rhadlings.

Nym, we have no control over the weather. This winter is more severe, but we will survive.

Master, the intruders found your parent's space capsule.

I wonder if the intruders they came from the same place as my parents.

"Look what I found," Mac said, holding up a bottle of twenty-year-old Scotch Whiskey. "I've been saving it, but I think it's time we had a treat. Sebastian, check the food supplies for nibbles. Andy, shovel some snow into the water tanks. I think we'll hunker down in the starship for a while."

Sebastian returned, his face ashen. "Mac, water from the gale has penetrated the hold and ruined the last of our dried food. We'll have to go hunting for some fresh meat soon."

"Shit, I'm not happy hunting those gigantic creatures, they're too big."

"What about the fat pig-like animals we saw rooting around? We could handle one of those."

"Maybe, come on, have a nip of whiskey. We'll think about hunting tomorrow."

It was minus ninety-four Celsius the next day, and the wind was strong, but not gusting. Three astronauts climbed into the remaining autobot and set off, leaving Sandy and Simon behind. They sped along, avoiding the lake. After half an hour, they spotted two small pig-like animals. Adam set the zapper to high, and Mac brought the autobot in close.

One animal fell, the zapper killing it, the other escaping unharmed. As big as a wild boar, it had a thick layer of fat under its long shaggy coat protecting it from the cold. Its blubber and meat would keep them alive for another couple of weeks if they were frugal, and its coat could provide warmth for future forays in this frozen world.

The autobot refused to start, the engine frozen solid while it sat waiting. "We can't stand around here. We'll freeze our arses off," Mac said.

Sebastian and Adam made a trapezoidal frame from dead branches that littered the ground. They strapped the animal onto it with vines and signalled they would drag it. Mac grabbed the super zapper. Abandoning the autobot, he led, head bent against the icy blast of the wind. The ground was solid underfoot, and the snow froze as it hit the surface. He forced his feet to connect to the slippery surface. Sebastian trod in the prints left by Mac's snowshoes. Although hampered by the burden, Adam leaned in close. Slithers of ice, like shards of glass, pelted their protective faceplates and suits. The thermo-readers in their suits recorded minus ninety-five without the wind chill factor, which would take off another ten degrees at least.

The wind blasted them with an intense, silent fury. Their footsteps echoed in their heads as each foot hit the ground. The surrounding silence was oppressive and depressive. Each astronaut concentrated on reaching the starship, one foot after another, attempting to blot out the pain. Mac veered onto the edge of the lake, attempting to get back faster, only another hundred paces to the warmth and shelter of their starship. He increased his step, leaving a gap. Watching where he placed his feet on the slippery ice, Sebastian tried to increase his stride, but his tired, stiff legs refused to respond. His breath felt ragged in his chest. Heads down, he and Adam continued to drag the animal. Hampered by the weight of their burden, their chests heaved.

A flicker of movement, Sebastian looked up. Massive jaws gaped as a gigantic creature, much larger than any they had seen before, broke through the crusted ice ahead of them. Opening its mouth wide, its teeth crunched Mac's shoulder, lifting him off the ground. Mac swung the super zapper around and pulled the trigger twice. The laser hit the beast in the chest. It opened its mouth, releasing him before it sank back out of sight under the frozen lake. Sebastian only had time to notice a long, hairy neck and sharp fangs in his peripheral vision before it disappeared. The ice closed around the hole and froze solid again.

Leaving Adam to drag the kill, Sebastian supported Mac. They stepped off the ice onto the deep snow, forcing their tired legs to respond as they struggled to cover the distance.

Sebastian, Sandy, and Adam hauled the animal into the starship. Although exhausted, they knew they needed food. Sandy took control. "I feel like a cave woman," she said, cutting off hunks of meat. She grilled some while Sebastian attended to Mac's shoulder. The injury was severe, a deep puncture from the tooth. Sebastian cleaned the wound and administered antibiotics and morphine. "Try to get some sleep, Mac," he said.

"Here, get that into you," Simon said, handing Sebastian coffee that smelled of whisky.

"What do we do now?" Sandy asked, noting the deflated demeanour of her friends.

"Fucked if I know, let's decide later," Sebastian said.

Adam produced a pack of cards, and they sat around playing and drinking the last of Mac's whisky. Nightmares of beasts, attacking and destroying the starship, filled their sleep.

The critically injured beast sent a distressed message to the clan as it sank to the bottom of the lake, slowly dying. Rhadern received the thoughts relayed from beast to beast. He hoped the death of the beast wouldn't cause the beasts to confront the intruders. If he could communicate with the intruders, he could explain the beasts meant no harm. The earlier killings were a mistake, a miscommunication.

The beasts were restless. Thoughts between them argued for and against attacking the intruders. The Beast Master concentrated to send a message to all the beasts. It took tremendous energy.

Beasts, I understand your concern. Don't retaliate. I will try to communicate with them again.

Summoning Nym, he rode close to the starship.

Exhausted, the crew slept until late. A watery sun hung in the sky, no snow fell, and the wind abated.

"Do you think it's warmer?" Sandy said, making coffee while Sebastian attended to Mac's wound. She turned on the scanner. An enormous beast stood a few metres away from the starship. Piercing red eyes locked onto the monitor screen.

"Holy fuck, Simon, Sebastian, Mac, come and see this. We're in trouble!" she yelled.

Four astonished faces peered at the screen. A chimp, draped in multiple layers of fur, slid off the beast's back. The beast glowered, its red eyes daring them to cause trouble. The chimp stepped closer to the starship.

"What do we do now?' Sandy said. Sebastian reached for the super zapper. Simon held up his hand. "Wait, I'm getting a message," he said, holding his head. The chimp's top lip curled, revealing large white teeth and pink gums.

Intruders, I am Rhadern, the Beast Master. This is my friend, Nym. We mean you no harm.

Simon frowned; he could hear the chimp's thoughts. He concentrated hard.

Beast Master, we are from Earth. We mean no harm either. I am Simon.

The chimp bowed low. *Welcome to Rhamendren, the land of silence.*

Mac grabbed Simon's arm. "What's happening? What are they? Are we in danger?"

"We're communicating through thought transference. He said he is Rhadern, the Beast Master, and this is the planet Rhamendren, land of silence." Simon explained. "He said they mean no harm."

Sebastian stepped forward, the zapper raised, ready to leave the starship and confront the visitors. "No harm! What about Pete, Reggie, and Will?" Sebastian staggered as a jumble of thoughts filled his head.

They were an accident, a misunderstanding. The beasts are a gentle clan. Intruders came before you and almost annihilated us. We thought you might do the same.

"Fuck that, they were my friends," Sebastian shouted at the monitor.

"Sebastian, calm down," Simon said. "Mac, do you want to confer with them?"

With a shrug of his shoulders, Mac sank into a chair. Overcome with pain, he didn't want to deal with the situation. Sebastian administered another dose of morphine. "You go, Simon, you can communicate with them," Mac said.

"I'll go too," Sandy said, strapping a ray gun onto her belt. "Just in case it's a trick," she said in answer to Simon's raised eyebrow. Noting the size of the ray gun and remembering the size of the beast, he smiled at her bravado. Adjusting their space suits against the cold, they exited through the escape hatch.

Sebastian watched through the monitor, ready to use the super zapper if needed, but he could tell Simon and Sandy weren't in danger. The beast prostrated its enormous body at their feet. The chimp grinned. Simon and Sandy extended a hand. The chimp clasped their hands in his. Sandy and Simon looked relaxed as they walked over to the beast. Sandy ran her fingers through its fur. Sebastian watched Simon touch the beast's horn.

"How do we know we can trust them?" he asked Mac.

"We don't, but we haven't any other many choices."

Sebastian paced the floor of the starship, only stopping to view the monitor.

"Well, that was interesting," Simon said, entering the escape hatch and shedding his thermal gear. "The space capsule we found belonged to Rhadern's parents. They were space chimps from America in the sixties. Like us, something catapulted them through space, probably into a wormhole. Nearly a hundred winters have passed since Rhadern was born."

"Can't be a hundred years, that's not possible," Sebastian scoffed.

"He said winters, not years," Sandy said. "The seasons are short. Rhadern said this winter is longer and is more severe. It's almost over. Soon the snow will melt, and we can take off. Ruben said the engines are okay."

Rhadern was telling the truth about the change in the weather. Less snow covered the ground. The sun lost its silvery sheen, replaced with a rosy hue which deepened a darker shade of red each day. Days became warmer, too, allowing the astronauts to venture outside in lightweight suits.

They made preparations to depart.

"Simon, is something bothering you?" Mac asked." I thought it would please you to get going."

"Two things: I'd like to have more time here to find out about this planet, and I feel we should take the chimp with us."

"We need to move on, but you can ask the chimp if he wants to come."

The next day Simon sent a message to Rhadern to meet him. The Beast Master rode Nym close to the starship.

Simon, would you like to ride Nym?

That would be fantastic.

Come, I'll show you more of Rhamendren

Kneeling on the ground, the beast made it was easy for Simon to clamber aboard behind Rhadern. A harness around the beast's neck helped the Beast Master control the direction his wanted to go, but there was nothing for Simon to hold on to except the shaggy fur. He forced his legs in, steadying his body and clenched the fur tightly as Nym lurched to his feet. Simon's heart tensed as he looked down. Four metres high the view was incredible, but frightening. He clutched harder and tried to relax enough to enjoy the ride. They passed trees, small green leaves sprouting from their enormous branches. Some tiny flowers emerging glittered in the sun. Eyes open in wonder, Simon relaxed and enjoyed the experience. A few dozen beasts emerged from nests to stare at them, their deep-set eyes disconcerting. Simon heart raced, imagining them wanting to devour him. Reading his mind Rhadern assured him.

They are just intrigued to see someone else ride a beast.

Arriving at Rhadern's cave, Nym sank to the ground allowing Simon and Rhadern to disembark. Fascinated with the ingenious way the cave's ventilation system worked, the Beast Master and Simon shared ideas.

Rhadern, we are leaving soon. Mac says you can come too.

Where are you going?

Hopefully home to Earth, where your parents lived.

Thank you, Simon. I know nothing of Earth. I will stay here with the beasts. I'm not sure how many more winters I can endure, but I am happy to share them with my friends.

Three more suns rose and fell before Mac called them together.

Simon sent a message to the Beast Master.

Rhadern, we depart in the morning. Farewell.

Disappointed there was no reply he checked the boosters and engine ready for take-off before falling into a fitful sleep.

A bright red sun filled the sky. With a heavy heart, Simon started the boosters and then fired the engines ready for lifted off.

"Mac, Simon, Sebastian, look!" Sandy yelled peering at the monitors.

Hundreds of beasts prostrated themselves on the ground. Rhadern, the Beast Master stood at the front. He raised his hand and waved.

Farewell my friends. Safe journey.

The starship took to the skies. Simon watched until the planet was just a tiny dot on the screen.

"Let's go home," Mac said.

From the Author

Rhamendren, Land of Silence, was written for fun. A reader of adventure and fantasy stories, Lynne Phillips discovered the world of science fiction when she went to high school and studied *The Day of the Triffids,* by John Wyndham. She became obsessed with science fiction stories. H. G. Wells, Arthur Clarke, Isaac Asimov being favourites, until in 1965, Frank Herbert wrote *Dune.*

Dune was one of the inspirations for Rhamendren, land of silence. Fascinated by the idea of the sand worms travelling under the sand and emerging to terrify people, Lynne always wanted to include the concept in a story. In this story, the creatures are more like hairy Loch Ness monsters which travel under the ice.

The idea of including silence in the story came about after reading the *Name of the Wind* and *The Wise man's fear,* by Patrick Rothfuss. The concept of a world of silence was intriguing.

Originally, the story was called Rhamendren, Land of Ice and Silence.

About the Author

Lynne Phillips lives in the Northern Rivers area of New South Wales, Australia. She only began writing in 2017; life was too busy before she retired. Her stories have been published by Zombie Pirate Publishing, Black Hare Press, Fantasia Divinity Publishing, Our Wonderful Anthology, Black Ink Fiction, and several online magazines. She enjoys exploring the craft of writing stories and the challenges it presents. She writes in most genres and likes her stories to be a bit off-centre. Her first love is writing for children and young adults. Her priority is spending time with her family, while her passions are reading, writing, and keeping fit.

Connect with her on:
https://www.facebook.com/lynne phillips.505

The Withering
by
Kat Farrow

The Withering

Cold singed Neela's flesh as she pinched the thin hard carapace of the effigy, making sure it was a solid object in this place of shadow and thought. Bone white and smooth, slightly larger than her face, it had a slight bulge for a nose and two rectangular slits for eyes.

She took it from the chicosk spirit's outstretched hands. It varied from the one the chicosk wore over its face, but that was its own. Over time, the mask would have molded itself to the spirit's own desire. Why that desire would be the face of King Jaluduth, one side melting in folds like the sides of a spent candle, she would not guess. But the unsettling sight distracted her from the vague arthropodic shape of her Underland guide.

Neela glanced up at the towering figure, its head nearly brushing the top of the tunnel. It gave a slow nod, encouraging her to place the mask over her face. The slight movement caused the tiny skeletal body dangling below the chin of her guide's mask to tinkle like hollow wooden chimes.

The mask she held had no skeletal body attached. She wasn't sure if it would grow one after she put it on, or if a visitor's mask never did. Her studies had found no record of seekers for several centuries, and the accounts of those who had gone before were vague about too many things.

There was no ribbon or strap to attach to the mask. Puzzled, she held it up over her face and felt a slight pressure, as if she had dunked her face into water. The mask stuck. She could feel the cold brushing her skin, but the mask itself hovered a finger-width above her flesh. Hooking a finger under the edge, she tugged. It would not come off. She thought it would not until she left the Underland.

If she left.

Looking back up at the chicosk, she heard a tinkling from below her own chin. With thin fingers, she brushed at the bottom of the mask but felt only the dry chill air of the passageway. Focusing on the chicosk, she realized the mask altered her vision. The guide's shape had become more solid, and she could clearly see its two long, multi-jointed arms and four legs. The more defined appearance was both more and less comforting than the dark, amorphous shape it had been.

Gaining her attention, it motioned her to follow. As soon as it turned, its body glowed, illuminating the dark passage in a soft blue light.

Neela dug her hands deep into her cloak's pockets, touching the small objects they contained. Their familiarity comforted her as she watched the rippling movements of the chicosk moving further ahead. With a deep breath, she freed her feet from the soft ash and sand of the tunnel floor and followed. This is why she had come. To seek answers. To seek help for her dying world.

The chicosk moved steadily, its head turning to check on her progress now and then. The soft glow it created lit the carved reliefs on the walls as it passed. Neela had seen many of the archaic symbols in her studies, several defying translation over the centuries. Intricate patterns interspersed the symbols. Many were complex versions of the prints used on the robes of the priests and royal family.

The chicosk's legs dipped in and out of the thick, sandy ash in silence. Its dangling bones tinkling only when it turned toward her. Neela's own bones clinked with every step, and every booted footfall made the slight shushing of sand passing through an hourglass.

As a child, Neela's grandmother had told her stories of the Underland. The place where thoughts were kept when not being used. Dreams, nightmares, inspirations, dread. They came and went as needed, but some became stuck or buried, forever lost to those who believed they had created them.

The chicosk guarded and cared for them. But there were other things. Things that fed off of them as much as tended them.

The legends told of a few brave souls who ventured into the Underland, seeking answers or lost knowledge. Those who returned had only sparse memories of the place and only received part of what they had been searching for. Neela had spent the past seven years combing the old scrolls for information to verify these legends. Long before she had the need of it. Before the deaths began.

Her people were starving, but it wasn't for lack of food. Something had changed in the plants. Or the soil. Or the water. It didn't matter how much you ate; you were never satiated. You never gained weight. Children never grew. Your body lost its ability to heal. And then, you began to Wither.

It spared no one but affected some more quickly. It was even said the royal family lay Withering. None had seen the king himself for over a year.

Neela had lost friends and family. Her grandmother, hale and hardy less than three years ago, was now a shade away from death. Neela herself had not felt the full brunt of the Withering. Yet. She still had strength and a sharp mind. Still had more flesh on her bones than most of the population. She didn't know why…unless it was for this.

Her chicosk guide stopped as the tunnel opened upon a large vestibule. A glowing mist illuminated the carved stone room, circling far above. A dozen passage entrances lined its circular walls, and above each entrance was a symbol.

This was one detail which had been consistent in the recollections of those who had returned. Neela was to choose the one she believed would take her to her desire. She had not expected a different chicosk to be waiting in each entrance. A new guide for whichever way she chose.

Neela brushed a lank strand of light brown hair that had fallen across her mask's eye slits. She tried not to grimace as she felt several hairs come free to drift down to the ground.

Moving away from her first guide, she began circling the room, reading each symbol. She was grateful she had spent so much time with the scrolls and polymaths. The symbols were in an ancient script. Only one gave her trouble.

Future
Past
The Way of Light
The Way of Dark
Life
Death
The Way of Giving
The Way of Taking
Spirit
Flesh
Thought

The last symbol looked like a combination of the glyphs for Nature and Imagination. She thought it might be an ancient glyph for *Magic*, but that didn't seem quite right.

In her studies, she had tracked down recollections from nine of the doors, but what they held now may have changed. Her quest was for something that had not been in those passages then. But there was no way to be sure.

Neela moved to the center of the room, closed her eyes, and slowly turned. There was a light, woody scent that seemed to mix with the vestibule's musty air.

She stopped where the scent was strongest and opened her eyes. The doorway with the unknown symbol was before her. She examined the chicosk guide looming just inside the passage.

Its gray mask was egg-shaped and the size of her whole torso. Deep, bark-like ridges ran horizontally, with eye slots as inverted triangles, roughly chiseled. Its tiny skeletal body appeared to be made of sticks. It glowed less that the first guide and appeared to have twice as many legs in the shadows of the tunnel.

Skin prickling, Neela took a hesitant step, then stopped. She had one chance. Sinking her hands deep into the pockets of her cloak, she turned and circled the room again, closer to each door.

Her fingertips passed over the objects she had brought. A small, seven-pointed bronze star, a silver coin, a thin glass vial of poisoned wine, a tiny, corked pot of honey, a zeluu nut, a carved wooden bead, a palm-sized sack of barley grain, and a braided strand of her and her grandmother's hair. She had already given a gold coin to the first chicosk, to allow her passage into the Underland. She hoped the remaining items would be enough.

When she again passed the doorway with the rough masked chicosk, her fingers brushed upon the zeluu nut. The smooth, oblong shell had turned ice cold.

Pausing, Neela turned to face the guide again. She pulled her hand from her pocket and held the nut out on her open palm. The chicosk's legs shuffled, but the mask remained still.

The strange Nature + Imagination symbol it would be then.

With a slow, silent breath, she moved closer to her new guide. She held the nut out an arm's length away from the silent being. Black spider-legged fingers reached out and grabbed the small nut. The mask nodded, stick bones clicking, then the chicosk's body rippled and turned, its glow brightening to a pale gold as it moved down the passage.

The ground grew damp and soft under Neela's feet as she followed. A heavy mist appeared low on the floor, pulling up in wispy curls with each step of her guide.

This tunnel did not have the carvings of the first. Deeply grooved, it looked as if long claws had run the length of it. Like the mask of its chicosk keeper.

The ground grew bumpy, as if disturbed by the roots of trees. But the mist hid whatever it was, and Neela kept tripping, causing her bones to clink and jingle. Ahead, a brighter glow illuminated the bobbing silhouette of the chicosk. That woody scent flooded her senses, and her skin felt a slight breeze tinged with moisture.

The tunnel ended and opened into an immense cavern containing an underground forest. A soft blueish light filtered down from high above a dense canopy. Purple and green glow-snails left streaks upon tree trunks, and small balls of colored light darted like fireflies around the overgrown foliage. Glowing fungus dotted the misty ground, and there were bushes with leaves longer than Neela's arm, bearing black flowers the size of her face. The breeze rustled leaves, but the odd forest had no sounds of birds or small animals.

Captivated, her eyes darted around the strange sights. Neela had read no descriptions of this place. She wondered if she would have been able to see any of it without her mask. She watched the path of two glowing spheres twisting around each other, then plummeting into a bush. Turning to seek others, she realized her chicosk was nowhere to be seen.

She was alone.

Recollections of the other passages taken had spoken of rooms with small doors, tables with objects to choose from, or a being to ask a question of. Here, there was no sign of the direction she had come from. No definite path to follow. No objects to choose from. No one to ask.

Her shoulders sagged, and a small sound of sorrow escaped her in a sigh. She pulled the braid of hair from her pocket and ran her fingers over the bumpy strands, taking deep, slow breaths. Calmer, she examined her surroundings more closely. She could see there was indeed no path to where she stood. No broken branches or bent leaves. The mists clung low against the ground, preventing her from seeing any footprints.

She crouched down and tried waving the mists back away from her feet, but the curls her hand movement created arched back and poised themselves like snakes about to attack. Pulling her arms in close, she slowly stood. The mists settled back down to their quiet swirling. She took a hesitant step and met no resistance from it.

She took another, then a sound made her jump, setting her bones tinkling. It was like the hoot of an owl, but very low and deep. She strained her ears listening as it echoed oddly, bouncing through the dense foliage.

The forest fell silent but for the light rustling of leaves, and she took another step. Then a bright orange dragonfly buzzed past her ear. It buzzed back and circled her, finally coming to hover a finger-width away from the nose bump of the mask. She went nearly cross-eyed, staring at its bulbous black orbs as it examined her. It was enormous, its body the length of her hand. The creature's wings beat a cold draft that whistled through her eye slits, making her blink.

It retreated a few feet and hovered. Neela took a step toward it. The dragonfly reversed its flight and flew a short distance but remained facing her. She turned to her left and took a step away from the creature. But before her weight had finished shifting, the dragonfly buzzed around her again. Circling her head twice, it stopped in front of her mask, waiting. It slowly flew back to the right, where it had been before, still facing Neela. She watched it, then took another step toward the flying being. It turned, flew a short distance, then turned back to her.

"Am I to follow you?" Neela asked, her voice cracking from disuse.

The dragonfly bobbed in the air, waiting.

Neela reached into her pockets again. Releasing the clutched braid, she fingered through the various objects. When she touched the tiny pot, it was cold enough to bite. Gingerly, she removed the small bit of honey and offered it to the flying creature on her open palm.

The hooting sound rushed around her again, making her jump and bones tinkle. Glancing around, she saw nothing but the odd foliage through her eye slits. Neela looked back at the dragonfly and saw it now held the small pot clasped with its legs. She could still feel the burning cold upon her palm where the pot had rested. She shook her hand and shoved it back into her pocket, searching for the reassurance of the braid, and nodded at her new guide.

The dragonfly bobbed once more and turned. It flew, darting, then pausing, to make sure Neela was following, leading her past trees whose gnarled trunks were wider than she was tall. It wove among black and red vines which dripped down from the thick intertwining canopy above. More of the glowing firefly-like orbs bobbed around the foliage, their different colored lights twinkling as they flitted in and out of the leaves.

Neela's muscles ached from so much walking. She had not been immune to the Withering, and she had spent much of her time in huddled research when not tending to her grandmother. Her breathing was becoming labored when she lost sight of the dragonfly as it darted behind an enormous tree.

Rounding the tree, she discovered a glade with a large stump near the middle. The bushes grew low around the edges and the mists thinned enough to see patches of the ground beneath. The dragonfly hovered in the middle of the clearing, waiting for her.

As Neela approached it, she realized what she had mistaken for a stump was an enormous owl. Gripping a fallen branch, the being was as tall as Neela. Its wing and back feathers were a dark smoke color, streaked with the glowing snail slime the tree trunks had. Its breast was pale and spotted with complete blackness. The spots had a depth to them, as if they were small tunnels of night calling out to be explored.

The great owl ruffled its feathers, and the dragonfly bolted, leaving Neela to stand alone before it. It watched her with deep orange-red eyes, pupils the same depth as its breast spots.

Neela's bones clinked as she shook off the entrancement they offered and began fingering her objects again. Two objects felt cold this time, the seven-pointed bronze star, and the carved wooden bead. The bead belonged to her grandmother, gifted by an admirer in her youth. Carved into the shape of an owl's head, her grandmother had kept it wrapped in a soft cloth, worn tucked into her waistband, until it was too loose to stay put. She had insisted Neela take it with her.

Neela offered the objects to the great owl spirit. The owl ruffled again, then shot one wing out and swept it over Neela's trembling palm. It resettled and waited.

Neela bowed low and said, "Great Spirit of the Underland, I seek aid for my people. They are dying from lack of nourishment and cannot gain it with food nor water. Even the animals wither and die. How can I help them?"

There was a slight rustling, followed by a chorus of hums. Then silence.

Neela waited for ten breaths, then looked up. There was no sign of the owl. In its place floated three of the glowing firefly-like beings. Stepping closer, she saw they were not insects, but pulsing spheres of light, the size of fat plums.

A deep voice rumbled through the clearing, running up through her feet and shaking her mask bones.

"CHOOSE ONE."

Neela gulped and bent close to examine the orbs. Their centers flickered like the flame of a candle, but each pulsed with a different color. The left one was a deep purple, the middle a pale green, and the last a brilliant orange.

She tried fingering the remaining objects in her pocket, but they gave no clues. This was to be her choice. She wished she knew what she was choosing.

Neela held her hand close to each one and felt a slight warmth emanating from the orange one. She grasped it gently, and it buzzed as its glow pulsed through her skin, making her hand feel its lost strength again. She stood mesmerized before remembering she needed to find her way back out.

Reaching the place she had stepped into the clearing, she looked around. The thick mists made her unsure of which direction she should try.

A small squeak from near her feet caused her bones to tinkle again. A dull brown rat the size of a cat sat back on its haunches, staring up at her.

Neela took a half-step back. When it stayed still, she said, "H-hello. Will you guide me out?"

The enormous rat made another tiny squeak and waited.

Neela felt through her pockets and discovered the small bag of barley was warm, not cold. She pulled it out and dangled it by its drawstrings.

"Will this work as payment?" she asked.

The rat's tail and whiskers twitched as it reached up.

Neela lowered the gift into its grasp. The rat clutched the bag with its sharp teeth and turned into the mist.

She followed.

The ground mists often obscured the rodent, but the being would make occasional jumps, breaking the surface of the gray clouds to mark the way.

Neela was well worn by the time they reached the tunnel entrance. The rat waited a few feet inside as she caught her breath.

When the rat squeaked twice, Neela nodded.

"Yes," she said. "I'm ready."

The soft orange glow of the globe was of little help to illuminate the pitch-black tunnel. She kept the barest touch upon the scarred wall as she followed the squeaks of the rat, stepping with care over the bumpy floor.

Sooner, the dim light of the vestibule appeared ahead. Her steps became more sure as the passage floor evened out, and she caught the loping silhouette of the rat ahead of her.

She stepped into the open space of the vestibule. All passages but the entrance tunnel were now sealed with either rock or immense wooden doors. She glanced around but could not see the rat who had guided anywhere. Her trip had not been as perilous as most of the recollections she had studied. She hoped she had chosen correctly. Whatever the orange sphere was, she hoped it would be of help for her people.

She moved toward the unmarked tunnel, but before she had taken three steps inside, her first chicosk guide reappeared, blocking her path. Neela's bones jingled with her sudden stop. Looking up at its melting mask, it appeared more ominous than before. The being seemed to stare at the globe held in her hand.

Keeping a tight grip on the globe, she rummaged through the remaining items in her pockets again. When she touched the silver coin, its cold made her gasped.

Pulling it out with her free hand, she offered it to the chicosk.

"I—I'm ready to leave, now," she said, her voice quivering a little.

The chicosk had been following the movement of her hand which held the sphere. Now, it tilted its head toward Neela's face, and after a moment's hesitation, took the proffered coin.

It turned and started down the passage, its glow not as bright as before. Neela followed, eager to free herself of the Underland.

As the long dark of the tunnel closed in around her, she heard a soft squeak. Neela glanced over her shoulder. The opening of the vestibule was a distant, dim spot the size of her thumb. As she turned back, the chicosk's glow ceased.

Neela froze as her eyes sought the warm glow of the globe clutched in her hand. It was faint now. Fainter than in the previous passage.

Something brushed past her, and a wave of goosebumps ran through her entire body. Her pulse pounded in her ears and her bones made a slight tinkle as they settled from her sudden stop.

Neela felt a slight breeze against the back of her neck. Something grabbed her around the waist and threw her against the wall, face first.

Her mask protected her head, but she heard it crack. She slumped to the sandy floor, her whole body shaking from the impact. Neela held the sphere up before her to see her attacker.

The chicosk bent down over her, the pale orange light reflecting eerily over the rippled folds of its mask.

Neela pulled her knees close into her body and coughed. "Why?" she asked.

The chicosk raised its arm, poised to strike.

Neela felt her strength waning from the collision with the wall and so, so much walking. The sphere pulsed in her hand, its warmth comforting. On instinct, she thrust it toward the chicosk's eyes, and it emitted a brilliant blinding light. She drew her arm up to shield her own eyes and heard the chicosk stumble back, slamming into the opposite wall.

The squeak came again, and Neela shivered as the rat guide brushed past her folded legs. It turned toward her in the fading orange light and gave two quick squeaks.

Neela struggled to her feet. The moment she was up, the rat ran. She stumbled after it, guided by its cries in the dark, her left hand brushing the wall reliefs to steady herself. Clutched in her right hand, the globe flickered as if about to go out.

A distant scrapping sounded behind her, spurring her to move faster, but the ashy sand pulled at her feet.

A small light grew in the distance ahead. Her way out.

She pushed her shaky legs onward, trying to gain ground ahead of the approaching scrapes. Her head pounded, her ribs hurt, and bruises throbbed. She knew she would not heal from this. Her only slim chance was to break free from the Underland with the sphere. She was uncertain of what would happen then.

The scraping grew near, and the rat ran back past her, squeaking wildly. It nipped at her heels, urging speed.

The light from the entrance had grown enough Neela could see where the soft ground became more solid. She pushed herself to a stumbling run.

The air changed, becoming fresher as she neared the light. Sounds of life echoed dimly from outside.

Just as she reached the entrance, something caught her leg. It pulled her back and down. She slammed to the ground hard; the air burst from her lungs.

The chicosk rolled her onto her back, pinning the hand clutching the orb, and punched her mask hard.

A crack echoed in the entrance, and the scattered bird song of the outer world ended.

A chunk of Neela's mask broke off, revealing one violet eye.

Her vision split between the vision of the mask and the sight of her own world.

She saw the chicosk preparing to strike; the sphere pulsed in her hand.

With her free hand, she reached up and grasped the chicosk's dangling skeleton, and yanked hard. The bones came free and disintegrated in her clenched fist. The chicosk released her hand and Neela drove the throbbing orb into the right eye of the chicosk's mask.

The chicosk stumbled back, emitting a piercing squeal.

The glowing globe melted into the mask and light shot out of both eye slits.

Neela drug herself backward with her elbows, watching as the chicosk scrabbled at the mask, trying to free itself of the light. Then it collapsed to its knees, and the mask fell away, revealing the face of King Jaluduth.

Neela blinked. She could see his face clearly with both her masked eye and her free one. It was her king. His face was not half melted like the mask. Instead, a heavy growth of beard sparsely covered deep scars across the right side of his face.

Her masked eye saw the king's face upon the dark spindly body of the chicosk. Her free eye saw the king in his own body, but his skin was soot black and rippled under tattered clothing.

The king gasped and squeezed his eyes shut. When he opened them, their whites kept a soft orange glow around his deep brown irises. He glanced out of the Underland's entrance, then focused on Neela.

"You...you are from my city?" the king asked.

Neela nodded, pulling herself closer to the entrance wall.

"You worked with the polymaths, didn't you? Did you come to the Underland seeking an end to the Withering?" the king asked.

Neela nodded again.

The king closed his eyes, then his left shoulder twitched violently. When it stopped, he said in a strained voice, "I, too, came. I know not how long ago. But this thing consumed me."

Neela's masked eye could not help but stare at the chicosk body.

The king caught the slight movement of her mask and shook his head. "No. This is not one of the chicosk. It is one of the others. It holds my flesh captive. Feeding off my mind and emotions, until it ripped my soul from me." He looked at Neela, the orange glow of his eyes softly pulsing. "You must have returned it."

Neela tried to sit up straight, but the soreness and pain crumpled her back against the stone. "I was offered a choice of three spheres, your highness. I did not know one of them was you."

"I am grateful nevertheless," said the king. "What is your name?"

"Neela, your highness."

"Neela. I cannot break free from this thing, Neela. It has consumed too much of me. As I fought it, I learned it was the thing causing the Withering. It desires to be above with us. To feed off of us."

A grimace of pain flooded the king's features and his left leg jutted out at an impossible angle. He gasped, then panted off the pain until he could speak again.

"It seeps a slow poison up into the roots of our crops so it can feed off the thoughts of sorrow it creates. It grows stronger, every day." King Jaluduth paused, glancing out the entrance into the forest. "I do not think it is strong enough to survive out there yet, but it soon will be. I grieve for the sake of the world if that should happen."

Neela coughed, drawing the king's attention.

"Did it—we do that to you?" he asked.

Neela nodded.

The king met Neela's eyes and the orange of his own pulsed dully, fading.

"I am truly sorry," he said. "I cannot keep it back much longer."

Another pulse of pain shot across his face. Panting, he said, "You…you must do something for me. For our land. It is much to ask, but you were brave enough to come to the Underland."

"W-what is it, my king?" asked Neela, her voice trembling slightly.

"If you can, you must destroy us both to free our land of the Withering. I won't be able to hold it back much longer."

Neela gave a weak smile beneath her mask. She could barely move and the king—King Jaluduth himself—was asking her to kill him.

She shifted, trying to ease her pains. Her hand fell against something hard in her cloak pocket. Clenching her teeth, she wiggled her hand inside. Somehow, the small vial of wine was still intact. Poisoned wine. The vial felt warm as sunshine. She pulled it out and showed it to her king.

"This is violet wine, your highness," she said. "It…it is a very special wine. I believe you have a fondness for it?"

She watched the king's haggard face closely. Meeting his eyes, she nodded slowly.

"Yes, Neela," said the king, his left eyebrow cocking. "It has been a favored drink among royalty for centuries."

She knew then that the king understood. Violet wine had often been a last request of dying monarchs of the past, laced with things to make the rulers passing quick and relatively painless. She hoped the first would be true but doubted the last.

"I offer it to you as a gift, your highness," she said. "To ease your pain and suffering."

She held the vial upon her quivering palm and extended her arm as much as she could.

The king nodded and pulled his twisted body toward her. He reached out, grasped the vial, and retreated. Panting from the effort, he looked toward the entrance of the Underland. They were but a few feet from the opening and the woods beyond.

"Thank you, Neela," he said, not looking at her. "I shall drink it in the sunlight, I think."

Neela watched the king pull himself out of the tunnel and prop himself against a tree facing away from the Underland. He convulsed once, nearly dropping the vial, then stilled enough to pull the cork and down the contents in one gulp.

A moment later, her masked eye saw the chicosk's many legs jerk and writhe. She turned away, wishing she could close her ears to their shrieks and the thumps of flailing limbs slamming into the tree trunk.

She coughed and cringed at the pain in her chest. She stared into the darkness of the Underland tunnel, taking shallow breaths as she waited for the sounds to end. Her eyes caught a slight movement in the darkness before her, and a shiver racked her, making her flinch.

The rat appeared a moment later, bounding toward her and stopping at her side. It rested back on its haunches and squeaked.

Neela's split vision showed a rat of two colors. The mask's eye showed the dull brown fur she remembered. Her own eye saw fur that shimmered like silver.

"Thank you," she said to it, and tentatively placed her hand on its back. The fur was soft, like that of a well-fed cat, and she stroked it gently.

The rat moved closer, then hopped over Neela's legs and sprung out into the sunshine of the outer world. It turned and squeaked at her again.

"I have no strength, little one," Neela said. "I am broken, and I will not mend."

It hopped toward her and back several times, finally stopping an arm's length away. Neela looked out toward the tree the king had rested against. All was silent, and she saw a jumble of limbs, human and chicosk, in a tangled heap. The trunk hid the king's torso; the wood missing large chunks of bark up and down its surface. Traces of red glinted along the edges of the deep cuts.

Neela could smell the rich, clean scent of the forest. She closed her eyes, inhaling as deeply as she dared.

The rat squeaked again, and Neela reopened her eyes. The rat stood a short way out of the entrance, sunlight shimmering on its fur and dancing through the leaf shadows around the animal. She felt so cold now, and the sunlight was enticing.

"All right, little one," she said. "I will try."

She turned and lowered down to her elbows. She pulled herself along the hard ground, her knees slipping as much as pushing her closer toward the rat. It wasn't far. The stone entrance was only a body length away and the patch of speckled sunlight only a bit more. But every inch filled her body with pain as the movement shifted her cracked ribs.

Her mask fell away as she cleared the entrance, but she did not dare stop until her nose nearly bumped into the rat. She stared at the glossy black eyes and silver coat with both of her own violet eyes. It leaned in and touched her nose with its own, then bounded away a short distance.

The ground shuddered, and Neela looked back at the Underland entrance. It had sealed itself with tall narrow stones like long moss-covered teeth.

Panting, Neela curled up on her side. Her bony fingers shaking, she slid her hand into her cloak pocket one last time. Pulling the braid out, she clutched it with both hands.

"I am so tired. I shall sleep now," she said to the rat. "Will you stay with me?"

The rat hopped in close, then circled until it laid in a small ball resting against Neela's chest. It stayed with her until Neela took her last shallow breath. Then, gently grasping the braid in its teeth, it bounded toward the city.

From the Author

I've always been intrigued by Japanese cultural masks, and I am a fan of "No Face," from Studio Ghibli's *Spirited Away*.

When an anthology call went out with a theme of "masks" I started creating this story. I was bound by word count limits, though, and couldn't finish it the way I wanted. When the story didn't make the final cut, I decided to add the things I thought were missing. I'm much happier with this version.

About the Author

Kat Farrow grew up skinning her knees and listening to the wind among the rabbit trails and red rocks of the Four Corners area of the western U.S., and currently resides in the mountains of northern Utah.

A multi-genre author, her works range from fantasy, sci-fi, mystery, historical, and children's stories. She has short stories appearing in *Happy Holiday Historicals* (Camden Park Press, December 2021), LTUE's benefit anthology, *Parliament of Wizards* (February 2022). and *Witches of a Certain Age* (Camden Park Press, June 2022). Her first children's novel is scheduled for release in 2022.

Find out more about Kat at LoreWeaver.com, her works for children at SpindleSpark.com, and follow her on Facebook @authorKatFarrow.

Susan, Too

by
Stephen L. Antczak

Susan, Too

I knock twice on the wooden door, my knuckles raised for a third knock. It opens before I can knock that third time, and there HE is, looking up at me, although it feels to me as if I am looking up at him.

"What do you want?" he asks sharply.

"I need…" I'm not sure how to say this, even though I've been rehearsing what to say for a while now. So, I just blurt out, "I need a place to stay."

"Find a hotel," HE says and begins to close the door.

"Oh, do come in," a woman's voice says in an English accent, with warmth.

The door opens further.

HE sighs and walks away.

"Would you like some tea?" Susan asks.

Before I can respond, a gunshot rings out, and I realize that HE has shot me in the chest. I see him standing just beyond his wife, holding a Colt revolver. I stumble backwards out the door and turn away so HE won't shoot me again because I know HE's not the type of person to shoot someone in the back, but I collapse and bleed out in his driveway.

"I don't have anywhere else to go," I say as Susan scalds the kettle before putting in the tea and boiled water.

"Sure you do, kid," HE says. "I can give you names, addresses, a letter of introduction, and bus fare."

"Are you hungry?" Susan asks.

I nod.

HE sighs.

"Look, kid, you don't want to stay here. I'm a monster. Ask Susan!"

"Oh, you," she says to him, affectionately. She reaches out and touches my forearm with her fingertips. "HE's not really a monster. He just likes to think he is."

"Lots of people think I'm a monster," HE says.

"Yes, dear."

HE sighs again.

"I'll be in my office working," he says. He turns to go, then turns back to look at me, his expression hard. "*Working.*"

Before long, the angry *clack-clack-clack-clackety-clack* of a Royal marches down the hallway and into the kitchen.

"Cream? Sugar?" Susan asks. I nod.

Sipping the sweetened tea and looking into Susan's kind, blue eyes, I fail to realize the *clack-clack-clack* has halted. HE swings an iron mace into the back of my head, the blow so hard it knocks my left eye out of its socket, and my face slams down onto the kitchen counter. I die as HE finishes me off with a skull-crushing second blow.

"Biscuit?" Susan offers. She has arranged a selection of tea biscuits on a tray.

"Yes, please," I say.

I can hear HE emit a loud sigh from his office, even over the loud and rapid *clack-clack-clacking* of his work.

"Now, tell me what's going on," Susan says.

I sigh.

"I don't know what's going on," I say. "I don't know why I'm here."

"I don't either!" HE yells from his office. *Clack-clack-clack-DING!*

I try a biscuit. It's moist yet also crumbly, and tastes like pure, unadulterated Heaven.

"You had a dream," Susan says.

"Yes, but after—"

"You read the story."

"Yes."

HE comes out. Now he looks interested.

"Which story?" HE asks.

I glance at him, then at Susan, then back at him.

"Oh, that one." HE nods. "Yeah."

"I'm a time-traveler," I say, even though it feels silly saying it aloud.

"We're all time-travelers, kid," he says.

"I wanted to come back and tell you—"

"Tell me what?" HE asks.

"I think I might be like you," I tell HE. "A monster."

"You're not a monster," Susan says. "I'm sure of it."

"I'm   the   monster   here,"   HE   says.

"You're not either," Susan says. "No one here's a monster."

"But I've done monstrous things," HE says.

I nod.

Susan sighs, and says, "Haven't we all?"

I suddenly feel strange, and then the world goes all topsy-turvy and I hit the floor hard, whacking the side of my head on the hardwood.

"Did   you   poison   the   tea?"   I   hear   Susan   ask.

"Who me?" I hear HE retort.

Everything goes black, and I die in spasms as my guts feel like they're being burned up.

"What's geosynchronous orbit?" HE asks me.

I blink. Not a question I was expecting.

"Bah!" he waves off my apparent stupidity. But I'm still thinking: Is HE asking me *what* it is? Is HE asking me how far above the orbit it is? The path it traces like a dotted sine wave around the Earth? I don't understand the question.

"How long have I been here?" I ask.

"One cup of tea and two biscuits, so far," Susan says. "Would you like another?"

"Yes, please." She pours another for me. I look at it with no intention of drinking it. I just don't want to leave.

She adds milks and sugar.

"Thanks," I say. I still have no intention of drinking it or even sipping it.

"I'll be right back," HE says. "I want to show you something." He heads down the hall to his office.

"How many more times is he going to kill me?" I ask Susan.

"Oh, don't you worry about that," she says, waving it off. "HE doesn't mean anything by it."

HE returns, this time wearing a tall, conical wizard's hat, electric blue with gold stars and crescent moons, a cloak in the same pattern, and carrying a tall–taller than him–gnarled wooden staff.

"How old is Jeffty?" he asks.

"Five!" I yell my answer.

"Wrong!"

HE seems cruel, then. I'm not wrong. Am I?

I'm burnt to a crisp by a lightning bolt that snaps out from the staff. But this time, I don't die. Like a cartoon I sit there, blackened from head to toe.

"Ouch," I say, because it really did hurt. Like a sonofabitch.

But I'm not dead.

"Ah, crap," HE says, then turns around, shoulders slumped a little, and shuffles back down the hall.

"That should do it," Susan says.

"Do what?" I ask.

"Eventually it stops working and he's forced to recognize that this isn't his story."

"Ah, okay. It's your story, I guess."

She just looks at me.

"It's yours," she says after a moment.

"Right, right." I nod, realizing the truth of it.

"You have a Susan, too, don't you?"

"Yes," I reply. But then I feel the need to tell her more. "The story HE wrote…I always wanted to, well…but I didn't think I could be that.

Or do that." Shit, I don't even know what it is I'm trying to tell her. "I read it and worried that HE was me. You know?"

"As I said, he's not a monster," Susan tells me. "He's a writer. And it's just a story."

"It's not *just* a story!" HE yells from his office.

Susan smiles.

I don't tell her that's not what I meant. I never wanted to be a monster. I never wanted to do monstrous things. But, if I did, I'd want it to be just a story.

Well, maybe not *just* a story.

But, a story all the same.

I die in my sleep, next to the woman I love, realizing I'm just as lucky as HE was.

"Thank you for stopping by," Susan says at the front door. "I'm glad you did. It was a pleasant visit. Well, except for all the killing. I'm really sorry about that. It would be lovely if you could stay longer, but I understand that you have to go now."

"Yes, I do have to go now," I say, though I don't really want to go.

"We all do eventually, don't we?"

I step through the threshold to the outside, the world. I turn to say something, I don't know what, but the door closes with a firm, heavy wooden *thunk* of finality, followed by a click of permanence.

I arrive home and insert the brass key into the lock. I hear a dog emit a short, not-quite-convincing bark from inside. I open the door.

"Hey, you're back," Susan says from the sofa, where she's reading a book, her blue eyes now looking up at me. I can tell she'd fallen asleep and my opening the door had awakened her. I realize I'm calling her Susan in my mind, and it makes me smile.

The dog remains on the sofa at her feet, but his tail thumps into the cushion rhythmically.

"Why are you smiling like that?" Suzi asks.

"Oh, just glad to be home," I say.

A long time after we'd met, I wrote HE a letter telling him how much I'd liked "Susan," and how much I'd enjoyed our meeting, even if he probably didn't remember me. HE replied via handwritten postcard thanking me for the note about "Susan," and taking umbrage at my suggestion that he might not remember me, as only HE could, pointing out that, yeah, maybe he was old, but he wasn't yet senile.

From the Author

I developed a love of science fiction early on during the 1970s, and very quickly became exposed to the works of Harlan Ellison. I also decided I wanted to be a science fiction writer very early, even before high school, but it wasn't until college that I became interested in the social aspects of the genre in terms of going to conventions, meeting other fans, and meeting the writers. Aside from meeting comic book artists at small comic shows in south Florida, my first introduction to the social world of science fiction was the 1986 Worldcon in Atlanta. It was there that I finally got to experience the physical presence of the names that, for me, were imbued with the essence of science fiction, culminating with Ray Bradbury and Harlan Ellison.

I eventually had several, and generally pleasant, encounters with Harlan and his wife, Susan, over the years. When I read his story "Susan" in F&SF, I decided to go and write him a fan letter telling him how much I enjoyed the story, and the postcard quoted in "Susan, Too," is what he sent back. I wrote it more to play out the fantasy of meeting him and Susan at their house in Los Angeles, something I never actually did, and to try and capture the rawness (to me, anyway) of Halran's writing and also his personality. Perhaps it is more a vignette than a true story, and a number of my first readers didn't understand it, but I like to think Harlan would have.

About the Author

It almost seems that Stephen L. Antczak was destined to become a writer of fantasy, horror, and science fiction, seeing as he was born on July 20th in Salem, MA, and graduated high school in 1984. Over the years, he has written dozens of short stories, some comic books, some novels, some screenplays, and even a play or two. Some of these have been published or produced. He has also attended dozens of conventions and comic book shows over the years and met many of his favorite writers. He is currently working towards a PhD in psychology.

Taxi

by
G.A. Miller

Taxi

He looked at the expanse of the desktop, all the personal touches gone now. The battered stapler, the dented cup holding numerous pens, pencils, and a dull letter opener. How many envelopes had he opened over the years with…?

"Hey Dave, got a minute?"

Dave Ericson jumped at the sound of his managing editor's voice behind him, as wrapped up in memories as he'd been.

"Sure, Paul. Sorry, I guess I was woolgathering there."

"You have every right," Paul Miller laughed, "after all the hours you've sat at this desk. Hell, it used to hold a typewriter once upon a time, didn't it?"

"IBM Selectric." Dave sighed. "Thing was a tank, never skipped a single letter on me."

"I know you're not one for the whole cake and noisemakers thing, and the paper stopped handing out gold watches a long time ago, but I wanted you to have this."

Paul handed Dave a small box, surprisingly heavy for its size. Dave looked up at him and smiled.

"Well, go ahead and open it, willya? *Some* of us aren't retiring today, you know."

Dave opened the box which contained a USB drive and a large copper coin set in foam. The coin was engraved with a skull and the words Memento Mori inscribed on the face.

"Memento Mori?" Dave asked.

"Yeah, it's Latin. Means *remember that you must die.*"

"That's a hell of a sendoff," Dave grimaced.

"It's supposed to be a reminder to live while you can, dummy. Go see the world as a tourist for a change, instead of chasing wars and riots. Live a little! And if you really want to relive your glory days, that thumb drive has every story we ever ran with your byline on it. I had the geeks put it together for you."

"Hey, thanks Paul. This is really thoughtful."

"Oh, before I forget… What's your password for your desktop? They're gonna need it to clear it off."

"McIntyre70."

"You gotta be kidding me… Your password is a Scotch?"

"Ever tried a 50-year-old single malt, Paul? It's like your first woman. You *never* forget it."

Paul laughed loud enough to make a few heads peek out from behind their screens in the bullpen.

"So, what are you gonna do next? Got any plans?"

"Not really. With Kate gone and the kids grown and on their own, I'm alone now. I was thinking about maybe selling the house, getting a small RV and doing some traveling. Aim at the sun and leave the snow behind me, that kind of thing."

"Sounds like a dream. Once upon a time, I wanted to drive Route 66 all the way out and back, but we know how that turned out. You gonna miss writing under fire?"

"Nope. I may still do a little writing when and if I feel like it, but making a deadline is not something I'm gonna worry about anymore."

"Well," Paul held out his hand, "go on and get the hell out of here before I start yelling at them to make *their* deadlines. Enjoy life and stop and say hi now and then."

"I'll do that, and thanks again for this, Paul." Dave held up the little box as he shook Paul's hand, "I appreciate the memories and the thought behind that coin."

Paul headed back to his office as Dave walked to the lobby, exchanging waves and goodbyes with the reporters at their desks. Alone in the elevator, he slipped the box into his jacket pocket and pressed the L button for the lobby and began thinking.

RV? He thought, *where the hell did that come from? Still…it's really not a bad idea.*

He walked out of the building and began to turn toward the subway stairs at the corner and paused.

Last working commute, he thought. *Splurge a little, get a cab!*

He walked to the edge of the sidewalk and had just raised his hand to hail a cab when a gleaming yellow Checker cab turned the corner and pulled over in front of him. He opened the back door and slid onto the spacious seat, a throwback to another era.

"Good evening my friend! Where can I bring you tonight?" the driver asked with a wide smile.

He looked to be about Dave's age, maybe a little older. He glanced at the ID mounted on the dashboard; the driver's photo and the name Joe Pheriman.

"Oh, I'm sorry. I was admiring your cab. I haven't seen a beauty like this in a very long time."

"Thank you. She's my pride and joy, and I take good care of her. It's nice that you appreciate her too."

"You know, I'm not really in a rush to get home. Would you mind driving out of the city and heading north along the coast, or are you too busy tonight?"

"Never too busy for my customers." He smiled. "Everyone is always in so much of a rush, but not me. I rather enjoy being where I am, instead of worrying about something that hasn't even happened yet."

"You have a refreshing view, Joe. More people should be like you."

"I wish they were too," Joe said as he turned the large metal flag down on the meter and merged smoothly into the early rush hour traffic. Dave looked at the mechanical digits on the meter, then glanced at the leather hand loop mounted above the door, admiring the attention to detail in this beauty. It had to be a restoration, lovingly done, looking like it rolled out of the showroom and right to where he'd been standing. The only detail that wasn't period correct was in the dashboard. Where there would have been an AM radio with chrome buttons and large knobs for tuning and volume, there was a flat black rectangle, looking like an LCD screen.

"So, tell me, my friend. What does a well-dressed man like you do for a living?"

"Well," Dave glanced at his watch and smiled, "as of now, he does nothing. Today was my last day as a reporter for the Sentinel, and I am now retired."

"My congratulations! And a reporter! You must have amazing tales to tell. I have a great deal of respect for writers; I love to listen to their stories."

Joe tapped the dashboard above the rectangular panel.

"I can't read while I drive, but this reads them to me. I have many stories in here, more than I need for even the longest rides. It broke my heart to change out the original radio, but the stories make up for it."

"Do your passengers enjoy them too?"

"Oh, I don't usually listen with passengers inside. Wouldn't be polite. People either like to talk or stay busy with their phones these days."

"Young people can't seem to look away from their phones for a minute, you're right. I turned my work phone in today, and I don't miss it at all. This," he held up a well-worn flip phone so Joe could see it in the mirror, "is all I need if I want to make a call."

Joe's smile beamed in the mirror as he nodded his head.

"You have my respect. You see things that so many miss while they stare at their phones. That's why *you're* the writer, and *they're* the readers."

The cab stopped at a light, the ramp to the highway just ahead. Joe turned and gave Dave an appraising look.

"Does a reporter like other people's stories? Not news, but regular stories for listening to?"

"Well, sure I do. The reason I got into journalism is because I loved reading so much. Why do you ask?"

The light changed and Joe watched the road as he approached the ramp, his directional already on.

"We have a long ride to the coast, and I wondered if you'd like to hear one of the stories I have here." He tapped the dash over that panel again. "They're not overly long, like a novel, but I find them interesting."

"You know, that sounds good. Nice, easy ride while we enjoy a story. Please, go right ahead."

Joe smiled broadly as he tapped the screen with his fingertip and it came to life. Soon, a deep male voice began speaking; the perfect voice for a narrator…

It was unusually crisp and clear, the kind of day when it seems you can see for miles, with no haze to obscure the view. I used to call days like this *'Postcard Days'*, back when we actually mailed those to show people the nice places we'd been in our travels.

Entering the city park today was like walking into a wonderland, the lush greens and bright flowers more vibrant than they'd ever appeared in the past. I paused for a moment, just taking it all in, then walked slowly onto the path that I took every morning.

I normally paced myself, pausing at the same spots to rest, but today I took my time, admiring the pristine landscaping. The cleaning crew really outdid themselves, no trash or debris anywhere to mar the scene, so I kept walking. I finally slowed down, my knees complaining that I hadn't rested yet, demanded a break.

The park was undergoing renovations, most of the benches sporting wet paint signs, but there was one available with another old timer sitting on the end, his newspaper open.

"Pardon me, do you mind if I sit here for a while?"

"Please do, make yourself comfortable." His smile, as he peeked over the top of his reading glasses, was both welcoming and somehow familiar, although I was certain we'd never met.

He was a husky fellow, a perfect model for the grandfather role in a Norman Rockwell painting. He wore a short sleeved white shirt, with his eyeglass case and a sharpened pencil pointing up in the pocket, presumably for the crossword puzzle.

"Thanks. Seems I need to break up my morning walk and rest more and more these days."

"The years have a way of catching up with us, don't they?"

"I'll say! When I was young, I felt invulnerable, as if I could go on living the fast life forever. Guess it's finally time to pay the piper."

"Now there's an apt phrase you don't hear very often."

"Oh, my dad was full of those old sayings. Funny, they seem to be more relevant as time goes on."

"I've always felt that youth doesn't appreciate the wisdom offered by their elders until they've begun to experience life enough to recognize the value for themselves."

"Well, that's certainly true in my case. I find myself wishing I could go back and start over but keeping what I've learned through the years."

"There's that wisdom with age speaking," he chuckled.

"We look to be around the same age, you and I, so I'm sure you know exactly what I mean."

"Oh, looks can be deceiving, but I thank you for that."

"I apologize, I'm interrupting your morning."

"Not at all. It's nice to pass a little time with someone who walks through the park and takes the time to look and appreciate all that's around us here. So many young people miss the world around them because they won't look away from their telephone screens."

"That's for sure. It was refreshing to see you reading a newspaper, something I almost never see any longer."

"I get all I need from my paper," he said as he smiled and opened it back up.

We settled into a comfortable silence, he looking at his paper and occasionally making notations with his pencil and me just enjoying the day.

The park was alive with birds and squirrels foraging everywhere, but I was surprised there weren't any other people on such a beautiful day. I'd expected crowds, joggers, tourists, young mothers walking their children in strollers, but it seemed my bench mate and I had the park to ourselves for the time being. Even the city noise seemed distant, the music of the birds filling the air instead.

"It's somewhat magical without all the distractions, isn't it?" He startled me out of my reverie, seeming to read my thoughts, and smiled at my surprised expression.

"Oh, you're easy to read," he continued. "The contented look on your face says it all, just as plain as the stories in the paper."

"You seem to read people pretty well."

"Something you learn to do over time, Tom."

"I *thought* you looked familiar when I first saw you. I apologize though, I can't recall where I know you from."

"We've never met, no need to apologize."

"How did you know my name then?"

"It's my business to know people."

I glanced at his newspaper then, and instead of the usual columns of stories and advertisements, it seemed to be comprised entirely of lists, some in foreign texts that I couldn't read, unlike any paper I'd ever seen before.

"Who *are* you?" I asked, more intrigued than uneasy.

"I've gone by many names over the years. Call me Joe, if a name eases your mind."

"Forgive me for saying so, but I think I need to wake up from the most vivid dream I've ever had in my life. That you seem to know me in a perfect day in a park with no one else around can't be real."

"Well, that's how most people react." He chuckled. "But it's real enough, I can assure you. It's simply something you only get to experience once in a lifetime, and that's why it feels so surreal. It is pleasant though, isn't it?"

His voice had a calming effect, despite the odd circumstances.

"It's very pleasant, I agree, but I don't understand…"

"Relax Tom. It'll be clear soon enough, no need to rush."

He smiled again and returned to his paper, making notations with the pencil as he turned the pages. My mind was swimming with random thoughts and ideas, trying to figure out what was happening.

After a while, he folded his paper and returned his pencil to his pocket. He looked at the park around us and asked me a question.

"How are those knees of yours doing now?"

I hadn't even realized they stopped hurting.

"Funny, they feel fine now. Better than usual, as a matter of fact."

He nodded, as a man does when he already knows the answer to the question he'd posed.

"Let's walk a little, you and I." He got up, folded his glasses into the case and tucked his newspaper under his arm as I stood to join him. We set off on the path leading into the main part of the park, a walk I took every morning, ever since my doctor got on me about losing some weight.

We hadn't walked far at all when we rounded a turn and came to a fork in the path, the two branches heading in opposite directions. I stopped, surprised, Joe right beside me.

"I've walked this path in the morning for years now, and I don't recall *ever* seeing this fork before." I spoke softly, amazed by this odd day I was experiencing.

"This day isn't like all those others, Tom. Tell me, do you remember what your father gave you a long time ago, when you were still very young?"

"Yes, I sure do, but…how on earth do *you* know about that?"

"That isn't important. Do you have it with you?"

I reached into the pocket of my sweatpants and took out the well-worn Franklin silver half dollar I'd carried all my life. It was a 1950, the same year I was born, and my father told me to always have it with me in case I ever found myself needing a coin for the ferryman. I laughed it off as superstition at the time, yet I've carried it as a good luck charm ever since.

I handed the coin to him, and he nodded and looked closely at it, admiring the engraving.

"Beautiful craftsmanship back then, when men took pride in what they designed with their hands. Thank you, Tom. You want to continue that way." He held up his hand and pointed to the path heading off to the left.

"You're not coming?"

"No, I'm just the guide, you might say. The journey is yours from here on out."

"So…you're saying I'm…"

"You went to sleep peacefully last night and had what they call a myocardial infarction as you slept, basically the ticker stopped ticking. You had no pain at all."

"But you don't look like, I mean I thought you'd…"

"Oh, the robe and scythe? Please, in this day and age I'd be locked up in a second as a lunatic or a terrorist if I looked like that. Besides, there are good reasons why it's called popular fiction, with the emphasis on *fiction*," he said with a wink.

"That's a lot to process, especially in so beautiful a setting, Joe."

"The end isn't always bitter, Tom."

"I'm glad for that. So, the left path?"

"Yes, the left is where you want to go," he said as he extended his hand and I shook it.

I set off down the path, filled with a sense of wonder, of peace… and curiosity about what else might be inside Joe's remarkable newspaper.

After a moment's silence, Joe reached up and tapped the panel, which went dark again.

"Did you enjoy the story, Dave?"

"How do you…" Dave caught himself and looked carefully at Joe. He matched the description of the man in the park perfectly. He glanced back at Joe's ID card again and murmured "*Pheriman…Ferryman?*" As Dave gaped, Joe glanced at him in the rearview mirror and winked.

"Come on now, this *can't* be real," Dave murmured, "that was just a story, a fiction. Things like that don't happen!"

"To most, no… they do not, you're absolutely right. Why, you know that firsthand from all the places you've been and the stories you've covered."

"But… Why me?"

"Your talent. Your stories weren't just a summary of facts and numbers, they gave humanity and respect to those involved in the incidents you wrote about, and in so doing, made many of your readers more sensitive to how others feel. You weren't *just* a reporter. You were a standout in your field."

"So…are you telling me…"

"Oh, I'm afraid so, Dave. You didn't really decide to take a cab tonight, you took the subway like you always do, and there was a signal failure in a tunnel. The motorman was going too fast when he rounded a corner and ran into a parked train ahead. Your train, I'm afraid."

"And I always sit in the last car…"

"Yes, the closest to the stairs when you reach your station. You'll make the headlines again tomorrow, but as the subject rather than the author this time. At least it was instant, in your case, and you didn't suffer at all."

"What happens now?"

"I believe you have something for me, Dave, just like Tom did in the story we enjoyed. Yours isn't a dollar, though."

"That coin from Paul," Dave whispered. "What did he call it again? Something in Latin?"

"Memento Mori. Which is meant to say *Live while you can,* although the actual translation is *Remember that you must die.* And you lived a tremendous life and gave a great deal to many."

Dave slipped the box out of his jacket pocket and opened it. He removed the heavy coin from the foam and reached forward and gave it to Joe. Joe glanced at both sides and commented on the beautiful craftsmanship, then slipped it into a slot at the top of the meter box. All the digits on the meter rolled back to zero and the flag raised on its own.

"Thank you, Dave. Sit back and relax. We're almost there now."

From the Author

As I approached writing "Taxi," I wondered why do we always picture the specter of death as the Grim Reaper, a robed skeleton bearing a large scythe? Why couldn't the final guide be more of a friendly, grandfatherly fellow, one we'd be naturally drawn to, willing to spend some time talking and exchanging stories and pleasantries?

And along came Joe, the perfect example of what I was imagining. And what better venue for comfortable conversation than in a taxi cab, particularly one of the classic Checker cabs that used to prowl the avenues back in a bygone era?

I hope you enjoy meeting Joe and hearing the story he has to share.

About the Author

As a decades long career in the technical field was approaching the end, G.A. Miller decided to finally approach the blank page, an idea he'd toyed with for many years. 2017 marked his first acceptance in a publication, with the short story "Bequeath" making its debut in the inaugural issue of *Hinnom Magazine*, published by Gehenna & Hinnom publishers.

As time passed, more and more tales made their way into a number of publications, both print and online, and then 2019 marked his entry into self-publishing. Two collections of short stories and a novella appear on his Amazon Author page, and a brand-new novella was released in October, 2020 to join the growing collection.

Web: https://anitabob.com/welcome/

From the Editor

Thank you for joining us on this journey. It takes courage to step into a book when you don't know what you're going to get, even if it is the third in a series. (Maybe especially then!)

Often authors are required to make their story fit in with a group of other stories, yet, somehow, their story has to stand out at the same time, or it won't get published. Sometimes, when authors go down that path, they end up with great stories that no publisher wants, solely because the story no longer "fits in." Whether that is with expectations or with other stories, it can be a death knell for a great story.

The Particular Passages Anthologies are curated and edited with a light touch, so if you see a difference in grammar, punctuation, or spelling styles, that may be why. We are excited to give authors a chance to share a story they like, the way they like it, without trying to make it "fit in." As an editor and a publisher, I love reading these stories and not having any idea what the next story will be or even what to expect from the story I am reading! As a reader, I hope you found that kind of excitement in the stories of this anthology as well.

If you liked an author's story, reach out and let them know. The *best* way to make sure your favorite authors write more stories is to tell them you loved one of their stories. (Not to mention it will make their day!)

If you liked this kind of anthology, and would like to see more of them, please let us know. Comments to us, or to our authors, on our social media, websites, or in an email all work. That is the best way to make sure we do another one. The second-best way is to tell other people about the anthology, so that they buy the book, too. The third best way is to leave reviews anywhere you frequent online, including on your, and our, social media. Seriously, that helps *a lot*.

In the spirit of these anthologies, in the search for great stories in unexpected places, I wish you great adventures in your searches, and I hope you find the best things that just don't quite fit in anywhere else.

Sam Knight
6/14/2022

Additional Copyright Information

www.ingramcontent.com/pod-product-compliance
Lightning Source LLC
Chambersburg PA
CBHW020822260626
47169CB00003B/793